Ower

The Picture of Joe Roc

A Portrait from a Different Time

Owen Lennox

J.P. Grinion

First published in Great Britain by J.P.Grinion 2007
Eastgate House, The Street, Cressing, Essex.

ISBN

A CIP catalogue record for this book is available from the
British Library

This book is available from J. P Grinion.
www.jpgrinion.co.uk

To my wife, Pamela; and my daughters, Alicia, Amelia and Zara.

"There's no art to tell the mind's construction in the face."

Shakespeare: Macbeth

The Picture of Joe Roc

by

Owen Lennox

Chapter One

Picardy 1895

The smell of bread baking stirs ancient memories, feelings of well-being. As Madame Delaroche waited with her son in the small patisserie, her face half lit by the flickering, popping, gas mantle, the ovens from the back shop warmed them.

The baker came out wiping his hands down the front of his apron.

- "You wanted to see me?"

Madame Delaroche wasted no time.

- "I heard you wanted an apprentice."

Monsieur Lenoir knew of Madame Delaroche. He knew her husband Francis, a short man with a large beard, out of which came a larger than average bass tenor voice. The voice was much prized by the choir of the little twelfth century cliff top church in Varengeville sur Mer.

The baker attended the cliff top church; Monsieur Delaroche's often late arrival could be heard as he stumbled up the choir stall steps. Although Monsieur Lenoir felt the bass tenor lacked breeding he liked him for his voice and his good nature. The Delaroche family were farm labourers who, although natives of Varengeville, now lived in Dieppe a few kilometres along the coast. The winter had been slack and they were hungry. Joseph the eldest of three sons was small and thin for his age.

Monsieur Lenoir looked long and hard at the pair of them; the strong good-looking woman, stout with coal black hair, her gold earring glinting in the gaslight. He knew her pride would not permit her to ask a second time. The boy had regular features, though starved-looking, his thin face accentuated his large eyes but the baker saw honesty in those eyes and he considered himself a good judge of character. His two sons had been killed in the Franco-Prussian war and he and his wife were getting old and needed an extra pair of hands.

- "I can't pay much but he'll not go hungry"
- "Merci monsieur. Au revoir."

Madame Delaroche turned and opened the door without a word of farewell to her son; it was as if she wanted to get out of the shop before the baker had time to change his mind. The bell above the door rang as she left and a blast of cold morning air hit the room as it swung closed.

Joseph and the baker stood looking at each other. A tear was forming in Joseph's eye as the baker took the boy's cap off his head and rubbing his cropped hair said,

- "What do I call you?"
- "My name is Joseph but my friends call me Joe."
- "Ah! Like the English. Come on then Joe let' get you an apron."

An all-embracing feeling of belonging came over the small boy and a look of amazed privilege spread over his reddening face. The winter was well established when Joe started at the patisserie. He had been used to the hard labour and the long hours working on farms with his father and two younger brothers Andre and Julian. The work at the bakery was a pleasure in comparison. Joe did not like the farm work; he was a sensitive child who always felt cold, wet and hungry. His clothes were often damp, dirty and his hands calloused. As he had stood in the baker's with his mother he had fallen in love with the smell, the warmth of the place, the emotion in his eye had been born of the joy of anticipation.

Joe was not the physical type; he hadn't shown the same interest in labouring as his two younger brothers and was of little use to his father who saw him as eating more than he was worth. With Joe working at the patisserie there was one less mouth to feed. Joseph had not inherited his father's strength or voice, but he had his mother wits, he was quick to learn and Madame and Monsieur Lenoir liked him.

His working day started at three in the morning and was over after the midday meal following the Angelus, the wine they drank with this meal made Monsieur Lenoir sleepy and now that he was older he slept longer.

The different working hours took a little time to get used to but as the days lengthened with the approaching spring, Joseph thought himself very fortunate. Andre and Julian did not envy Joe; they both liked the fresh air and the dawn to dusk farm work and thought Joe's hours were unsociable, but working while others slept and sleeping while they worked suited Joseph and he thrived. He took to the trade and over the next few months assimilated the baker's knowledge and experience. Joe was a natural and being ambidextrous he handled the dough with ease. By the time twelve months had passed he was able to do all the work of the patisserie. His bread was as good as Monsieur Lenoir's and some thought it better than the masters; his cakes were lighter and more moist. Some afternoons Joe would experiment while Monsieur Lenoir slept. Monsieur Lenoir was pleased with his apprentice's enthusiasm and took pride in his own ability to pass on his skills, he said,

"You know you are a good teacher when your student is better than you."

Madame Lenoir took Joseph under her wing. Each afternoon she would spend a couple of hours teaching him how to read and write. Madame Lenoir was a patient and thorough teacher and within a few months her diligent student was able to write his recipes in a book. Joseph started taking books home along with his little parcel of bread and cakes. The rest of the family was not much into reading but the cakes were a welcome treat. Joseph's new position pleased both his family and the baker but he was the most pleased, he was earning his keep.

After work, Joseph would walk home along the cliff tops past the farmland that drops down to the edge of Dieppe. On the way he might collect a turnip or onion depending on who was about. These little finds supplemented his small wage, which he gave to his mother. Madame Delaroche picked up bits of fish from the quayside, where she sold her shellfish, with these and the leftovers from Monsieur Lenoir's oven and the little extra money Joe provided meant there was often meat on the table; the Delaroche family ate very well.

Madame Delaroche was a good cook. The meals she made were a tribute to her invention. Their main meal was at eight after which Joseph went to bed. He had to be up at two and walk to Varengeville; his working day started at three.

One summer's day while walking home through the long meadow grass that covered the cliff tops over Pourville he started to run. The tops of the grass lashed his bare legs as he sped on his way. The clouds of soft pastel shades scudded across the blue sky. He started to whirl himself around, arms outstretched, faster and faster, his package tied with string spinning at the end of his hand like a sling shot, he tipped his head back and watched the sky and clouds swirling in circles. Then stopped, and wobbled on his feet from the dizziness, standing still as the landscape kept on moving. In the distance, on the edge of the cliff, as his eyes began to regain their focus he could see a man, with a canvas on an easel, who was painting.

Looking at the painter Joseph was reminded of a story his father had told him about a man that he had seen painting on the same cliff top some years before. Francis said he stopped scything for a while and went to watch the man paint. The artist didn't notice him as he was like a man possessed, as if it were his last day on earth. Suddenly he stopped and walked to the edge of the cliff. He looked down, down to where the breakers raced each other up the beach; crouching, he clasped his hands behind his head. Francis said he heard the painter quietly sobbing.

The cliffs overlooking Pourville are majestic, with a savage beauty. Their chalky whiteness is a sheer drop into the crashing waves. People often went there to kill themselves, an easy place to disappear. Fearing that the painter might jump Francis turned and walked away leaving the scything for the following day; he said, "A man's grief is his own business." Later that evening he saw the flame-haired painter, drinking absinthe outside a cheap cafe in Dieppe.

- "Stay away from artists, they are all mad, they think because they can paint fruit they can eat paint," he told Joe.

But the story of the man painting with such frenzy fascinated Joe. Why would painting a picture arouse such passion?

Joe was curious about these people who came to Dieppe to paint; they had enough money not to work but not enough to dress properly. They spent their time in the poorer bars and restaurants, as if being poor was something to envy or the latest fashion. These tortured martyrs, these daddies' boys playing at poverty, mocked the struggle the real working people had to endure. The ordinary people of Dieppe found them patronising but ignored this and their drunken camaraderie, their false friendship. The locals were friendly and welcoming to these strangers and the custom they brought with them to the shops, the markets and the restaurants.

Most of the painters that came were French, from Paris, but some were English. They came to Dieppe because of the coastline. Joseph appreciated the dramatic splendour and the unique sense of place but had always associated the area with hard farm work. Now with his free time he could enjoy the day's soft spring breeze. It was not the same as the wind that raked the place in the winter, the wind, laced with ice, enough to cut you in half. Joe knew both faces of this schizophrenic place, this day it smiled, the light blinding him with its crystal clearness, the scent of its meadow was intoxicating. On a day like this Joe understood the attraction the cliffs held for these leisurely painters who spent a few hours a day with their paint boxes, making their pictures, if the weather was right. Joe didn't begrudge them their self-indulgent lifestyle; he liked them as they brought colour and gaiety to the town.

As Joseph quietly neared the artist who was too absorbed in his work to notice his approach, he paused, unseen, to look at the painting. The painter stopped what he was doing and looked at Joe in surprise.

- "What do you think?" He asked abruptly.

His French was impeccable, but he was a foreigner, Joe could tell by the clothes he wore.

- "I like it." Joe replied.

- "Why do you like it?"

- "It's different from the others."

- "Others! Which others, you've never seen any of my work before?"

- "The other painters who come here, to Dieppe, there are lots of painters in Dieppe."

- "I suppose there are. Art imitates art and artists imitate artists, they follow each other around like some family circus."

- "Do you mind if I watch?"

- "No, not at all be my guest."

Joe opened the bread and pastries he had wrapped in a cloth and he offered some to the painter. The artist seemed eager to stop and wiping his hands took a piece of bread. They sat down and chatted as the painter opened some wine and got out some cheese, tomatoes, sardines, olive oil and salt that he had brought they shared each other's food. The painter had his own bread but it was dry.

- "It gets lonely up here on your own, all this standing about, my feet are freezing, this fresh air painting is all right for some but I think I prefer working in the studio," he said, taking a chunk out of the bread and chewing heartily. "Your bread is better than mine," he continued, "What's your name?"

- "Joseph."

- "I'm an expert on bread Joe and yours is good," the painter spoke with easy familiarity. "Where did you get it?"
- "I made it; I'm a baker, I work for Monsieur Lenoir in Varengeville."
- "I know Varengeville."

The painter told Joseph that his name was Walter and Joseph introduced himself. They talked as they ate. Walter bemoaned that the light kept changing and the scenery kept moving. The impromptu lunch had made Joseph sleepy so he bade his farewell and Walter congratulated Joseph on his bread again,

- "You're a good baker, for one so young."

Joseph returned the compliment as he left saying he thought Walter was a good painter then headed home for an afternoon nap and then his third meal of the day. He had never eaten so well in his young life and felt things could only get better.

Summer moved into autumn and Joe grew with the seasons. The pantry of the Delaroche family was full as Christmas approached. On Christmas Eve Monsieur Delaroche harnessed the horse and cart to take the family to Varengeville for High Mass. The cart was mainly for Monsieur Delaroche as the rest of the family had to walk each time they reached a hill, of which there were few but long and steep. Walking over the tops was half the journey. It was a cold evening and the wind whipped in from the sea. The church was a little warmer, it stopped the wind and the heat from the congregation took the chill out of the stone walls. There was a cafe with a large fire where Monsieur Delaroche warmed himself and loosened his vocal chords with a few glasses of Cassis before following the family to the church. Then, missing the odd step in the dark, he climbed to the choir stalls to lend his lung-power to the sung mass that had already started.

The journey home after mass seemed quicker and the meal of oysters and bread washed down with a good white wine left the family dozing by the fire content in the knowledge that there was no work on Christmas Day.

Over the months leading up to Christmas Joe had seen Walter a few times. He was always pleasant and had come into the baker's shop on a couple of occasions. Walter lived in Dieppe and could easily pass for a Frenchman, when it pleased him and an Englishman, when it pleased him. His father was Danish and his mother Irish and he had been brought up in Belgium and England and he was at ease in either language and spoke several others tolerably. He was staying in a rented apartment, not far from Joe's house near the Church of St. Jacques.

That Christmas Day Joseph and his two brothers were walking the short distance to the harbour to watch the ships. As they walked down Quay Duquesne Walter caught hold of Joe's arm.

- "Just the man I want to see. You couldn't loan me a couple of onions could you?"
- "I'll try!" said Joe. Andre and Julian looked on, Joe told them he would catch them up and headed back home.
- "And some bread if you've got any, Joe," Walter shouted after him.
- "I'll try."

When Joe got home his parents were still in bed. He helped himself to a couple of onions from the string that hung on the back of the pantry door and two bars of bread from the breadbasket. He ran back to where Walter was waiting, full of gratitude.

- "You've saved my life; I've got some people coming for dinner tonight. I'll pay you back tomorrow."
- "It's OK, "Joe shouted as he ran off to catch up with Andre and Julian.

The quayside creates an atmosphere all its own; the ghostly mist; the damp cold that clings and pervades every part of you, seeping into the muscles, bones and sinews; the sucking sound as a wave subsides from a hollow in the harbour wall; the screech of the gulls as they search for an easy meal. The noise of the wind as it whistles low carrying the stinging corrosive salt that burns your face and stiffens your hair. The grudging respect the sea seems to have for the shore as it advances and retreats. The three boys hastened the sea on its way throwing stones as if to wound the fathomless body. As they played their games they looked out to the offing where an England bound ship buoyed up by the tide steamed out of sight, the haunting sound of its foghorn moaned in the distance like a last breath. Their talk was about the strange place and people that lay beyond the horizon and in their beachhead battles they fought imaginary wars with that old enemy over the sea, till hunger sent them home.

The next day was a workday and Joe was up and off in the early darkness with his oil lantern to show his footfall. While he walked his thoughts were on the ocean. A foghorn snored its way to a deep-throated crescendo, a warning through the thick air enough to rouse those dozing in the early morning. Nothing was visible, just the sound proclaiming the enormous power moving slowly towards its berth. Joe picked his way through the wet grass.

When he arrived at the bakery Madame Lenoir answered the door. This was not normal; the pallor of her face stood out against the black dress she was wearing, a shiver went down Joe's spine. He followed Madame Lenoir through to the back room and she motioned for him to sit down. Joseph had already guessed what was coming and he wasn't wrong. Madame Lenoir told him the baker had had a heart attack and had died earlier that morning. She asked Joseph if he could carry on as usual. He wanted to help, to continue as normal. That morning he made the same amount as would the two of them. After the Angelus bell had tolled Joseph went up the stairs to see Madame Lenoir. A steady stream of people had been into the shop to get their orders and pay their last respects. It was lunchtime and he went to the bedroom door. Through the crack of the half open door he saw the baker, lying with his arms by his side as if he were dozing. The cool winter sun had warmed away the mist and bathed the room in light. A beam of sunshine glinted on particles of dust as they danced in the silent room. The sombre figure of Madame Lenoir in her widow's weeds knelt at the bedside; head bowed, silently mouthing a rosary. Joe slowly pushed open the door and stepped unheard into the room to pay his last respects, the undertaker was tying the bow at the neck of the shroud. Joe stood for a short while then being unnoticed left quietly, not wanting to disturb the scene.

When Monsieur Le Conte had finished dressing the corpse he offered Madame Lenoir his condolences and left her to her grief. He took Joseph by the arm as he led him down the stairs. Monsieur Le Conte knew Joseph; but had never spoken to him before. He had always dealt with the baker when he had ordered bread and pastries for funeral parties. Now it was the baker's turn. The undertaker didn't want to bother Madame Lenoir so placed an order with Joseph for the following day.

On the day of the funeral a thin layer of snow covered the crisp earth, the whiteness of the covering reminded Joseph of a dusting of icing sugar, appropriate he thought. Those who had black wore it and stood out like painted figures on paper. Madame Lenoir had given Joseph a suit that had belonged to one of her sons and she said he could keep it. It was too big but he liked it and knew he would grow into it. He felt the part in his new suit but his old brown boots with his toe coming through spoiled the look. The cloud stayed low as if out of reverence as the priest, Monsieur Lenoir's friend and confessor buried the baker in the small graveyard of old church in Varengeville perched on the white cliff tops.

Over the weeks that followed Joseph kept the bakery going. Madame Lenoir who had always been a kindly woman with a ready smile, could not hide the sadness of her loss, she had lost her two sons at Metz and now her husband. Joseph knew the seasons in the same way he knew about life and death, working on farms from an early age had taught him that death followed life as surely as hope followed despair. Madame Lenoir was an old woman and although she might keep it going for a good while Joseph knew she would not keep the bakery.

Over the past twenty years Varengeville had become increasingly fashionable with the rich Parisians who bought up the land and built grand houses on the promontory with views of the sea. They used them in the summer when the heat and the stink of Paris was at its height, the breeze off the channel was a refreshing relief. The owner of the Hotel de la Ville, on the front in Dieppe owned such a house. Joseph knew him by sight as he'd served him a few times when he'd come into the shop. Joseph knew he would need a new position sooner rather than later and decided to speak to the hotel owner. Joseph lacked the courage to approach Monsieur Chavannes. Each time he came into the shop Joseph meant to speak but couldn't and was filled with remorse at each lost opportunity. Normally a gentleman of Monsieur Chavannes' standing would not go into a shop but this was Varengeville not Paris. He liked to mix with the locals and always gave his regards to Madame Lenoir.

The spring had just begun. Joseph felt Madame Lenoir would not keep the bakery much longer. Outside the shop Monsieur Chavannes stepped out of his carriage, the bell on the door rang. Joseph served him two éclairs, while he was wrapping them he plucked up the courage to talk to the hotel owner.

- "Pardon me Monsieur Chavannes but it is unlikely that Madame Lenoir will keep the bakery much longer and I may be looking for employment in the near future. Is it possible that there will be any vacancies at the Hotel de la Ville?"

Monsieur Chavannes looked at the boy the way one person looks at another to make them feel uncomfortable. Joseph didn't feel uncomfortable he was pleased with himself. Monsieur Chavannes could see it and his face betrayed a slight smile.

- "I don't deal with the staff but I'll pass it on, give my regards to Madame Lenoir."

The bell rang again as he left. Joseph's eyes followed him as he got into his carriage and headed for Dieppe.

The following day Madame Lenoir handed Joseph a letter.

- "Monsieur Chavannes came to see me last night" she said. "He wants to buy the bakery; he said he is willing to take you on, but in a different situation. I've written you a suitable reference, you can read it if you wish."

Indeed Joseph could read it she had taught him well. He opened the letter and read about himself in glowing terms: reliable, punctual, hard-working, willing to learn...

- "Monsieur Chavannes said to take the letter to the manager of the Hotel de la Ville, a Monsieur Decker, today at five o'clock and he will see what he can do for you." Madame Lenoir was pleased for Joseph but her pleasure was tinged with sadness knowing it was a farewell. She was going to live with her daughter in Chamboucy.

She embraced Joseph and he kissed her on both cheeks. As he was leaving she told him to wear his black suit.

The suit seemed to fit him better, and at five o'clock he asked at the reception of the Hotel de la Ville to see the Manager. He was shown to the office and ushered in.

- "Wipe your feet!" shouted the manager, "Come over here, you've got something for me?"

Joseph wiped the brown boots that he'd just polished with candle wax, and strode purposefully across the Persian rug and handed over the letter. The Manager read the letter, folded it up, put it back in the envelope and handed it to Joseph.

- "I have an opening for a trainee confectioner you can start tomorrow. There will be a deduction from your wages for your clothing. You will get your breakfast and midday-meal here. You start at three in the morning. Don't be late. Good day!"

Joseph took back the letter bowing slightly as he walked backwards towards the door. The manager paid him no attention and continued with his paperwork as though the interruption had never occurred. Joseph couldn't remember leaving the Hotel or running home. That evening he had more food on his plate and an extra glass of wine.

- "You can have a lie-in tomorrow." his father said.

The Hotel de la Ville was only a ten-minute walk from their house.

Joseph arrived early for work next morning and the confectioner set him to work; he told him how much bread he wanted. Joseph didn't ask for any directions and the confectioner, who appeared taciturn, didn't offer any.

As the weeks went by, Joseph - kitted out in his oversized whites - found the confectioner not to be as cold as he first thought. Alfred was thoughtful but witty, his quiet manner and steady approach to the day's work was in contrast to chefs and commis shouting and reacting to orders. Alfred's work was planned and prepared the day before and the two of them worked in the relative peace of the early morning before the kitchen became a frenzy of activity. The two confectioners often sat in the bakery at the end of the midday meal, Alfred casting barbed observations in the direction of the bustling kitchen as the sweating cooks marshalled the food from pans to plates.

- "It's not a bad place to work if you don't mind the sight of blood and the smell of burning flesh."

The shouting and loss of tempers were as common in the kitchen as in a family. As Joseph saw more of the kitchen, and the people in it, than he did of his own family, it began to feel more like home with the warmth, the good humour and the food; it was like a second love affair.

Joseph had arrived with skills; he wanted to be the best. He and everyone else could taste that he was not just good at his job. Alfred passed on his knowledge and experience and as Joseph soaked it up like a sponge, he began to fly. As he grew as a confectioner he also grew into his whites and the black suit Madame Lenoir had given him. The brown boots of the farm labourer had worn through beyond repair and been exchanged for a cheap pair of sabots. Each day as he walked home he looked in the cobbler's shop window at a pair of smart black shoes, Oxford caps. He wanted those shoes. He had been saving money from his wages and almost had enough.

The April weather was pleasant but still changeable and Joe's feet were often wet from the rain soaked cobbles as he walked home in the early afternoon. One day, as he walked, head bent to the rain, Walter called to him from across the road,

- "Joe, how are you? Long time no see!" Walter took a franc from his pocket, "That's for the bread and onions."

- "It's too much."

- "It's been a while, I've been away and you've earned a bit of interest. You did me a big favour and I'd be insulted if you didn't take it." Walter got hold of the boy's hand and pressed the coin into the palm. "Refuse nothing but blows Joe."

Joe thanked him and walked off nonchalantly with a smile on his face, the walk broke into a run.

Next day the shoes were on his feet, part of a deceased wardrobe the cobbler had bought in and repaired. Smart and the right size; clothes were starting to fit him.

As Alfred and Joe sat drinking their coffee, Joe's feet were on a chair showing off his new shoes; Monsieur Decker came into the bakery. He stood there looking down his nose. Joseph felt uncomfortable; he took his feet off the chair and shuffled back in his seat.

- "Do you have any trousers to go with those shoes?" he demanded.
- "Oui, Monsieur!"
- "You can work this afternoon, we are short of waiters."

Joe knew they were short staffed. Three waiters had got the Packet Boat to England the previous night; they had just received their call up papers for military service. England seemed more preferable to them than the army.

Joe was back in the hotel at two o'clock and was instructed to do what Patrice, one of the waiters, told him. Joe had a fair idea what to do. He was quick on the uptake, and he had watched them before, watched and remembered. The bar of the hotel was noisy, lively, full of smells and sounds, shouts and laughter. The atmosphere was heavy with the taste of the smoke from Gauloise, the smell of red wine and black coffee mingled with the aroma of food from the restaurant. This heady cocktail assailed the senses encouraging the punters to eat and drink with abandon. The voices mingled with the rich smell of the place and swirled like the curling blue smoke from the yellow cigarettes. The back of the room seemed a good distance off as Joe struggled with the large tray laden with coffee, absinthe, beer and wine. Holding the tray high above his head he made his way through the crowds which stood in groups. Some tossing banter back and forth, some listening or distracted. Snatched patches of conversation crackled in his ear as he fought his way to the far end of the room. Through the clamour of the crowd Joe heard his name being called.

- "Joe! Joe! Over here."

It was Walter. He was sitting with four or five other men, dressed as a gentleman, in keeping with the others in the company. Joe hardly recognised him as he was normally in the habit of dressing like a fisherman.

- "Monsieur," Joe enquired?
- "What's this Joe, a change of career?"
- "No! I'm just helping out for a bit of extra cash. Three of the waiters left for England last night."

One man in the company wearing a coat with an astrakhan collar spoke up in good French.

- "A cold place England but I can recommend the margarine and the weak tea."

The company laughed - a private joke no doubt - but the man's laugh was ironic; it belied the rheumy look to his eyes dark against the paleness of his skin. His nose had pinked with the heat from the room and the Cognac.

- "No place for a Frenchman!" said Walter.
- "Nor a Greek!" cracked the gentleman much to the amusement of the in-crowd.

Joseph was despatched to fetch drinks for the assembled company. On his return Walter said,

- "I've just been telling my friends that you're the finest baker in France."
- "Confectioner," Joseph corrected good-humouredly.
- "Ah! Bread the staff of life. I pride myself on being a bit of an expert on bread, and water of course," said the gentleman in the coat.

The laughter broke again as the good fellowship piled on,

- "Here's to the bakers," he said, as he threw coins onto the tray. "Come on Robbie and you Charles, a toast to the bakers of this world."

All the men tossed money on the tray.

- "That's for you my little confectioner friend and keep the drinks coming."

The humour was lost on Joseph, unlike the money, which was greatly appreciated. Joseph's affection for the English grew along with his wealth.

The place was busy, and Joe moved from table to table enjoying the convivial atmosphere where laughter was tossed in the air out of a hum of constant chatter. The night wore on, early morning crept in slowing, softening the sound of the crowd that lessened as the drunk, the lonely and the unfaithful drifted into the night air, dispersing like the smoke that blurred the ceiling. The waiters stacked the chairs and swept the floors, their activity contrasted to the indolence that barely moved those whose senses dulled by drink slowed their reactions to that of a tableau. Some lacked the impetus required to get them on their way while others just luxuriated in their own contentment. By two in the morning the place was empty. Joseph's body ached with a craving for sleep, he had been awake for almost twenty-three hours, and his head was numb. He went to the kitchen, made himself as comfortable as possible on the floor and was soon asleep.

The waiters remained in the bar and divided out their tips, as was their custom. Each got fair shares, the grafters, the grinners, the slow and the sullen, no one complained, some in their hearts were grateful, some resigned, some begrudging but they were equals, some days you did well, others not so well, it worked out evenly in the end.

At three o'clock, Joe was woken by Patrice.

- "I thought you'd gone home," he said. "We are sharing out the tips. Where're yours? "

Joe instinctively handed him the five francs in assorted change and Patrice went through to the bar. It was empty. Patrice waited a while then went back into the kitchen. He gave Joe one franc in change.

- "It wasn't a good day for tips today, you did OK! You want to take it up full time. Sleep well you've got to be up in an hour comrade."

Daybreak didn't come 'till three hours after Joe had started his day's work. He worked like a marionette but his good practice and the thought of extra money kept him going. The early light had turned into day and Joe worked through his tiredness like an automaton. The dough was kneaded for the correct amount of time; the texture was his guide not the clock, both hands working simultaneously. The dough proved on the shelves. The smell, the look and the feel of it said when it was ready to be knocked back. Left to prove again then shaped and flashed with milk. The oven gave forth its perfume. Joe and Alfred moved like clockwork in unhurried symmetry not speaking, they passed each other, walking around as if in an elaborate dance. Flour was thrown in arcs that caught the first glimmer of sunlight, cobs and plaits were formed with a flourish of artistic panache. At break time Joe shook with the shock of the strong bitter taste of black coffee.

- "You make a few centimes in tips last night eh! Joe?" Alfred enquired.
- "I got my share."
- "What do you mean you got your share? Whose idea was that?"
- "Patrice's, that's the way it works, isn't it?"
- "No! You do a one off; you keep your own tips. How much did you have?"
- "Five francs."
- "How much did Patrice give you?"
- "One franc."
- "He's probably pocketed the rest. He's always been a bit slimy. I'll ask the other waiters."

The pastries were made with renewed vigour as Joe lost his tiredness and seethed instead with indignation. He fantasised, ideas and plots of violent revenge, as words repeated themselves, racing through his head, and he felt hurt, betrayed and cheated. It wasn't so much the money but more because he felt he had been made a fool of. What he hadn't known he hadn't missed, but with his new education as to the ways of the waiters, he now felt the violation of a victim. As his fatigue returned his anger increased, he asked himself, why had he been so stupid? Why had Patrice stolen from him? Maybe because he could, the answer came back. How could he get his money back? Joe wondered as he slammed closed the oven door.

Alfred had a word with the other waiters. They knew nothing of Joe's money. Patrice had pocketed it. When they confronted Patrice, he laughed it off as some big joke.

- "I know nothing of this money; the boy must have been dreaming. Five francs on his first day as a waiter, don't be ridiculous."

Later in the bakery Joe asked Alfred.

- "How can I get my money back?"

- "It's his word against yours. The way I see it there are two ways, diplomacy or violence. With diplomacy you explain the situation that what he did was wrong and ask him to give you the money back. With violence you beat him up and take the money off him."

- "Which is the best way?"

- "Diplomacy is always the best way, but you may have to be prepared to compromise and settle for only part of the money. In reality there is little or, no chance. The second way, violence, maybe, but you risk losing your job and your teeth, anyone fighting will be sacked and besides that he would probably beat the living shit out of you."

- "What else can I do?"

- "Learn the lesson, put it behind you, otherwise it will only make you miserable."

Joe changed from his whites and went into the Bar for a drink. He sat down and called Patrice over.

- "I'm sorry sir I can't serve you, you're under age."

- "I'd like my money back."

- "I'm sorry sir, I don't know what you're talking about; you're going to have to leave."

- "OK Patrice, I understand, get me a glass of wine and there'll be a tip in it for you."

Both boys saw the humour of the situation.

- "Certainly Sir."

- When he returned Joe threw a franc on the tray. "Keep the change"

- "Thank you, Monsieur."

A wry smile passed between the boys, amused at their role-play. The cheap wine was bitter to taste and as the alcohol flushed round his brain it doubled his tiredness but quelled his rage. Joe hoped the show of bravado might have put Patrice on his back foot. He quickly tossed the rest of the wine down his throat and got up to go, while he still could. His concentrated walk took him to the door where the cold air woke him enough to get him home and to bed.

Joe felt better when he woke and over dinner he told the family what had happened. Out of the general discussion and outrage Andre made a suggestion.

- "You give me one franc and I'll get your five francs for you."
- "And how would you do that."
- "Alfred gave you two options. You've tried option one, I will use option two, I'll beat him up and take the money off him."

Joseph looked around at the silence of approval that surrounded the table.

At length Francis spoke.

- "I know that boy and his family, they don't forget anything, the money is not that important. Keep away from grudges Joseph," he looked at Andre and pointing at him, said. "and you, don't get involved."

Having said his piece the father returned to his dinner.

- "I want no more said on the matter," he added.

The two boys glanced at their mother who gave them a knowing look.

Joe, in his suit, and Andre, wearing his rough farm clothes, walked along the deserted cobbled streets. They stood in the alleyway opposite the Hotel de la Ville. They didn't have long to wait before the waiters started to leave the building, said their goodnights and went their separate ways. Andre set off walking towards Patrice, as he passed him, he threw out a fist that hit Patrice in the ear with such force it knocked him against the wall. Andre quickly thrust his forearm under Patrice's chin pinning him against the wall and he butted him. Patrice's nose burst open as Andre kneed him in the groin. Holding the back of Patrice's hair three short punches went into the cheekbone, jaw and mouth. Patrice fell to the ground stunned by the suddenness and violence of it all.

The yellow gaslight glistened on the rivulet of red blood coming from Patrice's nose and lip. His breathing was laboured as Andre sat on his chest with one knee on each of his arms and went through his coat pockets. Andre took all the change, half a packet of Gauloise and a box of matches before standing up. Joe walked from the alleyway and stood opposite Andre looking down. Andre gave Joe five francs and pocketed the rest then took out two cigarettes, lit them and passed one to Joe. Joe took a drag and watched the blue smoke rise.

- "We share our tips here," Joe said. "Thanks for the smoke see you at work tomorrow."

He dropped the cigarettes and matches on Patrice's chest, stepped over the prone figure and he and Andre walked home. The gentle rain was steaming on the gas lamp making it sizzle.

Nothing was said but it soon became apparent at work as to what had happened. Patrice was not well liked by the other waiters, they were wary of him and although Joe was not one of them he was given a grudging respect. The feeling amongst the staff was that this business was not yet over. Alfred didn't beat about the bush.

"You've made an enemy there Joe, he's a sly one you better watch your back."

The days moved on and Patrice affected an obsequious manner as he danced through the bar with an ingratiating air. Joe and he avoided each other as much as possible which wasn't difficult, there was no need for their paths to cross.

Chapter Two

Dieppe

One afternoon as Joe left work he saw Walter with a painting on his easel, he was painting the Hotel. After exchanging pleasantries Joe sat and watched for a while, they didn't say much, Walter was concentrating on his work. Joe respected his silence; he was fascinated by the loose marks of paint applied so deliberately. As a chill came into the air, Walter looked to the sky. In the near distance rain clouds were building as he carried on painting. Joe lit a Gauloise and smoked while the light dimmed altering the colours, the shadows disappeared. Walter painted on as if by memory as the scene changed. Reference was made to previous marks and his palette had been more or less set before he had left his apartment. The low key of his colours let him concentrate on the drawing. He painted till the rain caught up with them and made it impractical.

- "What I could do with now Joe is a nice cup of tea. Do you fancy a cup of tea Joe?"

Joe agreed and they picked up Walter's stuff and hurried through the rain to his digs.

Walter's apartment was small, on the top floor of one of the narrow streets off the harbour. There was a window facing north. The flat was dark and cold. Not the apartment of a rich man. Walter lit a paraffin-stove as Joe considered where to put the bag of paints he was carrying. The room was a mess, paintings, drawings and photographs littered the place. Walter put a pan of water on the gas stove. The ovens at the Hotel were gas as well unlike those at the Lenoir bakery. Joe missed the smell of the wood, but not having to chop it and wait for the oven to heat up saved time. Walter showed Joe a photograph he had taken of the Hotel a week or so before. Colours were already mixed on another palette and a canvas was squared up with a drawing of the Hotel enlarged from the photograph.

- "I work in the evening, that's the advantage of having gas light. People think I laze all day, and I suppose on occasion I do but that's because sometimes I work all night. Look do you recognize this street?"

It was a street next to the Church of St Jacques near where Joe lived. While Joe looked at the paintings Walter went off and made the tea. Joe had never tasted tea before but did not want to appear rude or provincial. The brew was light brown and aromatic as he drank it his face curled.

- "I'm sorry do you take lemon?"

- "No it's fine, just the way I like it."

- "Just as well, I don't think I've got any lemon."

The room filled with the scent of bergamot, a scent new to Joe, the aroma mingled with the smell of paraffin, oil paint and linseed oil. Joe sat in a large worn leather chair, with the stuffing oozing out of it, and decided to develop a taste for tea, it seemed sophisticated. Joe saw a photograph of a nude that had been dropped on the floor.

- "You have a camera?"

- "Yes, a drawing can be made much quicker with a camera, and more accurately. Just as well really, the prices I sell my work for I need to produce as many as I can."

Walter pulled a portfolio from under the chaise longue that was scattered with discarded clothing. The portfolio was full of drawings, in pencils and chalks, of buildings and nudes. The women's bodies, prone and abandoned, were of great interest to Joe.

- "I did those in a brothel in London."

The sentence bounced around in Joe's head. This apartment was the most exotic place he had ever been. The pictures of women were the first naked women he had ever seen. London had always fascinated him; he wondered what it was like, he'd seen the boats leaving for Newhaven. Newhaven to Joe meant London and they left every day not a hundred metres from where they were sitting. The closeness of London tantalised Joe, the most important city in the world. He was of an age where sex was never far from his thoughts and the word brothel and London together made for a heady mixture.

Joe's eyes fixed on a life painting in the corner of the room; he stared at the nude figure with the intent curiosity of his awakening manhood. Walter took this fascination for an interest in painting.

- "You interested in painting Joe?" he asked.

- "Yes, I'd love to be able to paint."

- "The trouble with painting is you can't eat it. I'll do you a deal Joe, I'll teach you to draw and paint and you can teach me to bake bread and cakes the way you do."

- "OK."

- "We'll start on Sunday after Mass. You finish early on a Sunday don't you?"

- "Yes."

- "I'll give you the money for the ingredients."

"OK."

It was all arranged. Joe asked Walter how he sold his paintings. Walter told him he used to sell in London but the few he sold didn't fetch much money so now he sent his work to an agent in Paris. The paintings went for a bit more and at least they generally all sold. He took them down in batches of forty every few months and picked up his wages from the last lot. It was a hand-to-mouth existence and hard work but it was the life he had chosen. He had tried being an actor and found he was better suited to painting. His father had been an artist doing drawings for a newspaper. So being an artist did not seem as strange a profession to Walter as it did to Joseph.

That Saturday evening Andre, Julian and Joe were playing with a ball in the street when Andre came up with an idea; he knew there was a bare fisted fight at Pourville the next day. The boxers fought for a purse, but the real money was in the gambling. Two young men would strip to the waist and slug it out amidst a circle of onlookers. Joe was interested in the boxing but knew he was going to see Walter. Andre convinced him that he could make some money on the local boy a lad called Les Quinnet. Andre explained that the two men were well-matched so the best they could hope for was evens; a small bet wasn't worth it so Joe gave Andre and Julian four francs. Andre made the stake up to five. With all their business settled, Joe went off to bed, the next day he would start to learn how to be an artist.

The smell of fresh ground coffee greeted Joe as Walter opened the door.

- "I thought we'd have a coffee before we start."

It was obvious Walter had just got up, his shirt was still hanging out, the buttons of his waistcoat weren't done up, he was unshaven and his hair was all over the place. Joe had never been one for staying in bed, he couldn't understand the attraction, there was so much living to do and each day held its own mystery. The apartment being a small mansard attic, it was already quite warm and a gentle breeze moved the dirty net curtains that hung at the window. They sat in the tatty armchairs and drank the thick black liquid. Walter lolled his head back after the first sip, he held the cup close to his face and let the aromatic steam drift up his nose, a sigh of utter relief groaned from his chest as the coffee hit the spot.

- "A heavy night last night Joe, but no matter let's get on, I'll just finish my coffee."

Walter noticed that Joe's coffee was untouched.

- "Don't you like your coffee," he asked.
- "I prefer it with milk in the morning." Joe replied.
- "Typical French eh! Help yourself; we don't stand on ceremony here."

Joe heated some milk; soon they were ready to start. Joe took Walter at his word, there was no ceremony. Walter had never patronised Joe, and Joe treated him in kind; as two aprons were produced their relationship changed, Joe was in charge, and with his apron on he adopted a mantle of authority - he was in his element. Before they could start they needed to clean the kitchen, it was only small but filthy. When it was clean and tidy Joe measured the ingredients, stressing the importance of measuring.

- "It's alright for chefs to guess their ingredients but to be a baker, a patissier, a confectioner it is an art, chefs are just tradesmen."

The arrogance and expertise of the boy impressed Walter, his ability demanded respect. After Joe had shown Walter each stage of the preparation Walter was told to do the same. It was the way Joe had been taught explaining each step as he went and writing it out so Walter would not forget. The morning went quickly. For lunch they had the hot bread rolls they had made and a vegetable soup that Joe had thrown together. They ate at the table with the windows to the veranda open. The gentle sounds of a quiet Sunday's activity wafted up to their loft. Through the slit at the end of the narrow street a portion of the harbour was framed and beyond that, the sea and beyond that, the sky. A cigarette and a coffee finished the simple meal.

"The simple pleasures are often the best," said Walter who was more awake now and ready to fulfil his part of the bargain.

The first lesson Walter taught Joe was that artists were neat, tidy people who worked cleanly. The evidence of Joe's eyes didn't bear this out. It seemed the contrary to Joe. The pans he had found in the kitchen had had the remains of past meals dried in them, with green circles of furry mould on the top. These were close neighbours to a cast iron 'bain marie' half full of rabbit skin glue size. Walter used it for priming the boards and canvases that were stacked against the walls. The glue had to be heated and mixed with chalk to make a gesso. There was a jar of linseed oil, sun drying, on the windowsill and a stone jar of turpentine stood on the floor. In the sitting room every surface was taken up with the paraphernalia of painting and books and newspapers the detritus of a bohemian lifestyle sprawled about the place. Neat, clean and tidy, it was not. The sun strained through the grime on the windows and struggled on past the greying net curtain. Walter picked up his palette.

"Look." he said. "All of the colours are set out in order so as you don't have to search for them. White is pivotal, coming down this side are the warm colours starting with the coolest warm and finishing with the richest. Leading away from the white on the other side are the cool colours. I work with a limited palette mostly earth colours with a good red, blue and yellow. The paint is mixed in the middle of the palette and I always keep it clean."

The number of paint rags scattered around the room testified to this.

- "I always try to keep the paint clean otherwise it gets muddy and dirty and no one likes dirty pictures. But before we start painting Joe we need to be able to draw."

Walter set up a tinted board on a table easel and started drawing a skull that he had placed there. He drew with a small brush using Burnt Sienna thinned with turpentine. He used a cloth and turpentine to rub out any mistakes. The skull was quickly sketched out, and then starting from the centre he built up the drawing in detail. After a while he stopped, changed the board and told Joe it was his turn. As Joe had been watching, the anticipation of getting started was overwhelming but he understood the importance of good preparation, it was the same with baking. He understood the rudiments of learning, you look, you listen, you imitate and the more you practice the better you get. Walter told him,

- "I don't start with the painting until I am happy with the drawing. Paintings go in three stages, when you start out you think it's going to be the best painting you've ever done, then it doesn't go to plan and you feel like throwing it out of the window. If you don't throw it out of the window you eventually end up with something satisfactory. But it is always a compromise; you never get the painting you imagined so you start again and have another go. When people ask me which painting is my best I always tell them the next one."

Joe worked for about an hour. Walter made the odd comment but generally left him to work it out for himself. Walter busied himself by squaring up a photograph of a street near St Jacques, a horse and cart outside a shop. He then squared a canvas to scale and started drawing the image onto the canvas. Joe was too engrossed in his own drawing to notice what Walter was doing. After a while he sat back and looked at his own work.

- "I think that is it."
- "If you're happy with it then stop, you don't want to overwork it."
- "Regardless, I have to go, I told my parents I'd be back for four. Will I be able to finish it later?"
- "Of course you can, I'll leave everything where it is. Pop in when you're free."

Joe knew it wouldn't be moved, why should it he thought, everything else appears to remain where it falls. When Joe got home the sparse tidiness of his house made him feel bigger. Andre and Julian were in high spirits, Les Quinnet had won but it wasn't easy it was touch and go, fourteen rounds, but the other man had finally failed to come up to scratch.

\- "Just as well," said Julian.

\- "Quinnet was almost finished."

They laughed, talked, ate and drank and divided up the winnings. It had been a good day Joe had worked hard and was tired. His bed was beckoning but knew he'd be on time next day he was a good riser.

Over the next week Joe called in on Walter a couple of times, and with his help, he finished the painting. Walter would talk about mixes, and colour relationships, high key and low key as if he were talking about music. The skull was painted with a limited palette of blue greys, time passed quickly when Joe was painting, he had a strange sense of, being, and time just went by. The feeling was similar when he was experimenting with new ideas for cakes. The two activities seemed to complement each other. He felt it had something to do with being creative, his success gave him confidence and he wanted more. He wanted to live and experience everything. Although his face was still young his fine features were losing their childlike feminine look, his slender frame grew taller, more muscular but still carried its youthful grace. As he stood back from the painting he had made he could see the pattern and structure Walter had been talking about. Sunday's drawing had been blocked in with three tones using a wide brush. Walter had said always use a brush bigger than the one you think you need. The finishing off with a small brush had been minimal, the painting had been made easier by spending time getting the drawing right. He was pleased.

Joe understood the power of money. It was a tool that could be used. He'd been hungry, he'd been cold and his clothes and shoes had been ragged. Money had taken him one step away from what he had been, money would give him respect. He knew he could never be a capitalist like Monsieur Chavannes but money would go some way to give him the pride and independence to be any man's equal. He saved as much as he spent. He dressed quite dapper, his hair was thick and fair but the scented oil that slicked it back made it look darker.

The times, like his appearance, were changing; the equality, liberty and fraternity of the revolution were slowly coming. People would still look down their noses at him but he resolved to look everyone in the eye. He knew his worth but didn't see his time at work as selling his skill, it was a pleasure, and he felt privileged. The harder he worked, the smarter he became, the more money he made. Albert told him,

"A man would wear out a few pairs of shoes before you'd meet a better confectioner than you, Joe."

Honest praise from a fellow professional is a rare beast and it boosted Joe's confidence.

Joe took to going out in the evenings and socialising with the young bloods that hung around the harbour drinking and talking. Conscripts and sailors spoke of where they had been, their exploits, their fighting, their gambling, and their women. The boys were older than Joe, some were fishermen others worked on the ferry. The company was rough and ready and losing a few francs on the turn of a card was part of the excitement. On bad days, when the wild weather raged outside, Joe sat with them in the cosy smoke filled bars on the quayside drinking warm beer.

As the weeks and months passed Joe applied himself he got smarter and worked harder, his reputation grew, and he was well thought of in his trade. Joe kept the other side of his life private, his ability as a painter was developing but that was different, it was loafing and never going to make him a living. Painting was a luxury, a hobby, but it was also knowledge, it was a different way of thinking and Joe knew that all knowledge was useful and being able to think made you smart.

Listening to Walter talk, Joe learnt that the artists that flounced about Dieppe were mostly of independent means, they didn't have to work, they played with their paints. They socialised together, drank too much, anguished over nothing. Fawning praise concealed envy as they bitched behind each others' backs about lack of talent. Walter professed to be different, he was part of Dieppe, and he lived in the town and didn't just visit like the others. He also sold his pictures. Walter knew all the artists as they came and went but assured Joe that he didn't pass derogatory comments about their work. He drank with the local people mostly the fishermen down by the docks.

When Joe went round to Walter's apartment on a Sunday he always tried to make something different, croissants or pan au chocolate but Walter preferred the breads, a brioche or a chapatti; they worked out cheaper and Walter was, after all, buying the ingredients.

When they painted Joe was Walter's contemporary. Walter with his palette encrusted around the edge in the old paint, standing out like ancient jewels. He worked on several paintings at the same time. When the light changed or the painting wasn't working he would change canvases. Walter talked of places and people, about an American artist called Whistler who had taught him to paint. Although Walter never derided Whistler's work and always spoke about him with affection Joe picked up that Walter's opinion of his master wasn't as high now as it had been. Walter laughed as he spoke about Whistler's posing, his self belief, thinking that he was creating great art, his dandy dress sense and his social pretensions. Joe found this very strange, he had seen Walter out with his friends from Paris, buyers, and hardly recognised him he was so well-dressed. Joe didn't know if it was hypocrisy or acting or just that this Whistler had taught him well. Walter said he preferred Degas to Whistler, saying his drawing was better. Joe had vaguely heard of Degas and some other painters who were trying to be different. Walter said he knew Degas and had worked with him when he was in Paris. He told Joe that Degas didn't want to be lumped in with these other painters; he just wanted to be Degas and make good pictures. Paris sounded glamorous to Joe but there was that other place in Walter's life, London.

London excited Joe's imagination; it had a darker side, more strange and exotic. Walter spoke of his friends in Camden Town, good painters, living in poverty in squalid conditions in this run-down area of London. They used prostitutes as models. A lot of artists did, Degas and Lautrec did, but the brothels of Montmartre sounded far less seedy, cold and drab than those of Camden Town. Camden Town was near Whitechapel where Jack the Ripper had murdered several women. The murders so horrific they had heard of them in France, the gory detail of the murders rivalling those of the Rue Morgue. Joe loved listening to Walter's stories and came to equate painting with being degenerate and risqué. It was daring, not at all respectable, peopled with bizarre characters full of their own self-importance.

Whenever Joe got the chance he would try to get a look at some of the work of the artists that painted in Dieppe. One day he saw Walter sitting outside café Tribuneaux drinking Benedictine with a friend. Joe had picked up a bit of English from Walter. What his friend spoke sounded like English that had been put through a mangle. It turned out that he was an Australian; Walter introduced him as Charles Condor. He had some work with him which he showed to Joe. Joe made the right noises, but he wasn't impressed and went on his way. He remembered the man's face from the day he had worked in the bar, he had been with Walter then and with the man with the Astrakhan collar.

Joe had done a few still life paintings, and a couple of self-portraits but he knew Walter used models, and wanted to have a go. Part of being an artist meant that you could see women without any clothes on. It might not be the only reason for being a painter but it seemed to be a good enough reason to Joe. He asked Walter if they could work from a model, saying that he was as good as that Australian painter.

- "That's not saying much," was Walter's reply. "When you can follow a simple formula painting is easy, anyone can do it, the art is giving it that little something else. And to keep on doing it, most painters give up; it's too hard for them. You're not an artist unless you are still painting when you are over forty. And unless your family is rich you must be able to sell your work, and to do that you must sell yourself. You have to become the buyer's idea of what an artist is, and paint what the buyer thinks art is. You have to make the buyer think he is clever, has good taste and can recognise a bargain. Most men buy paintings to show off and impress their friends, it appeals to their vanity but most of the time they don't know what they're looking at. Most women buy paintings to match the curtains. The real connoisseur is buying a piece of your soul. If you are lucky as a painter, you are not dictated to by fashion; you become the fashion, and then can do what you want. You don't need to sell, people will buy. Next Sunday you will have a model."

Joe had managed to keep his Sunday activities from his parents. They thought his hours on a Sunday were longer than they really were and didn't complain when he brought home fresh bread and sometimes cakes. Joe always managed to make more than Walter needed. Joe knew his parents did not approve of artists; painting pictures was not a proper job. They knew Joe knew Walter. But Walter was accepted; he was ordinary, he spoke like the Picardy, dressed like them and drank with them.

Joe knew differently, there were two sides to Walter. His time as an actor hadn't been wasted, the world was his stage and he was playing several different parts. Some days the fisherman out on the boats, some days the dandy, other days the bohemian artist. To some people he was Walter and to others he was Richard.

Sunday came round and Joe was eager to get to Walter's apartment. When he arrived at his squalid rooms the model was already there. She was tall with a graceful figure; her long flaming hair was a burnt gold that framed her freckled complexion.

- "Today I want to draw Madame Villain in the peasant costume of the local fishwife, we draw first then we eat," Walter said.

And they did, two easels were set up and they both worked in chalk pastels. Walter worked at a furious pace, standing, crouching, leaning back, tilting his head, squinting then forward to the easel, totally absorbed in what he was doing. Occasionally he would rest, look at Joe's work and comment or change a line or tell him to look again at a certain area, check an angle or a proportion. After two hours Walter was satisfied, he saw the model to the door Joe heard him say,

- "I'll pay you later" as he touched her arm and kissed her.

Walter had his cookery lesson and they ate the results. Joe said he knew the model she used to collect shellfish with his mother.

She had a few children, her son Titine was a friend of Julian's. He told Walter that his mother didn't like Titine who was a bit wild on account of not having a father. Tintine's father had been a fisherman who had drowned along with another man a few years ago. His mother had kept the boat and hired men to fish, now she had three boats and sold the best fish in Le Pollet. Joe said his mother didn't like the way she got on with men and hung around the bars in the evenings. Walter seemed to know all this. He shrugged,

- "You have to feed your children."

On his way home Joe felt let down, his week of anticipation of seeing a naked woman and then drawing from his little brother's friend's mother with all her clothes on was a disappointment. He wasn't too hungry; having eaten so late, then realising he had left his apron at Walter's he headed back to the apartment. The door was open, he announced his arrival

- "It's only me, I forgot my apron."

- "It's hanging on the peg."

- "Thanks." Joe got the apron and was leaving.

Just outside the door he heard Walter say to someone else.

- "Has he left?"

- "Yes" came the reply."

Joe recognized the voice, his curiosity was aroused. He quietly sneaked back along the landing and looked through the crack of the half-open door that led to the sitting room. The model was in the same pose as before. Walter was finishing the earlier drawing. Joe was about to leave when Walter changed the drawing.

- "Now we can start the life study," Walter said.

The model slipped off the stool she'd been sitting on; taking off the black shawl she loosened her tight waistcoat, unbuttoning it from the bottom. Her head was lowered and as she opened the waistcoat she raised her eyes and smiled seductively. Her large breasts hung loose inside the camisole, Joe could see the hard nipples against the soft shirt. She undid the bow at the top of the shirt and pulling it teasingly out of the skirt crossing her arms she lifted it over her head her breasts bounced and swayed as she shook her hair free and threw the garment over the chaise longue. Joe's cock was hard in his trousers and his mouth was dry, she had a fine figure, meaty without being fat. Her hands went around the back of her skirt throwing her chest forward she struggled to unbutton the skirt.

- "Come here I'll help," Walter offered and as he went over she turned her back to him.

He undid the button with ease and the skirt dropped to the floor. His right hand moved across her belly as his other hand fondled her breast. Slowly he pushed his hand down inside her petticoat. She rolled her head back as he kissed her on the neck. Joe wanted to leave but his feet wouldn't move, his thighs had turned to jelly.

- "You've got me all wet," she said, "you're going to have to do something with that prick of yours."
- "And I thought you wanted to save it till later."

She turned round and lifted her arms round Walter's neck. He looked down at the bow holding her petticoat and loosened it, her eyes locked into his and she smiled, it dropped to the floor. She kicked off her sabots and stood bare footed and naked. The fading light from the window caught her form. Walter undid the buttons on his fly and putting his hands under her thighs lifted her on to his stiff prick. Her chin rested on his shoulder and she groaned as her arms tightened around his neck. Joe's cock exploded in his trousers. He couldn't move until the spasms had stopped. He watched as Walter walked with faltering steps to the chaise longue where they fell laughing. Joe used their commotion to quietly back away from the door and out down the stairs.

In the morning the fish quay at Le Pollet was a living thing crowded with bodies, those buying and those selling. Fish wriggling in buckets, women filleting and seagulls ever open to the opportunity to steal a scrap screeched low overhead. Madame Delaroche had been out early and saw the sun rise as the tide had receded. The heavy baskets of mussels and oysters had been lugged to the fish market on the hand cart where she stood in the throng yelling her wares with the other fishwives. The banter was fierce going backwards and forwards, heavy laden with innuendo and accusation. Laughter ran along the flagstones under the arches and round the harbour wall. The line between laughter and tears was thin and ragged. Augustine Villain looked tired and drawn; she'd been up since dawn helping to unload the catch from her boats after she had left Walter's bed. She was a young woman handsome and strong. She was filleting fish as she was selling them.

- "The speed you're going, Villain, the fish will be off before they're sold," called a voice standing behind a basket.

Much laughter ensued as another wife chipped in.

- "If you're getting paid by the kilo you'd make more money selling your own fish."

The cackles of mirth rang from the women when another jibe was tossed in, the laughter rose up on another wave.

- "You should be wide awake the amount of time you 'models' spend lying on your backs."

Augustine Villain had borne their jokes in silence. As a single woman with a family the money was more important than the bitching. But the opportunity was too good to miss.

- "We models work very hard for our money you want to ask Madame Delaroche's son. I was modelling for him yesterday."

No sooner the words left her lips than a slap from the right hand of Madame Delaroche, as hard as leather and as cold as a cod, hit Madame Villain full in the face. The shock woke her out of her lethargy and the instinct of the fighter took over. Madame Villain wasn't the equal in strength of Madame Delaroche but the ferocity of will stored up through loneliness and injustice of a hard life made her a match for any creature God made. Turning into the bigger woman, head down like a bull her left hand grabbed at Madame Delaroche's throat. The right hand with the filleting knife flashed across the sky towards her face. Madame Delaroche moved her head and the knife went into her gold earring, feeling the knife stuck, Madame Villain jagged the blade down and ripped the earring through the lobe then pushed Madame Delaroche back where she knocked over her half empty basket of mussels. As she fell to the ground her ear poured with blood. Madame Villain stood rock solid.

- "Touch me again and I'll kill you," she said brandishing the knife.

The waves still splashed and gurgled on the harbour wall and the seagulls still called out but for a moment everything seemed silent, time moved like a slur for a moment, then raced to catch itself up. Villain backed away wiping the blood from her filleting knife on her apron as the crowd looked on. The drama over, they went back to their business. The women descended on the wounded Madame Delaroche like a well-rehearsed troupe. Cold water was applied to the torn ear, a needle and thread soaked in brandy and neat stitches joined the cut. The golden earring was found, straightened and sewed back into place. The blood on her neck, jaw and face were wiped clean. The anger Madame Delaroche had felt towards Villain was misplaced. The heat of the moment had inflamed her passion and she had responded to defend her family's honour. She knew Villain had acted in kind and the wound was as much her own doing as Villain's. But mostly it was Joe's doing. Cleaned up she put the shellfish back in her basket and walked over to Madame Villain. This time there was no surprise attack or instinctive response.

- "Keep away from my son."
- "I do as I please, your son likes drawing, and I don't think he's interested in the other."
- "I don't like him hanging around the likes of you."
- "Why? In case I damage your reputation? We know your reputation. Joseph is old enough to make up his own mind what he does."

- "I've told you keep away from my son. Next time I won't be coming at you with an empty hand."
- "And you'll know where to find me?"

Madame Delaroche went back to the business of the day and continued to sell her shellfish before taking her smouldering rage off home.

Joe was in bed, warm and safe when a hand grabbed him by the collar and lifted him bodily from his slumber and threw him across the room where he landed on the floor.

- "Where were you yesterday?" his mother demanded.

He stood up in shock and three punches followed the words, a right, left, and a right again his face spouted blood, from his mouth, nose and a small cut in the white of his eye.

- "Don't lie to me," she said, and went downstairs.

Joe got dressed and followed her into the kitchen; he filled the tin bowl with cold water and rinsed his fattening face. The blood coloured the water. He dabbed his face carefully with a towel and sat down at the table with his mother. She poured him a cup of coffee he added milk and sugar and stirred it; he thought the sugar would calm him and stop his shaking. Blood dripped from his nose forming spirals in the milky drink.

- "I was round at Walter Sickert's apartment he's been teaching me to paint."
- "Was Madame Villain there?"

- "Yes, she was modelling."
- "Was she naked?"
- "No!"
- "What did you do?"
- "I did a drawing. I've been going round there for a while, mostly I paint apples, oranges, jugs and things, I've done a couple of self-portraits and I paint or draw buildings from photographs. Yesterday was the first time I have drawn from a model."
- "Model, she's a whore! You don't go round there again."
- "You've ignored me most of my life and now you're telling me what I can and can't do!"
- "You live under my roof you do what I tell you."

Joe looked properly at his mother for the first time and noticed her blood soaked clothes and the stitches in her torn ear.

- "What happened to you?" He asked.
- "Madame Villain said she'd been with you, so I hit her and she cut me with a filleting knife."

Joe would have liked to think his mother was defending her son but he knew it was her own honour that was at stake. He drank his coffee and took his sore face back to bed. He came down when the others were in and had already started eating; the atmosphere was warm and jovial but went quiet when he took his place at the table. Andre started,

- "So you're a bit of an artist then are you Joe?

Papa has told you about those people, they don't know a proper days work from a punch in the eye, whereas you do. Still, you had a women round there."

- "Shut up," Madame Delaroche shouted abruptly, "it's finished, let it lie."

Andre and Julian started laughing again.

- "I know Titine Villain. Is his mother really a whore," asked Julian.

- "How else do you think the widow woman keeps him in shoes," replied Andre.

- "I told you to leave it."

- "She is a hard-working woman; her fish are the best in Le Pollet. That's how she keeps her family fed and clothed. How she spends her time and with whom is her own business. I've always found her friendly and polite. She's known that painter for a long time. She's not a whore, any woman who can work and bring up her family on her own deserves your respect not your sniggers, and even if she were a whore what would you rather her children go hungry with no shoes."

The father had spoken. Madame Delaroche rose from the table and patted his shoulder as she went to the kitchen to get the salt.

Joe ate his dinner in silence, the distance between him and the rest of the family, a distance he had always felt, was apparent, his mind was made up. Life had more to offer than he would get in Dieppe.

-      "I'm leaving at the end of the week." he said.

Julian's fork remained in his mouth as he turned and looked at Joe's swollen and bruised face. Madame Delaroche broke the silence of the table.

-   "You don't have to go."

-   "The time is right. I want to go and work in Paris I've learned as much as I'm going to with Albert and I can make more money in Paris. I've got enough saved for a couple of weeks. If it doesn't work out I'll come back."

Having finished his meal Joe got his jacket and went out. Francis looked at his wife.

-   "He's right."

    That Saturday night the Bar Riche was buzzing, Joe had settled all his business with Hotel de la Ville. Albert had tried to persuade him to stay but when he realised he was fighting a lost cause, he wrote him a good reference. Joe told Walter the story of what had happened but he'd already heard it from Madame Villain. He told Joe that he would look after his paintings and drawings and gave him a letter of introduction to a friend of his, a Monsieur Dupoirier, who ran a small Hotel on the Rue des Beaux Arts. This was his last night in Dieppe and the wine was flowing. Joe had his suit on, his shoes polished, hair slicked back and a Gauloise hanging from his lip he looked every inch the young blade with his black eye and broken nose. His scoured the room through the smoke, the sawdust and bodies, he was on the hunt. He had bridges to burn and Bar Riche had a certain reputation. A girl looked straight at Joe; she was young and pretty and wore a fine dress. She walked across to where he was standing with his friends.

- "Aren't you going to buy a girl a drink, sailor?" she said.

- "I've been waiting for a man like you."

Joe bought her a drink. As they left together Joe had his ticket to Paris in his pocket and a beautiful young girl on his arm, he wasn't going home tonight.

Chapter Three

Paris

Joe had never been on a train before, it was clean, new and expensive and he felt rich, full of the optimism of youth. He was confident, there was no looking back. This is what he had worked and saved for. He was going to have a good time. He had slept later than normal after his first night of sex. Fumbling youth doesn't make for a great lover but his earnest endeavour had been treated with good humour. A professional is a better teacher than trial and error. He had plenty of time to get home pick up his bag and get to the station.

The journey was exhilarating, the speed thrilled him. There was some trepidation as the train travelled through the outskirts of the city he had only ever heard of. It was big and intimidating. As Joe stepped off the train he marvelled at the enormous engine, belching steam, the roars, the whistles and the hisses echoed in the cavernous glass and steel building. People busied themselves intent on their own purposes unaware of others, like so many parts in a huge machine keeping the city turning. He walked out onto the pavement leaving the cool shelter behind him with its evocative scent of sulphur like rotten eggs. The aroma of coffee, cigarette smoke and the sounds of the cosmopolitan city assailed his senses, he breathed in this heady mixture borne up by the warm dry air that reeked of freedom. Feeling awake and alive he set off in this strange city, that he felt he had known all his life, to find 13 Rue des Beaux Arts. He headed for the Seine; he wanted to see the river, the boats, to mingle with the traffic. Everywhere he looked there were horses, carts, carriages and men pushing and pulling and fetching and carrying; the choreography of chaos as if driven by an invisible metronome. Joe was impressed by the number of clocks on buildings and the watches constantly being pulled out of people's pockets, looked at, listened to, rattled, polished, put away. In the country people didn't keep time, the seasons kept time; things happened when they needed to. The time was for trains and, as Joe had learned, bakers. His was a precise art. He was now the possessor of his own pocket watch, a handsome leaving present from his friend and teacher Albert.

When Joe got to the river, boats of all sizes and shapes filled the waterway from bank to bank. The air was filled with the sound of the sails flapping and the shouts of the boatmen as they moved the water in different directions with their oars and paddles. Steam and smoke belched from ships chimney stacks. As he strolled alongside the bank taking it all in, everything was bigger and more numerous than he had ever seen and seemed to go on forever. Each road repeated the same pattern, more cafés, and more restaurants, enough to feed an army; more shops with more goods than people could need or want. Too much! Sparrows were everywhere feeding on horse dung in the roads. The river air carried the savoury tinge of sewage as it bore the waste of a city to the distant sea. Gulls squabbled over scraps amongst the rich odour. As the sun got hotter Joe found the Rue des Beaux Arts. Women walked past him with parasols up to keep the sun off their faces and the bird droppings off their fine clothes, a pomander on their wrists to keep the stink from their noses.

The Rue des Beaux Arts was cool with buildings five floors on either side. The Hotel d'Alsace wasn't large but Monsieur Dupoirier was, in girth at least. The Hotel was where Walter sometimes stayed when he was in Paris and Monsieur Dupoirier knew him well. After reading the letters from Albert and Walter, Monsieur Dupoirier looked up.

- "You're very highly recommended Monsieur Delaroche but I do not run a bakery here. Can you cook?"
- "Yes!" Replied Joe suddenly feeling intimidated.
- "I have an opening for an assistant chef, if you are interested."
- "Yes."
- "You can have board and lodging for a week to see how you work out, then we will discuss wages."

This suited Joe well. He was shown to his room took out his whites and started immediately. The Chef de Cuisine, Pierre, was a genial man who had worked for Monsieur Dupoirier for years. His favourite saying was we always get paid, sometimes, eventually. In spite of his haphazard way with paying wages Dupoirier was a fair and generous man, when he was solvent. It was the nature of the clientele who frequented Monsieur Dupoirier establishment that kept him poor. He was a soft touch for artists, artists that tended not to understand finances, theirs, or anyone else's.

Joe was a good cook he had a gift for food; age does not determine ability. If you are good enough you are old enough. Joe was an artist in the kitchen whether it was fish, fowl or pastry. His cooking, his invention and economy impressed Pierre, a man who gave credit were it was warranted. Joe was taken on and his wages agreed and backdated.

Joe had taken to working with food in the same way that Andre and Julian had taken to farm work. While they loved the physicality of the outdoor life, Joe would be found dreaming, staring into the middle distance. His disinterest earned him many a heavy clump around the ear or a kick up the backside and being sent off with his grandfather Henri to make the dinner. Joe liked being with his grandfather, he could live off the land and cook on an open fire. He had taught Joe how to trap and skin a rabbit. Vegetables from a kitchen garden simmered slowly over a low fire with cream and flour to make a thick sauce flavoured with wild herbs and soaked up with country bread. Wind fall apples were stewed and eaten with egg custard. Food tasted better for being eaten in the fresh air. Joe's grandfather loved outdoors, here he showed Joe how to cook hedgehog, caking it in mud and letting it roast in the ashes for hours then peeling away the hardened clay so the spines and the skin came away to reveal the tender succulent flesh. Birds, fish, shellfish, wild berries, vegetables, herbs, flowers were all abundant and free, they also tasted good, fresh and of the earth.

Using this acquired knowledge and experience gained from his grandfather and his mother, Joe conjured up dishes that Pierre had never dreamt of. Country food of Normandy soon fed the faces of the impoverished artists that filled the Hotel. Joe was in his element. He toured the markets and slaughterhouses of the vicinity. Soon he became known in the area, a part of the scene, shopping for the offal and cheaper cuts meat to dress up. His economy saved Pierre money from the kitchen budget, Joe got his cut to supplement Monsieur Dupoirier's ad hoc wage system and the takings from the restaurant grew.

One steaming August morning as Joe made his way to the abattoir he passed some sheep and cows as they were herded down the street. All of a sudden a young bull smelling the stench of death panicked and bolted through the open door of a primary school. The herdsman chased the animal, but it was terrified by the screaming of the frightened children and clambered up the stairs. Fearful laughter and squeals of self-preservation overtook the children as they ran over each other in their excitement to get out of the way. Two herdsmen brought the young animal under control on the upstairs landing. The bellowing beast echoed through the corridor like some mad orchestra as the men, pulling and pushing, managed to get the beast back to the top of the stairs. There was a wild look in the animal's eyes as it confronted this alien environment. The sound of shit and piss as the animal let go sent the children into fits of hysteria.

A slaughter man had been sent for and after he manoeuvred his horse and cart through the crowds outside the small school he produced a long length of rope to attach to the bulls nose ring. As the slaughter man held the rope at the bottom of the stairs the two herdsmen whacked, pushed and poked the bulls' arse. Slowly the animal's front legs were got onto the top stair and more men joined the tug of war. The rope tightened forcing the animal to make the first few steps but its legs not designed for descending stairs caused it to stumble and slip in its own urine. The man on the end of the rope ran out of the way as the ungainly beast crashed down. Mad with pain and fear the young bull thrashed about trying to stand up but one of its legs was broken, its vocal chords strained a shrieked discord, its eyes wide with terror and disbelief. The slaughter man, careful of his safety, came round the animal avoiding its short horns and straddling the beast tied a rope round the bull's shoulders. The other end was attached to his Percheron horse that had been released from the cart, using a lamppost as a lever the horse was led down the street. The horse's head was held as it slowly dragged the bull into the road. Once on the street the struggling animal was dispatched with a single heavy blow from the spike hammer. Blood from the animal's head ran thickly in the gutter as it shuddered with its last breath. The crowd that had gathered, and jostled each other to watch the dramatic execution slowly dispersed with mumbled chatter back to their mundane lives. A few people stayed and watched as the carcass was hauled onto the back of the cart. Horse and cart reunited made their way to the slaughterhouse. The crowd gone, Joe could see down Rue Jacob; a distracted figure caught his eye, a man standing alone, looking vacant, oblivious to what had taken place. Joe recognised the man as the guest from the Hotel, an Englishman. Monsieur Melmoth, who was standing in front of a restaurant he must have just come out of, was crying.

As Joe made his way to the abattoir his thoughts were unaccountably disturbed by the Englishman. A shovelful of sheep lights and intestines had been thrown out of the sliding double doors to keep the flies off the slaughtered meat, the sight of them, warm and steaming on the cobbles, snapped Joe out of his reverie. A pig had just been hung on chains and its throat slit. The blood was being collected in bowls then transferred to a barrel where a man with his arm shoulder deep in gore stirred it so it didn't congeal. Another man poured in quantities of oats and handfuls of salt and pepper. The pig's intestines had been washed and were ready to be filled to make the black pudding. Joe wanted to try a dish using tripe but couldn't resist half a side of pig. It was too much for the D' Alsace but he would cut it up and sell what he didn't need round the doors. He also asked for some black pudding and waited till it was ready.

Back at the Hotel Joe regaled Pierre and the other staff with the story of the bull in the school.

"You should have seen it," he said, at length to the bemused listeners. "Yeah! Maybe you needed to have been there."

His audience unimpressed melted away.

"I'll tell you who was there," Joe continued, "that Englishman who sits in the corner, Monsieur Melmoth."

"He's Irish," said Pierre.

"He's not like any Irishman I've ever come across."

"And you've come across a lot have you?"

"I've met a few at fairgrounds and horse fairs."

Joe was intrigued, the Irishmen he'd seen were rough and ready types. They had dug the canals and now they were all over France laying the tracks for the railways. They were known for their drinking, fighting and roast beef. It was an Irishman called Devlin who had nearly beaten Les Quinnet at Pouville. Andre and Julian had been worried, he was a much smaller man, but ferocious. He carried on fighting long after his cause was lost. His face swollen, wet with blood, tears and snot turned him into a grotesque. This Irishman Melmoth didn't look like a fighter; he had the mannerisms more like some once grand old women, who had fallen on hard times. His face was pasty and podgy. He stood with his hand on his hip holding his cane and gloves in one hand and a scented cigarette in the other. He seemed vaguely familiar, but Joe couldn't imagine where he might have seen him before.

Joe set to work and made a marinade for the tripe and cut it into small pieces. He used a tarragon white wine vinegar and extra virgin olive oil, a squeeze of lemon, some honey, black pepper, sea salt and English mustard ground in a pestle. Plenty of chopped garlic was added and it was left in the cellar with a cloth over it. He then made a batter with cornflour and beer and left it to mature for a few hours. It wasn't needed till the evening.

Just before the dinner Joe spooned some beef dripping, so white it looked iridescent, into a deep pan and fried the tripe that had been coated in the batter. It was served with a creamy onion sauce and new potatoes boiled in mint; parsley was added as a garnish. Albert had always taught him that presentation is as important as the food.

Pierre inspected the plate, before it went out the touch of green of the parsley, the cream of the sauce and the golden brown of the batter.

- "It looks good enough to eat Joe." He tasted a bit. "I'm sure if you cooked shit it would taste like Ambrosia."
- "It looks good, it tastes good and it was so cheap even Dupoirier can afford it, and tonight, Monsieur Chef de Cuisine, when I have been paid I will go out in Paris and be young." Joe added with a smile on his face.

When the guests had eaten Pierre and Joe took what was left and ate it in the restaurant. Melmoth was still sitting in his corner smoking a cigar and his fat white hand cradled a large brandy

- "Compliments to the chef," he said, without turning round.
- "What was it, I hope it wasn't snake?"
- "No Monsieur, It is the speciality of the house, a country delicacy from Dieppe." Pierre replied.

Joe noticed the coat hanging by the door, it had an astrakhan collar. He remembered where he had seen Melmoth before; he was the man wearing that coat in the Hotel de la Ville with Walter that day. Walter had done a drawing of Melmoth, a quick sketch, Joe had seen it in Walter's apartment, and the drawing had a sad pensive look to it. Joe remembered it because it looked like it had no eyes, sunken as they were into its head. He was gaunt then and his hair was long. The hair was shorter now and his face was fat bloated with drink, the coat that had swamped him then now looked like it was made for a much smaller man.

- "Pardon Monsieur, Joe ventured, "Are you acquainted with Monsieur Sickert?"

Melmoth turned his large head slowly and eyed the young man with a quizzical look.

- "And you '*mon brave*' how are you acquainted with Mr Walter Richard Sickert?"

- "I know him from Hotel de la Ville in Dieppe, I used to work there. I saw you there once; I've just recognised your coat."

- "How low can a man go, that his coat is more recognisable than he is," he said as he rose slowly and made his way to the chef's table.

- "It's lucky I still have that coat, most of my other clothes were stolen in Naples."

He sat uninvited and continued in a distracted manner. As he did so, he occasionally used a lace handkerchief to dab a suppurating boil on his neck that was being irritated by his collar.

- "It's a while since I've seen Sickert, although I did write to him some time back, I sent him a poem, not heard from him since, just a thank you note. Of course I understand his reticence it's the artist's role to play with fire, but it is the nature of the element to burn the careless, and it is, after all, contagious and destructive. Walter has danced in the flames and has not yet been consumed. He repaid my kindness to him and his family, with a drawing."

- "I've seen the drawing in Monsieur Sicket's apartment."

- "In his apartment! No whiff of scandal I hope?" Pierre laughed.

- "He was teaching me how to paint."

- "Is that what they are calling it now? Not *showing you his etchings*?"

- "Yes I have seen some of his prints." Pierre laughed more.

- "No I mustn't, Walter has too robust an appetite and never to my knowledge did he dally with the dilly boys. Besides my rudeness may offend you, as I feel it offended Walter. I think I overstayed my welcome in Dieppe. No? I have a vague recollection of Walter mentioning a talented baker's boy, who painted with a natural ability, and baked bread like it was manna from heaven."

- "Oh! He's very good," said Pierre.

- "It's only justice that a baker has recognition above the poet."

Melmoth rambled on in a hypnotic monologue about art, beauty and youth, the glories of Rome, Pompeii, Herculaneum, philosophy, love and death. The speech had the rehearsed spontaneity of an actor. Then he stopped a distant look came into his eyes. He started again,

- "I was in the Rue Jacob today, I saw two boys with their mother, and it reminded me of what I have lost."

He drank their wine as if it were wages and left to find another audience to entertain and drink more from the poisoned chalice. The departure though measured, seemed sudden. Like any good performer he left them wanting more. Pierre was bemused, it was not usual to sit and talk with guests, especially ones who had mutual friends with the under chef. Jean Dupoirier was sitting in the shadows; he must have heard the conversation. There was sadness about him, but no hint of reproach. Instead, he came over and started clearing their table. This was not normal behaviour from the proprietor, Pierre and Joseph were surprised and uncomfortable; the three men finished clearing the table together without a word.

The months ran on from summer to autumn. Monsieur Melmoth was civil with Pierre and Joseph as their relative positions demanded when he was sober and more convivial when he had had, or needed, a drink. He told them the alcohol dulled the pain of an ear infection, but what other hurt or hurts it dulled he didn't say. Over the weeks the ear infection got worse and he took to his bed. There were many comings and goings of visitors, a couple of Englishmen booked into the hotel, but it was Dupoirier who waited on the sick man even to the point of administering injections of morphine. Joseph was touched by his generosity of spirit.

At the end of November as the nights grew longer and took the warmth from the days, a melancholy set in. Everyone in the hotel knew Melmoth's time was coming to an end. The quiet acceptance that accompanies death took up residence. A Passionist monk was sent for, an Englishman. He arrived in his distinctive black, with the cross of the sacred heart pinned to his cassock, to administer the last rites. Melmoth, a Protestant, converted to Catholicism on his deathbed and died later the same day. Apparently it was syphilis, the ear infection was the outward sign of an internal decay that had started many years previously and had exploded with foul smelling debris from every orifice. Dupoirier organised, attended and some say, paid for the funeral. Joe and the rest of the staff thought this odd seeing that Melmoth had left a very large unpaid bill.

Paris was a buzz to a young man whose only ambition was to pleasure. The Exposition Universelle had opened in the April and Joe was one of the crowds of people who marvelled at the spectacle. Gaslight had turned night into day and now there was electricity. The Palace of Electricity with its facade in the shape of a fan lit up a chariot drawn by a horse and a dragon. Backed by the thirty pointed rays of a star, stood the fairy of electricity. 5,700 electric bulbs illuminated the palace on Sundays and holidays. The night was where Joe lived and worked. Electricity was the coming thing. The avenues and boulevards were starting to hum with the sound of electric cars.

Joe had met another young confectioner a Russian called Zee-Zee. Zee-Zee worked in a restaurant on the Boulevard de Clichy. He thought it was stylish to wear his hat at a rakish angle. He bought ties with stripes that matched the slant and started creating dishes that also echoed this penchant. Jelly was placed in a bowl then an edge was tipped till the first colour set, a second coloured jelly was added and tipped in the opposite direction and so on. Zee-Zee was young, flash, brash and confident. Joe thought he was a good enough confectioner but it was his style and panache that made him so popular. After all it was only jelly - he just gave old desserts a different slant so to speak.

It was a new century and the two young men had the most exciting city in the world at their feet. Joe had money in his pocket and was free as a bird. Both young men had an eye for the girls and there were plenty of them looking for a good time. Joe and Zee-Zee took full advantage of the situation; they were often seen at the Follies Bergere. They became friendly with Maurice, a singer, who was the same age as Joe. He would get them in backstage sometimes where the girls paid little attention to the young men and carried on with their dressing and undressing without embarrassment seemingly unaware of the effect it was having. There was a beautiful singer/dancer Mistinguette. She was the pinnacle of their desire. She patted them on the head, and kissed them on the cheek, leaving red lip shaped marks, then left by the stage door to an awaiting Lamborghini.

What the boys needed was something more tangible and the best place for that was at the Exposition. It was the attraction. People from all over the world came to marvel at the pavilions that stood in the shadow of the Tower Eiffel. Both Joe and Zee-Zee were snappy dressers and with their burgeoning facial hair and smart hats they could have been anyone. Young gentlemen up from the country, petit bourgeois, anonymous and reinvented, they played the part. They sat in the shade of the Tower lounging with legs crossed, smoking Gauloise, eyeing the rich young ladies. They played games at guessing the nationality of the different girls. Zee-Zee could recognize a Russian face from a distance, the broad cheekbones and generous smile. He would saunter nonchalantly up to them and feign surprise. Begging their guardians pardon he would engage them in conversation, "Don't I know you from, here or there?" dropping in the odd Russian word or phrase into his perfect French to let them think he was a tourist. Zee-Zee enjoyed his little games but Joe was more serious in his quest, he longed for an intimate relationship.

A month after Melmoth had died Walter visited the Hotel d'Alsace and took Joe on a tour of the seamier side of Paris. Next day Joe awoke with the stale taste of alcohol drying in his mouth, his tongue stuck to his palette, he had a monumental headache going on behind his eyes, and a vague recollection of wild music, people dancing on tables and fighting in the sawdust of a bar room floor. In the afternoon when both of them had recovered enough they went to the gallery Durand-Ruel, Walter had forty two paintings and six drawings in an exhibition. Also in the Gallery were some blurred paintings called *Nypheas* 'water lilies.' They were the work of the avant-garde painter Monet. Walter had arranged to meet Monsieur Degas there and when he arrived they were briefly introduced. Joe was still hung over from the nights drinking; it made the atmosphere in the gallery spiritual. He breathed in the ambience and felt a deep sense of calm. Walter had been good to Joe and Joe appreciated his kindness. He had befriended him as an equal, he praised and encouraged his artistic endeavours, neither his youth nor his lack of breeding were an issue, class didn't enter into it. He introduced Joe to Degas as a fellow artist. Walter would take Joe's advice as readily as he would dispense his own, he valued his opinion, and truth was worth more than flattery. Joe had looked at the paintings in the Gallery, they were indistinct dabs of colour that merged and blended into what was with some imagination supposed to be a pond of lilies. The barriers were down, this was art for the people that anyone could do, and the colours were fresh and bright not like the sombre browns of the old masters. The use of chemicals had made the bright colours cheaper. Joe looked at Walter then at the paintings, although

Walter's palette was limited his paintings still seemed light, the ones he had done over the summer in Venice came to life on the walls of the Gallery. Walter smiled as he discussed the work with Degas. Degas admired Walter's work, praise indeed from a master, but Degas like Monet was growing old and a new generation was already waiting in the wings. Looking at the artists as they talked Joe started to feel uncomfortable maybe they exaggerated the importance of what they did, Walter was just Walter, and some thought him crazy, dangerous maybe, different yes and daring, were these, the ingredients that made up an artist? Like the things Joe put together to make a cake; the flour, the sugar, the eggs, get the right blend, work to a recipe, was a painting just a formula? A painting didn't excite the senses in the same way a pastry did, the fundamental urge to satisfy hunger overruled everything the smell, the taste suddenly these snippets of life that hung on the walls left him cold, it was not his world he needed to get back to reality, he said his goodbyes and left. Walter was staying with another painter Jacques Emille Blanche in Auteuil so he didn't see him again.

Joe was late for work and Monsieur Dupoirier's displeasure was obvious by his attitude of sullen distain, his annoyance was tempered by his regard for Mr Sickert. Pierre's temper was less restrained. Joe disregarded Pierre and transformed his latent desire to paint into one to create great food from that day, and the weeks that followed, saw Joe as an artist with food, the colours the textures, the blend of flavours were all written down in his book. Joe picked up a recipe for coleslaw from a café in Rue Neuchapel that Walter had taken him to. He altered the mayonnaise slightly added a few herbs and made it his own. Joe was not cooking or inventing new dishes and desserts he was painting with food with presentations that fed the eye before the first morsel had been tasted.

One day Joe and Zee-Zee were hanging around the Exposition eyeing the girls, taking a glass of beer in a café, when two attractive girls paraded along the pavement in unseemly high spirits. Their disregard for convention was appealing to Joe.

- "Bohemia," Zee-Zee said.
- "Spain," Joe replied.
- "What makes you think that?" asked Zee-Zee.
- "The yellow scarf. A lot of Spanish girls wear them; you see them in the Rue St Dennis."

Zee-Zee was out of his seat and off. He sauntered up to the girls and introduced himself. The two Spanish girls consented to have a drink. Joe did not have the easy manner of Zee-Zee but as they chatted he offered to take them to the Pavilion de Art Modern. They strolled around the Gallery and Joe impressed them with his knowledge and understanding of the exhibits. He told them about Sickert, when he was working with him in Dieppe and how he had met Edgar Degas and seen Monet's new painting, The Water Lilies. Zee-Zee was incredulous, but said nothing, impressed by his friend's powers of invention. What was more impressive was when one of the girls, Germaine, pointed out a painting of a woman laying on a deathbed who was being comforted by a priest. On the wall hung a large crucifix. It was called 'Last Moments', and signed Pablo Ruiz.

- "He is a friend of mine, "she said, "I'm meeting him tonight in Montmartre, would you like to come?"
- "It seems I am the only one who doesn't know any of the artists here. Of course we'd love to come and meet your friend." Zee-Zee replied for both of them.

That evening saw them climbing the hill to a steamy little bar called 'Petit Pousset,' it was full of Spaniards. The atmosphere was of a party that did not seem so much to have already started more that it had not finished, this was the ongoing fiesta celebrating life, youth and vitality. The natural reserve of the French was missing; Spaniards touched, held and embraced life with abandon.

Pablo Ruiz was about twenty and looked like one of those bare knuckle fighters from Dieppe. He was short and thickly set, he had a black corduroy three piece suit with tulip collar, and his jacket was open as were the top two buttons of his white shirt. The wine and song flowed easily; the air was redolent with the smell of drink and tobacco. The strutting Spanish men seemed to supercharge the atmosphere with their testosterone, as the girls did with their beauty and cheap sweet smelling perfume. Pablo hung on to an attractive girl like she was his possession as he swayed with a drink and cigarette in hand. Joe and Zee-Zee fitted in easily with the Spaniards. As the evening wore on and the revelling slowed and quietened Joe was introduced to Senior Ruiz and his paramour, by Germaine, as a fellow painter.

- "Another artist, Paris is thick with artists there are more artists in Paris than there is dog shit on the pavement."
- "Senor, I am not an artist, I am a confectioner that is my profession. I haven't painted for a long time."
- "Don't apologise, art is not a profession it's a passion," turning, he shouted above the noise to a man with tousled black hair. "Carlos I've found an honest working man who has fallen in amongst artists!" Turning back to Joe he said, "A man who can put food on a plate and has money in his pocket is always welcome among artists."

The noise in the bar drowned out his words as the place moved, it swayed and jumped as it spilt its way into another song. The blurred night slid effortlessly into the cold of a blurred morning. The excitement of Montmartre was as a lure, as were the Spanish girls. Joe became a regular visitor to the cafes that dotted the hillside one of his favourite being La Lapin Agile, just down the hill from the new basilica Le Sacre Coeur. As a consequence Zee-Zee and Joe moved in the same circles as the Spanish artists and over the weeks and months they got to know them well. Germaine, who had introduced Joe to Pablo, was a model. Half Spanish she had a sense of fun more typical among the Spanish than the French. After she had spent some weeks with Pablo she had moved on to his melancholy friend Carlos. Pablo and Carlos were inseparable, like brothers. Pablo the painter and Carlos the painter poet had moved to Paris from Malaga via Barcelona in search of fame and fortune. They had found little of either, just a certain notoriety amongst the bohemians that hung around the artists' quarter. The inevitability of success surrounded Pablo as much as the vulnerability of failure shrouded his melancholic poet friend. Germaine lived with Carlos for a while but his morbidity brought on by the fear of losing her rendered him impotent. Germaine craved joy; Carlos bound up in his jealous misery stifled her, so she moved on. As a butterfly flutters mostly in the sun, she needed to bask in the sunshine of admiration. The loss of Germaine broke his heart.

One evening Joe was in the Hippodrome where Zee-Zee worked. While waiting for him to finish he was surprised to see Carlos. Carlos, he thought, was still clinging to his forlorn love for Germaine but she was in his company with her sister Odette and a few other Spaniards. One of them, unbeknown to Joe, was her new boyfriend, they were having a meal. Joe could see Carlos was in unusually high spirits, he assumed that he was back with Germaine, or was he just drunk again? As Joe walked over to where they were sitting to say hello, Carlos put his hand in his pocket and took out some envelopes, he passed one to each person at the table. He then took out a gun,

- "This is for you," he said as he fired the gun at Germaine.
- "And this is for me," he put the gun to his chest and shot himself.

No one heard the thump of his body as it slid from the table to the floor. Never had the place emptied so quickly. The types that frequented Le Hippodrome did not want to attract the attention of the police. Joe stood transfixed as a couple of waiters raced to assist the victims. Those at the table were open mouthed, too shocked to scream. One waiter, cradling Germaine's head in his arms, turned to where Joe stood.

- "Get them out of here," he yelled, "you get out of here I will handle this."

The young people responded to the order with a sense of relief. The old regulars were left to deal with the gendarmes. Two streets from the bar Joe leaned against the wall. The sweat turned cold on his body in the warm night air as his shaking hand lit a Gauloise. A hot choke of tobacco caught his dry throat and he coughed himself back to the real world. The image of Carlos shooting himself stayed with Joe more so than the shock of the girl lying bleeding on the floor. As he lay in his bed that night, his eyes wide to the ceiling, the sound of the gunshots still rang in his ears.

Next day Le Figaro was still full of the Dreyfus case. The fate of the Jewish Captain didn't interest Joe; he was more interested in what had happened at the Hippodrome. There was nothing in the paper and the restaurant returned to normal. Joe went back to retrieve his hat. It turned out that Germaine, miraculously, wasn't badly hurt, a flesh wound to the neck. The mad poet was dead and, by all appearances, forgotten.

Paris had everything Joe wanted at this time in his life but enough was never enough, his intention had always been to go to England. He wanted the easy confidence of the self-possessed wanderer. Walter had that style, that *panache* which was the currency he used wherever he was, and wherever he was he was charming and esoteric. People found him interesting and good company. The life of someone with a portable skill and a gift for languages was what Joe wanted. His life in Paris he spent on good times and girls. To have them meant he had to work. Fortunately Joe enjoyed his work as much as he loved to play. He developed in his craft, inventing new recipes practising his art with food. He knew he would never go hungry and would never be out of work. The need for his skill was universal he could take it anywhere, when it suited him. Joe wanted to move up the social ladder as well as the hierarchy of his profession. He needed to seek out new masters and to learn from them, he had a thirst for knowledge, an envy that drove progress, and courted disaster.

Joe had a prickly nature; he didn't like being looked down on. He thought his skill demanded respect. Those who disrespected him knew nothing and earned his contempt. He had a temper but could control it. He knew when to stay silent to keep people guessing. The places where Joe hung out had their dangers. Some people liked him others were suspicious of him; even disliked him, maybe he thought, they were jealous of his apparent success, the clothes he wore, his air of confidence, or perhaps his wealth.

His friends and acquaintances seemed to move in patterns that Joe couldn't follow. He enjoyed their companionship but felt different like an outsider. He had the ability to live inside his own head, to be alone in a crowd, content to observe and learn.

His intuition became finely tuned to danger, or prejudice and he walked away from uncomfortable situations preferring to keep his own company, rather than jeopardise his safety. There was more to life than the hedonistic pursuits of the young although much of his time and money were spent pursuing the good life there was something missing, a hollow feeling. He wasn't sure what he wanted. But he knew he needed to save and learn and then when it came along, he would recognise it, and be ready to take advantage. The fine suits he wore were a disguise, the building of an image, inside he was still himself. He had ambition, he wanted to achieve, and with some style. He wanted to be somebody, a person with respect, someone to be looked up to. Regardless of who he might become, he knew he could never lose the essence of who he was, but he was confused as to who he was. Something that Melmoth had once said, stuck with him,

- "You can only be yourself, everyone else is taken."

Joe thought he might move to London, maybe he could fit in, there? The city had a magnetic fascination for him. He had been learning English. An English teacher gave free lessons to anyone who wanted to join his al fresco class next to the fountain outside the Louvre. Certain areas in Paris had become small free academies for those who wanted to learn. Joe took advantage of this brief largesse he knew it wouldn't last for long. His mother always said no one would buy a cow if milk were free. He gained a rudimentary knowledge of English that he honed with the English dancers that worked the burlesque shows in the evenings and haunted the streets at night.

Walter saw Joe when he visited Paris, every six months or so. When they met the talk was of art and artists. Walter's work sold well in Paris, this was no surprise to him he often commented on the poor quality of what he saw in some galleries. He told Joe that he had once been introduced to a painter Paul Gauguin, who had been a stockbroker. Walter said,

- "After looking at his paintings, I told him to go back to the stock exchange."

Life for Joe was easy at the beginning of the new century. He was renting a comfortable apartment and was walking out with a pretty girl called Claire. She had been a waitress at the d'Alsace. Walter introduced her to a wild Welsh painter man with a certain reputation, who was looking for a domestic. He was a portrait painter; his paintings were done quickly with an easy talent. What his mostly English clients were buying into was the scandal, his dramatic style of dress and his outrageous lifestyle. He was married with a house full of children that he also shared with his beautiful raven-haired mistress. His sister Gwendolyn was also a painter and as weird and scandalous as he was. She had had a brief affair with the sculptor Rodin, but as she could not live with the idea it was over, she would strip off stark naked and wait for him in the morning in the garden of his studio. The old man was beside himself. Joe liked her paintings, but they were a bit boring, small, still, quiet and reflective, a bit like she was really. She had spent some time in a convent as a way of recovering from her breakdown. Her brother was generous in his praise for her work. His own paintings, the small ones which he seemed to dash off with no lack of skill and a good deal of bravado, appealed to Joe they were fresh, simple and full of life. His drawings also interested Joe; they were more sensitive and personal than the paintings and demonstrated a discerning eye. Joe sat for him once or twice. Augustus John was dismissive of his own ability, it was all too easy for him, he would rather spend his time in the company of women than work at a painting; painting quickly bored him.

Joe liked Claire and was spending an increasing amount of time with her. Since witnessing Carlos's suicide in the Hippodrome, Joe now avoided the 'low lifes' that hung around Montmartre and the Rue de Clichy. He was concerned about drifting into a relationship but it looked like that was the way it was heading and they started spending the night together. Nights of sweat soaked passion that only teenage desire and abandonment can delight in. As they queued one warm summer's evening outside the Opera House to see Caruso in La Boehme Joe felt a calm contentment, he was basking in the adoration of a pretty young girl who loved him beyond reason. She made him feel like he was somebody, she made him happy. He was not prepared to risk losing that feeling. His desire to hold on to a bachelor's life was waning. She made feel important and needed. Claire was good natured and easy to get along with, he could do a lot worse. Maybe this is what he had been waiting for, what he needed; maybe he needed to be loved?

Although his life was comfortable, thoughts about London still persisted. Now that Claire was working for an English family he thought there was a possibility they could go to London together. He would go to Dieppe and speak to his mother.

As he got off the train he was greeted by the smell of the sea air. The familiar streets of his childhood filled him with nostalgia. He remembered playing here as a boy with Andre and Julian. One time Andre had nearly drowned them when he lashed a raft together out of driftwood pretending to be Robinson Crusoe. They dared each other to steal fish off the old women's fish stalls. He walked round the harbour and the arches of the fish market. The wind-blown noises unique to the shoreline assailed his ears. Tonight he would be out on the town, a free man, unattached, money in his pocket, the local boy made good in the big city. Tonight the circus and fair were in town, there would be lots of pretty girls out and about, he would wear his best suit, and tonight he would own Dieppe.

His mother was pleased to see him, 'the prodigal son'? They swapped gossip stories and recipes. She put on a fine meal of good wholesome country food. Joe's father, Andre and Julian were all initially happy to see him but there was as always a difference between them and they had grown further apart over the years that Joe had been in Paris. Joe took his brothers upstairs to show them his new suit. Andre tried it on, it fitted well, if not a little tight. It looked odd on Andre, his face was nut brown and his hair long and sun bleached. Maybe Andre saw his brother, as a show-off who needed teaching a lesson, or perhaps it was just devilment, but with Joe's best suit on he said, -"This'll do for me," and he and Julian went out.

Joe didn't know what to do; his protestations were met with a laugh as the door was shut in his face. Andre was always handy with his fists and his reputation had grown in recent years, he was a well-respected tough. Joe thought they'd be back soon, joke over? But as the night grew dark a black anger and the pain of betrayal ate into the core of his soul. Joe's parents were angry but resigned to the fact. Joe could not be consoled. His indignation and sense of betrayal was not going to ruin their night so they too went out. He was left alone with his humiliation, a hurt so intense that churned his insides. Joe moved around the room, memorising the shapes and smells that had once been so familiar, ideas of vengeance formulating in his brain, then evaporated. He tried to regain his calm but the wild dogs that chased around his mind kept on returning to stir up his passion. Andre and Julian arrived back in the early hours of the morning, worse for drink and carrying a coconut. Seeing the look on Joe's face had a sobering effect.

- "What have you been crying about you big girl? You want your precious suit back?"

With that Andre took off the suit pulling the legs drunkenly over his boots stumbling back and falling on the floor laughing. No one else spoke; he threw the suit at Joe, trousers then jacket. Joe went upstairs brushed his suit down, folded it neatly and put it in his case on top of all his other clothes. As he was leaving the house his mother asked him to stay.

- "Don't leave with anger and hatred in your heart, they are your brothers".

- "I'll stay tonight but I'll go back to Paris tomorrow."

Joe spent the night downstairs seething with anger, unable to sleep. He could hear the drunken snoring of his brothers through the floorboards. At first light he was gone. He had been so consumed with rage the time had not been right to tell his mother about Claire. The train back to Paris was delayed; the guard told him that some poor soul had decided to jump on the line, so Joe went for a walk to the harbour. He sat on his case, tiredness made him feel unconnected, the sun was shining and a cool breeze was blowing onshore. From the dockside he looked out towards England, the Packet steamer was moored up alongside. The reasoning for getting married was overtaken with trepidation as if the devil didn't want him to be contented. The desire to flee, an impulse to assert himself, started to brood in him. To start again, to forget this humiliation and fulfil his destiny, do what he had always dreamt of. He would show them all. Their envy at his success, he would compound it, rub their noses in it. They need not worry about him and he would not worry about them. Overcome with a sudden excitement he went to the office and bought a one-way ticket to Newhaven. Within the hour the ship was underway. That evening he would be in London.

Chapter Four

London

As Joe walked out of Victoria Station he questioned his own wisdom at ending up alone with nowhere to stay in this foreign capital. He'd been used to speaking English with people who knew him but this was different, everything he said was answered with,

- "What mate!"

They then repeated what he had said back to him.

- "You want the railway station?" "You want a ticket to Aldersgate?"

It seemed they couldn't speak without involuntary movement, be it head, neck, shoulder, arm, legs or feet, turning and fidgeting. Some of them could stand still when they weren't talking so why all the jigging about as soon as they opened their mouths? Instead of making him feel uncomfortable, it made him feel superior; they were the ones who seemed nervous. Although he didn't understand the replies to his questions very well, he was communicating in a different language in a different country and it made him feel good. The smells and the noises were different like the air seemed thinner, he felt different; special, a man of the world.

Joe headed for Camden but ended up in Whitechapel where he found a small café. He looked around to see what the locals were eating. Bacon, eggs, sausage, mushrooms and fried bread seemed to be the order of the day so he sat down and waited for his plate. He watched a short fat woman cook for a while then tried to decipher the words in the newspaper that covered the table. A girl brought him his food,

- "You're new around here aren't you?"

- "Yes."

- "You don't want to be walking around here dressed like that and carrying a suitcase at night. Where're you staying?"

- "I was hoping to find some a hotel."

- "Are you stopping long?"

- "I hope so."

- "I know a woman who's got a room for rent, I'm sure she'd be interested in a respectable gentleman like yourself. She works in the pub round the corner, The Dick Turpin. Ask for Sally Atkinson, just tells her Mattie sent you."

Mattie was as good as her word and Sally took some time off to show him the room. Mrs Atkinson was a widow with three daughters. A respectable woman, as respectable as you could be in Whitechapel. The girls were polite and attending school, but kept their distance with the foreigner, as did their mother. She took a weeks' rent in advance, and gave Joe his own key to the house. She told him there would be a jug of fresh water and a basin in his room and that his chamber pot would be emptied and clean every morning. Joe could come and go as he pleased, but no women were allowed. The odd hours kept by those in the catering trades meant he wouldn't see much of Mrs Atkinson and her 'three graces.'

Myrtle Street was part of a recent development of flats put up for working people of quality. Mrs Atkinson's husband, recently deceased, had been a foreman at the docks before a chain had snapped and caught him on the temple leaving a small bruise on his ashen skin, and a small insurance policy with which to bury him. Mrs Atkinson and her daughters were one step ahead of the poorhouse, her job in the pub and the rent from Joe would keep their heads above water. Although Myrtle St was respectable enough, you didn't have to go far in Whitechapel to find life in its basest form. The streets teemed with every nationality on God's earth. Drugs, drink, prostitution, robbery, murder, all manner of iniquity sat side by side with a goodness only shared by those in the extremeness of despairing destitution. Every drop of happiness was grabbed hold of and drunk down with relish. This was a vibrant community, a society that managed on the fringes of society; it suited Joe's lust for life. He had a little money and few clothes and nothing else. He needed a job. He had heard Walter talk about the Savoy Grill; it was one of the few places he had heard of in London. He woke on his first morning in this strange city put on the suit that was responsible for him being there in the first place, and set off for the West End.

The daylight was just sneaking through the smoky air, as he joined the throng marching at a steady pace taking each member to their respective destinations. His eyes lingered on people to the point of rudeness. He was fascinated by the difference. Everything was new to him; the buildings, the clothes, the smells, the weather. This was a foreign country, a new beginning. Men walked in pairs and chatted, women carried baskets and hurried with some urgency while others stood on street corners with arms folded in studied idleness. Joe's journey took him from the squalor of Whitechapel with the beggars, drunks and prostitutes, through the City to Holborn and on to the

Strand where the marchers became better dressed and good carriages crowded the road. A shop selling silk ties was opening and Joe went in and bought an expensive one with an impressive tie stud. Looking himself up and down in the shop mirror he knew he had bought himself that extra ingredient, an important one. The tie made him feel good, it made him feel confident. The sun was warming the streets when Joe came upon the Savoy.

Receptionists are notorious for looking and acting as if they own the establishment they are fronting. Normally they are aspiring middle class men and you are trespassing on their territory, their look of disdain makes you aware of that. With these preconceptions in mind Joe approached the receptionist who, to Joe's good fortune, was French. Joe asked if there were any vacancies for a confectioner. Claude was a Parisian, but didn't seem to share the same contempt for the rest of humanity that characterised some Parisians that Joe had known. Joe had the optimism of a dreamer, he knew what he was, he was a confectioner, and a good one at that. He didn't seem to understand that other people might be unaware of his ability. After Joe had enquired as to any vacancies for a confectioner, Claude asked,

- "For a trainee?"

- "No! I am a confectioner."

Claude's eye of experience scanned the boy and decided to feed him to soften his disappointment.

- "Have you eaten breakfast?" he asked.
- "No!"

Claude took him through to the kitchen, the interview took place as they walked, it was perfunctory.

- "Where are you from? What is your experience?"

The easy professionalism of Claude gave way to the frenzy of the kitchen. Claude called the breakfast chef over and told him to take the boy's order. He was about to break the news that there were no vacancies when he said,

- "Sorry I wasn't paying much attention before; did you say you worked at the d'Alsace?"
- "Oui."
- "On the Rue de Beaux Arts."
- "Oui."

Claude knew of the d'Alsace.

- "I know the proprietor."
- "Monsieur Dupoirier."

Joe was puzzled as to why a small Hotel in the Rue de Beaux Arts was known to Claude. He put it down to Claude being a Parisian. It turned out that Claude also knew Walter Sickert. Sickert stood out amongst the artists that frequented the Grill, not least because of his impeccable French, convivial manner and exquisite dress sense. Claude was not so impressed by Walter's paintings; he considered them to be dull and seedy. Knowing Dupoirier and Walter Sickert seemed to be reference enough for Claude and, against his better judgment - another confectioner being surplus to requirements, especially one so young - he took him on.

There were mild protestations from the head confectioner, an efficient and practical cockney, but Claude far from being the receptionist was one of the under managers and had no truck with dissent. Millburn, the head confectioner, thought it was form to complain. Far from extra hands getting in the way, what it really meant was that he would have less to do and he liked that. The rest of the kitchen thought that Joe had only been taken on because he was French and that Claude fancied him. No quarter was given; Joe was sent out to buy new whites and started work immediately. In the weeks that followed he kept his head down and the bitchiness that had accompanied his arrival soon evaporated. Joe's output and contribution gradually established him as a member of the team and he gained a grudging respect that developed into admiration.

Claude took an interest in the progress of his protégé and often sent his appreciation of Joe's produce to the patisserie, but was careful in not showing too much interest in Joe himself.

The Savoy, being The Savoy, had a clientele from the upper echelons of London society. Joe was oblivious as to who these people were or what they did, unlike the trainee chef he had befriended. Bob was from Sunderland in the North of England and was always full of himself, he was much more friendly than the southerners and passionate about sport, especially Sunderland's football team, one of the best in the country. He knew everyone that came into The Savoy and held them all in varying degrees of disdain from 'soft southern bastards, bourgeois middle class twats, to the parasitic aristocracy and over-privileged minor royals.' He especially hated the monarchy and saved his most vituperate vitriol for that he called that 'clan of oppressors.'

Joe and Bob lived near each other and Bob educated Joe to his views on society as they walked to or from work. Bob's opinion on the monarchy was that they were an international band of work-shy thieves. He could confide his anarchistic philosophies in Joe because he was a Frenchman and a republican. Bob said that the French had guillotined their King, but we paid our taxes to keep our pampered Princes and Princesses in the lap of luxury while the proletariat struggled and died in disease-ridden slums and that the time will come when the workers will unite and throw off this burden.

Bob told Joe that the Prince of Wales often came to The Savoy with his cronies, 'lickspittles' and hangers-on to a man, whom Prince Edward used to sponge-off and abuse. They tolerated the embarrassment in their misguided belief that some kudos was to be gained by being in the company of the future King of England. This reflected glory tended to ruin those who were stupid enough to entertain this spoilt, 'man child,' the overgrown schoolboy. Even his mother despaired of his immature pranks and wouldn't let the halfwit meddle in the affairs of state. She was of the opinion he was only fit for making himself fat while carousing with his sycophantic acolytes. They entertain his boorish behaviour at shooting parties and turn a blind eye to his inappropriate sexual advances to their wives, daughters and guests.

The Prince was due to dine at The Savoy 'with his merry band of disciples and whipping boys' later in the year. To maintain his patronage it was customary to serve the bored man with something different so he was able to 'enthral his contemporaries that hung on his every ridiculous utterance as though it were sacred text.' Should the offering not please his highness, the perpetrator of his displeasure may not only face his wrath but also might find they were out of work and hiking down the road to lesser employment or worse, no employment. 'Some poor bugger out of work while that over-privileged dirty fornicator of a fat bastard who had some lackey to dress him, draw his curtains, and run his bath for him was kept in the lap of luxury. The time would come and soon when the rest of Europe would rise up and follow the example of the French and dump this discredited bunch. But they will not give up their power and privilege lightly, they will use every devious ruse possible to hang on to what they have taken from the workers, the wealth of the country, earned by the sweat of the working class.' The first country that would overthrow the monarchy in Bob's opinion would be Russia.

And it was true the East End teemed with the disinherited Slavs, Russians and Latvians. The Jews who had fled the pogroms visited on them by the establishment via the hated Cossacks. The social order was changing and Bob wanted to be a part of it. Joe loved to listen to Bob talk of revolution, he learned so many new words as Bob espoused the works of Karl Marx and the virtues of the Communards, but he was a talker, an idealist who spent more time having fun than rousing the workers to rebellion. Bob had arguments and conversations with loyalists, patriots and revolutionary anarchists, but his was a good-humoured banter that was rarely taken seriously as he said it with a smile and a laugh in his voice. Joe liked his company and that sharp edge that surrounded him. Joe didn't question the contradictions that Bob presented and when he did there was always a reasoned or amusing riposte.

As Bob had said the Prince of Wales and his crowd had booked a table for dinner at the beginning of the London season. A team from the kitchen was assembled to produce a meal fit for a future King. Exotic fruits and vegetables were sourced, novel ways of combining different flavours were explored, and opinions were sought as to the Prince's likes and dislikes. This was the time when reputations were made and lost. The head confectioner, Millburn, shirked the responsibility with the excuse that someone else should be given the opportunity for glory. Whereas the French enjoy other peoples' success the English with their Teutonic blood enjoy other peoples' failure. What rankled with Joe the most was the penny-pinching meanness of the English. If they could get away with using margarine instead of best butter, or single cream where the recipe asked for double, the answer was always 'no one will know', but he knew! Or, 'no one can tell the difference,' but he could! Meanness to Joe was ugly and dishonest and the most ugly and dishonest were those on the make. Those obsequious creeps with lots of pretensions and little ability that feed off the backs of the more able, and when they have extracted their nourishment they use them as stepping stones, not giving a backwards glance as they move on to satisfy a hunger that can never be sated. Joe would make the dessert. If it was a success the head confectioner would take the credit. If it were a failure Joe would get the blame.

So the mantle of responsibility was passed to Joe, the young inexperienced flash, fly-by-night, Frenchman. He was given a free hand and he assembled ingredients of quality with which to experiment. Although each experiment surpassed the last they didn't satisfy the young man, besides, he was enjoying the celebrity. Each refinement was still a variation on a theme and Joe wanted to create something new, different and surprising. The team eventually settled on the sorbet that Joe had come up with, served with exotic fresh fruits and cream.

Joe's best ideas came in the morning just before he woke. On the morning of the dinner he leapt out of bed wide awake with an idea so outrageous he had to write it down before he forgot. His suggestion to the other confectioners was so strange they thought it was some kind of Gallic joke. It was agreed to let Joe try it as an experiment after the sorbet. The evening came and the dinner was a riotous success. Joe's assembled team of confectioners were well drilled in the making of the sorbets and they emerged from the oven high and light with a perfect top. A triumph by anyone's standards but the *coup de grace* was to follow. Each of the three confectioners given to do Joe's bidding had their tasks; one had organised the making of the sponge bases that came out soft and light with that melt in the mouth golden brown texture. The fruits were those that had been chosen for the sorbet but soaked in fine French Cognac infused with oranges and demerara sugar to make syrup. Joe had bought in the finest Italian ice cream he could find, it lay in the cold darkness of the ice-box waiting its turn in the ensemble. Joe whisked the meringue to perfection. The oven was pre-heated and the dessert was assembled with military precision. The fruit salad was placed on the sponge base, the syrup soaked into the cake and the ice cream was spooned on top followed by the meringue. The trick was to cook the meringue without melting the ice cream. After a short blast in the hot oven the dessert emerged. The top had stiffened; the peaks of the meringue Joe quickly browned off a sprinkle of sugar with a plumbers blow torch, he drizzled Cognac on the top and lit it. It was taken to the table, flambé. When the fire died out and the Prince drove his spoon into Joe's creation his astonishment was obvious. He called for the confectioner and Joe went out to meet the Prince. The lavish praise from the drunken Prince and the applause from his companions were well-meant and well-received. Joe's face was wreathed in smiles as he surveyed the opulent surroundings. The applause from his co-workers as he returned to the kitchen made his heart swell, he had arrived, his reputation was secure, he was on top of the world, there was to be no going back. Later that year Queen Victoria died and King Edward V11 took the throne.

The cabs from 'Up West' passed Joe and Bob as they walked home from work, the anonymous occupants eager to sample the wicked pleasures of the night. Joe and Bob stopped off at different pubs on their way home and soon became 'faces' in the area. They were offered the things young men with money in their pockets get offered. If a pretty young woman who looked clean and needed some help with the rent, Joe would sometimes oblige. There was often a baby and a grandmother about, which dampened his ardour somewhat. Bob was less particular and spent freely regardless of the dangers of syphilis. Joe remembered Melmoth in Paris and his horrible death. Joe was a sensitive person and although he hadn't known anything about Melmoth, the manner of his death had scared him; it also made him feel strangely sad, in a regretful way, diminished almost. It seemed odd that the drunken Irish gentleman seemed to engender kindness from strangers, but was never spoken of by Sickert, who was his friend and kinsman. Melmoth's death had affected Joe in such a way that he was particular about the company he kept.

Joe had another diversion, as well as a young man's appetite for the company of women. He, like Bob, was keen on all types of sport and liked a bet. Bob had introduced Joe to a card school run by some eastern Europeans. Both of them enjoyed a gamble on the cards and spent many an evening sitting with strangers, winning or losing as the hands were dealt. Joe was a good card player and a sensible gambler, when he lost he lost only his stake and stopped playing till he'd saved it up again. When he won he'd put his winnings to one side to buy a new suit, good cuff links or maybe a cravat or have a night out at the theatre. He only played with his stake. Over time he acquired the trappings of a gentleman the types he saw dining in the Savoy. He had the watch and chain, the walking cane, the silver cigarette box and the hip flask. When the opportunity arose Joe and Bob would take in a race meeting at Epsom or Sandown Park. Joe would look forward to these occasions and spend like a sailor. Hung over, successful or not, Joe was reliable and never missed a shift. He enjoyed work, he enjoyed the company, the banter, he enjoyed life, he drank it in and wanted more. The card school that Joe and Bob attended had regular players and regular nights. Some of the players were young men but mostly they were older; Russians, Latvians, Chinese immigrants. Joe often bumped into the Slavs in Whitechapel library. There was a Jewish librarian who spoke

Yiddish with them. Joe understood a bit of Russian and was picking up some Yiddish. Some of the Russians spoke French although at cards the common language was English. The Slav drinkers drank vodka but the serious players like the Chinese, of whom there were a few, stuck to glasses of tea from a samovar on the sideboard. The air was always thick with the aromatic Balkan Sobranie, Black Russian and Turkish tobaccos. Joe's eyes would sting with the smoke as he left in the early morning, the daylight blinding his eyes. The early morning air would freshen his clothes as he walked to work. If he had played well his pockets jingled with the night's winnings.

The Slavs always seemed to have money but didn't appear to work apart from one man, Jacob Peters, a Latvian who was married to an English girl. He worked in an import-export business. Jacob didn't play cards but was often about; he was short and stocky with a pug nose. He had the undistinguished face of a peasant, but his gaze was that of the uncompromising hard man. Behind his dangerous eyes you could detect a fierce intellect at work. There was a Russian, a gambler, Peter Piakow, a painter who had studied in Paris. Joe had always been attracted to painters and when he found out that they had something in common they struck up a friendship of sorts. Peter was older and charming and, although he talked a lot, he never said a great deal except when he was talking about his paintings, paintings he never showed to anyone. He and Joe went to some galleries together. Peter said he found the pictures in the National Gallery to be stiff and brown, lacking in the vitality of the more modern work he had seen in Paris. The Impressionist colours he observed were more vibrant, brighter, the brush strokes were livelier and the subjects more accessible than the allegories and mythologies of the old Italians. Whereas Joe loved the old paintings and was in awe of their technique and style he thought it wiser to keep his own counsel. To him one type of painting wasn't superior to another, they were just different - coming from a different time, a different place, a different thinking.

Bob noticed this developing friendship between Piakow and Joe. There were plenty of dodgy people in Whitechapel but the Slavs ran the show. Bob had a suspicious nose and it was twitching. Hanging out with the Russian was a dangerous game and he warned Joe not to get too involved. Joe didn't have to wait long. The regular Wednesday night card game was in full swing when Joe arrived at two. By three he was well ahead and by five he was in bed drunk and penniless and Peter Piakow had his I.O.U. for £5 in his pocket. Bob and Joe talked about it at work, the samovar was spiked and the Russians had cheated. Joe confronted Peter that night. In a forthright manner he told Peter what he thought, stopping short of saying that they had cheated. Peter's friendliness was disarming but he was uncompromising.

He told Joe that he knew what he was doing and to take responsibility for his own actions. But to show Joe there were no hard feelings he asked Joe to do him a favour.

There was a race meeting at Kempton Park that week and Piakow asked Joe to place some bets for him at the track. He personally couldn't make it as he was going to a funeral. Peter said he could have ten percent of the winnings and when he gave him fifty pounds Joe's disbelief was tangible. It was too risky and when he refused the fifty pounds Peter persuaded Joe to take ten. Gambling with someone else's money and getting paid for it appealed as much to Bob as it did to Joe. The meeting was a success. Peter knew his horses better than he knew his paintings. Three out of the five came home and the two that lost were short odds and low stakes. The ten pounds had turned into thirty. Joe had taken advantage of Peter's tips and turned his ten percent into twelve quid. Bob had done better and made twelve pounds two shillings and sixpence. The pair of happy gamblers rolled into Whitechapel in a cab, suited and booted, both smoking cigars. Their conspicuous display of wealth, and obvious good humour as they made their way to the door of the Rising Sun was brought to a halt as Joe received a smack on the head from behind with a blackjack, knocking him senseless. Both he and Bob were robbed of their money.

A cynic might think that this attack which relieved the boys of their cash might well have been pre-planned. The Rising Sun was the designated meeting place to pay Peter his share. Bob had taken a beating but was fit enough to get Joe back to Myrtle St.

Mrs Atkinson was terrified by the Russians that came knocking at the door that evening. She showed them up to Joe's room. Peter stood over the bed and explained the situation. He wanted his stake money and the gambling debt. The alternative was Joe could do another little job for him. After they had gone Joe lifted himself into a seated position, his head hurt but his mind was clear. Whitechapel was a dangerous place, anyone could have robbed him, but in his heart he knew he had been set up. Peter wanted to own Joe for some reason, but to Joe freedom was his life; he didn't want to become one of them, to be used by them, part of their game, whatever it was? He knew what he had to do and he had to do it now, while the anger and indignation gave him the strength of the foolhardy. He got out of bed and inspected his suit. The sight of the blood on his collar increased his anger. The back of his jacket was covered in dirt off the road where he had fallen. He instinctively felt the gash on his head where the blood matted his hair. The cold water of the basin turned blood brown. If he was to meet his doom, at least he thought he may as well dress up for it. He took out a fresh shirt, high collar, and a clean suit. He stood in front of the wardrobe mirror, gloves in hand, his black cane under his arm and took out his silver cigarette case. He lit a cigarette and drew deeply on the smoke, it made him feel dizzy and sick. There was a knock on the door and Mrs Atkinson let herself in. She apologised for what she was about to say and told him he would have to go, she gave him back last week's rent, she said she did not want the likes of that Russian gentleman turning up at her house, not with her being alone with three daughters. Joe asked her what she knew about the Russian. She didn't know anything about him in particular, but she knew the Russians in the East End were responsible for most of the crime, the burglaries, bank robberies and street crime.

- "That's who'll have turned you over," she said, "You'd best go to the police."

Joe asked her to pack up his clothes saying he'd be back for them later adding that if he didn't come back she was at liberty to sell them.

- "Don't do anything stupid," she pleaded, "Go to the police."

Joe picked up the money from the table, counted it and gave her half back. Her eyes were wide and her face flushed he could sense her heart beating, pumping the blood into her red lips her chest heaved, she was breathless with anxiety. She was a young woman, in her twenties, Joe hadn't noticed how attractive she was, more so in her excitement. Joe's anger made him reckless and he grabbed her by the waist and pulled her towards him, he kissed her passionately on the lips, running his fingers through her hair holding her close and tight. Her lips fused with the pulsating blood, he could now feel her heart beating through her tight bodice. Both of them became enthralled in the passion of the moment, he pushed her back against the wardrobe mirror, his hands lifted her full black skirt and petticoats and loosened the bow around her waist, her cotton drawers fell to the ground. With one hand on her bare buttocks, the other unloosened his trousers and he entered her moist warmth, lifting her off the floor. The thrusting was short and fierce; she put her fist into her mouth to quell the yelps of uncontrolled climax as he pumped into her. Her shoe fell off and clunked on the floor. She thought the sound might disturb the sleeping children but didn't care or move except to heave a sigh, the release of long pent up frustration. As he let go she was panting, she smoothed down her dress and picked up her clothes as Joe put himself straight. Joe's plans had changed somewhat. He told her to get her mother to look after the children for a few days. He wrote an address on the back of one of his cards and told her to meet him there at two and to bring his suitcases, he told her again,

- "If I don't turn up sell my clothes."

- "Go to the police or run away please," she begged, "these Russians will kill you."

He combed his hair, kissed her on the forehead and went out the door.

What he had to do, he had to do now, and on his own, there was no Andre to sort it out for a few francs. What could he have said to the police? He had the same distrust of the police that all foreigners have. He didn't want to answer their prying questions or have them waste his time. He had to strike while his temper still gave him courage. He reasoned that the Russians had no reason to kill him; they wanted to use him, take money from him, and milk him like he was their cash cow. Joe was not prepared to be used, to suffer extortion, to be frightened into giving them money; his purposeful stride took him through the crowded street at a pace. He only saw the space in front of him, as he muttered his words of self-encouragement under his breath his concentrated determination was interrupted; Bob was calling him from across the road.

- "Joe! Joe! Joe!"

Dodging the horses and carts he danced between the traffic and people. He hauled Joe's shoulder to a halt.

- "What the fuck do you think you're doing man? These bastards will fucking kill you"
- "No they won't, they've got no reason to"

- "I know these people, they don't need fucking reason they'll do it for fun. You go there and you'll not only give them a reason you'll give them their fucking entertainment. At least let the coppers know what you're doing. I know this copper from Sunderland. Slip him a few shillings; he and his mate will have a walk down the road with you."

Joe was touched by Bob's concern and waited 'till he fetched the two policemen back with him.

- "I've told them what it's about; they've got no liking for the Russians. Give them two bob and they'll walk down the road five minutes after you've gone in the house."

Joe gave the Peelers a couple of shillings and set off again, this time more slowly breathing deeply through his nose. He turned and tipped Bob a wink as he disappeared around the corner of the pub, the 'Coach and Horses', and into Sydney Street.

Ivan who rented the upstairs apartment in Sydney Street used it as a drinking and gambling club, for Russian and Slav expatriates. The place was always busy with comings and goings day and night. Joe was recognised by the man looking out the window and the door was opening for him as he got to the top of the stairs. The smell from the broken gas mantle that burnt continuously made him light-headed and as nausea gagged in his throat, he took in the stale smoky atmosphere peopled with the pale ghosts of men who rarely saw daylight. Across the room Piakow was talking earnestly to Jacob Peters. Joe walked over to where they were. A silence followed his every echoing step. Peter looked up and smiled.

- "You've come to pay me!" he said.
- "No, you spiked my drink; you cheated me at cards and set me up at the race track like a patsy, then had me mugged. I owe you nothing and that's exactly what you'll get from me."

Calling a man a cheat, even when it's true, is not always the best thing to do, especially so with a man with Peter's reputation.

- "Sit down Joe"
- "No!"
- "Sit down." Peter repeated in a casual friendly manner that took Joe off guard and he reluctantly pulled up a chair and sat down.

Looking around the room all eyes were on him, he was going nowhere and this sudden realisation hit him square in the pit of his stomach. Peter took out a Colt 45 revolver from a drawer in the table.

- "We are going to play a little game." he said as he emptied the bullets out of the barrel.

He showed Joe one bullet before placing it in one of the empty chambers. He spun the barrel and put it in the middle of the table.

- "You go first, you like to gamble don't you Joseph? If you win you owe me nothing. If you lose you owe me nothing. If you don't want to play I double your debt. If you don't pay you know what I'll do."

- "No you'll have to explain that one to me."

Joe turned his head to look at the time on the mantle clock, the minute hand ticked round another notch.

- "I owe you nothing," Joe repeated as he leaned forward eyeballing Peter intently, "And before you say anything," his finger pointing in Peter's face, "Get your man over there to take a look out of that window."

Joe's finger moved to indicate the man by the window. Peter moved his head and gave a slight nod to the man by the drape. He pulled it across and said,

- "Polizia."

The gaslights were already being dimmed as Joe picked up the gun and threw it at the window. The glass shattered and in the confusion he was out of his seat, across the room and out the door. He bounded down the stairs two at a time and into the street. Bob was there,

- "Come on," he yelled as they made off as fast as they could run, the two policemen were running just as fast in front of them.

The fine drizzle cooled Joe's face as he raced round the corner, his heart pounding in his ears and the blood throbbing in his split head. No one had followed or chased them but there was urgency about them as they climbed into the hansom cab that took them 'Up West.'

- "What the fuck did you achieve by that you mad frog bastard?" Bob finally spat out through gasps.

They both laughed, shaking with relief, while glancing out of the window in their nervousness.

- "I tell you what mate, there's a collier leaving St. Catherine's dock tomorrow, I know some of the lads on it and I'll be on it on the eight o'clock tide. If you fancy it I'll see you there, it's called the Isis."

- "I think I'd rather be on the Thames at eight in the morning than be in it at eight at night." was Joe's reply.

- "Good on you man, I'm going to pick up some stuff and go there now." Bob said as he jumped out the cab.

- "Been a hell of a day mate, catch you later."

The hell of a day wasn't over for Joe yet as the cab trotted its way to his rendezvous with Mrs Atkinson.

Joe left her warm bed early to make his way to the docks, suitcase in hand. He'd left Mrs Atkinson with some money for her trouble and the promise to get in touch when he found out where he was.

Time was getting on as Joe struggled his way through the crowds to the Savoy. His heart was beating in his chest again as he took a cautionary look around the corner. Outside the staff entrance to the kitchen stood two well-dressed men with broad cheekbones and small eyes. He gingerly made his way round the side of the building and knocked on the kitchen window. It was opened and Millburn helped him as he climbed onto a couple of crates to get in.

- "Where've you been for the last couple of days, we thought you were dead?"
- "I nearly was mate." And he related the story.

Claude was sent for. Joe explained the situation and asked to be paid-up-to date. Claude sorted out the money and asked Joe how he was going to get out.

- "Through the front entrance?"
- "No! There are strangers loitering out front as well."
- "But they are expecting me to come in, not to go out."
- "Maybe, I'll get the cleaners to swill the entrance, carelessly, as they splash those men's feet you walk out, don't run. Best of luck". He shook Joe's hand.

Joe stood in the foyer and waited his moment. Claude hailed him a cab and as the cleaners splashed water around the feet of the men outside, Joe walked out, suitcase in hand, the cab door was opened. As Joe waited for the driver to start the engine he lit a Gauloise, his hand was steady, he turned and looked at the men as the taxi pulled away. The two men outside made a point of complaining to Claude about the lackadaisical attitude of his cleaners without a trace of European in their accents.

The docks were heaving as he looked for the ship, Isis, amongst the mass of boats loading and unloading along the quayside. Above the noise and shouts Joe heard Bob's familiar northern accent calling him,

- "Joe, Joe! Where've you been mate?"

Joe threw his bag onto the boat and jumped on; as the ship started to move away from the mooring. The Isis edged its way down the Thames, to the open sea.

The crew consisted of the captain, his mate, an engineer and a couple of stokers, small well-muscled men, shirtless and black with coal dust. Joe took in the grey land blanketed under its grey sky. The monochrome picture painted in a watery mist. Hot tin mugs of sweet milky tea burnt Joe's mouth as they sat in the cabin full with the smell of coal, heat and smoke. They played cards, drank whisky and told stories. Joe told Bob about the Russians outside the Savoy, Bob seemed perplexed, but made no comment. He removed his shirt and took a shift with the stockers, Joe offered, but as a paying passenger the crew wouldn't hear of it. That night Joe and Bob slept on the floor of the cabin, they woke up stiff, cold and sickish with the motion.

The whisky had made his mouth dry and there was the acrid taste of coal smoke on his lips. Joe cleared his sore head by washing his face in cold water on the deck and breathing in the early morning mist. Breakfast was good, bacon, egg and sausage. The taste mixed with salty air was fantastic. It tasted of escape, salvation, freedom.

The collier made slow progress as the hull was stowed with crates of tin toys from Hamburg. There was no point in making the journey back unloaded, so the crew made a few extra quid, as well as the money they made from their two passengers, by taking another cargo back with them. Some of the colliers shipped barrels of urine to be dropped off in Yorkshire, to be used in the making of alum. The Captain used to tell the crew it was wine but everyone knew by the smell. The joke was that they were taking the piss out of London.

The steel grey sky followed them up the coast. The afternoon saw them passing Middlesbrough and the Hartlepools. Before long they were turning between the two new piers into Sunderland.

Sunderland appeared to be part of the sky in its greyness, shrouded in a ghostly fog that muffled the sounds that came in and went out of focus as the Isis slid by, sucked, as it seemed up that deep river, inexorably onwards. Joe had seen working towns and ports before but not like this one. Built on the sea with one route in and one route out there appeared to be no distinction between the areas where people lived and worked. Houses stood next to shipyards and people lived in the docks, their washing and children intertwined with the forges hammering and horses hauling. Joe stood on the deck his hair stiff with sea spray and took in the sights and sounds of this hive of activity. This was the engine room of the British Empire, this was where the ships were built and where the coal that fuelled them was hewn and sent round the world to the coaling stations in the South Pacific, St Helena, Gibraltar, and The Azores.

The small boat made its way up the centre of the river, the heart of this twenty four hour town. They passed under the famous bridge made totally of iron, this modern piece of architecture held Joe in awe, fascinated as he was by the lattice of its structure that patterned the sky. It reminded him of the Eiffel Tower only not as big but infinitely more useful.

Within what seemed like moments they had cleared the industry and could see some green fields of Southwick and Deptford straddling the river. The boat docked at Ayre's Quay, was secured and the men marched up the hill with indecent haste, eager to spend the extra cash their impromptu guests had provided. The men of the ship Isis were known to like a drink and before long they were bending their elbows as quantities of warm brown Vaux's ale was disappearing down their necks. After they'd slaked their thirsts they drifted off to their families.

Joe ended up falling asleep in the chair next to the fire in Bob's mother's house. Bob's mother Elsie looked like a mother should, short, round and wearing an apron. The house was close to the Ship Isis pub. As Joe was to find out everything in Sunderland was close at hand. Joe woke up to the smell of home baking. He was next to the warming fire of the blackened range.

"Here's a cup of tea son?"

Mrs Hill placed a mug of sweet white tea and a stotty cake stuffed with ham and pease pudding on the cracket next to the fire. When Joe had finished his 'bit bait,' Bob came in and said he'd been sorting a few things out. Now it was time to catch up with a few old mates and he hurried Joe along. It was Friday night and there was some serious drinking to be done. They trawled around the taverns and alehouses, on a pre-determined route, where the entertainment was as wild and spontaneous as the laughing and the flirting. The openness of the people cheered Joe and filled him with hope, he'd found a safe haven and the fears and the worries that had beset him of late melted away. This was a new beginning, for the first time in his life he felt like he belonged, he'd found a warmth and friendship, a home. The grass appeared greener in the North.

Chapter Five

Sunderland

Joe soon fitted into his new lifestyle. His digs were in Salem Street, just on the prosperous side of High Street East. He had a new job at Edward Binns, an up-market department store with an expanding bakery and restaurant that catered for weddings and the like. Ships captains and their families, who occupied the desirable properties of Hendon, frequented the place. Having a French confectioner added kudos to the establishment, and Joe's gateaux were a big hit with the ladies of the town.

On Sundays, in the summer evenings, the promenade along the sea front was the place to be, people thronged the Cliffe Park in their Sunday best especially the young and available, where it acted as a marriage mart. Joe and Bob found this a delightful pastime, eyeing the young women who walked slowly and primly along the cliff top, apparently oblivious of the attentive males. One such evening a gaggle of what looked like sisters strolled past the bench where Bob and Joe were seated. One of the sisters looked back over her shoulder; the quick glance was followed by a huddle of heads and the audible, "It's him."

- "I think I'm in there Joe me old son," said Bob."

The girls had stopped and the, 'should I, should I not' body language was resolved when the one who'd looked back came over to Joe.

- "Excuse me but are you the baker from Edward Binns' restaurant?" she asked.

It turned out that Rose - she wore a brooch that had her name in gold letters on black onyx - and her elder sister Polly were in service to a Miss Lomax in Athenaeum Street. They saw him every day as he passed on his way from work. Rose made sure she saw him every day.

- "Oh!" Joe exclaimed as he realised who she was, "You're the girl who knocks on the window and waves."

Soon the two young men were engaging the elder sisters in conversation as they all walked towards the tram stop at the top of Sidecliffe Road.

Rose was a petite girl, verging on pretty but more the handsome type with strong features and a determined look to her eye. She had an air of confidence, a cheeky cockiness that compensated for her lack of height. She had been beguiled by the cut of Joe, as he had walked past Miss Lomax's basement window, always fashionably dressed. Now she was smitten by the sound of his voice with its lilting French accent. Joe could sense the effect he was having and spoke French on purpose, as Rose was about to board the tram.

- "Rose, voulez vous promener avec moi ce Dimanche?"
- "Yes!" She replied as she leaned back from the platform holding on to the pole and with one hand on his shoulder kissed him on the cheek.

Rose sat next to her sister Polly, who was shocked by her sister's boldness; all the girls were a buzz.

- "Eh! Our Rose you should be ashamed of yourself coming on to a stranger like that. What did he say to you?" Polly asked.
- "I don't know, something in French but he'll be there next week"

He was there next week and the week after that, on the third week Rose had permission from her parents to invite him for tea.

The Madden family lived across the Silksworth Row near the pub the Ship Isis. They had two houses in the Ayre's Quay

Road, numbers eight and nine. Paddy and Mary lived in number eight with their ten children, Rose was the seventh. The house overlooked the Gill Cemetery towards Bishopwearmouth Church. Number nine was rented out for extra income. The Madden house had a front parlour behind which was a large bedroom. The kitchen was at the rear of the house with another bedroom above it, in the yard was the washhouse and the toilet.

Joe was shown into the parlour, a small coal fire burnt in the heath and the round table with a white tablecloth on it was set for four. Rose's mother Mary brought in a tray of tea and cakes followed by Paddy Madden, uncomfortable in a shirt and tie. Both Paddy and Mary were Irish and spoke with a brogue that Joe found difficult to understand. The stilted conversation and stiff surroundings were to no one's taste. The atmosphere was lightened by the impish inquisitiveness of Kitty, the youngest child who came in on the spurious pretext of telling her mother something. The timorous approach of the youngest was followed by the bolder interruption of the two eldest Hugh and Jimmy. They introduced themselves and said that they were going over the Ship for a pint.

- "Do you take a drink Joe?" Hugh enquired.

Joe had his seat pulled back, napkin off and was down the road taking his first draught within minutes.

- "Seems like a nice enough fellow?" observed Paddy.

Jimmy and Hugh were about the same age as Joe and the young men got on well. Two other brothers Jack and Joe turned up to get their father a jug of beer and they all went back to Ayre's Quay Road. This time, Joe was marched straight down the long corridor into the kitchen, the heart of the house. The kitchen seemed small, packed as it was with an assortment of people of various ages. As well as Jimmy, Hugh, Joe and Jack there was Polly, Tommy, Harry, Lizzie, Annie, and Kitty. There had been an Agnes, but she'd died a couple of years previously. A coal fire was burning in a large, lead black, iron range as the chatter was tossed back and forth in the cosy room, a bottle of Bush Mills was passed round, and Rose started playing the piano accordion. The comfort of the room, the drink and the music made Joe sleepy; he had an early start next morning as much as it grieved him to leave the burgeoning party he bade his farewells. Before he left he asked Paddy if he could take Rose to a show at the Garrison Field the following Saturday.

- "You can get three tickets, Polly would like to go as well." he replied.

Joe had no problems getting the tickets for 'Buffalo Bill and his Wild West Show'; the cowboys wore outfits that Joe thought very southern French. There was trick riding, and trick shooting from a cowgirl called Annie. The climax of the show was when the Redskins in war paint, with headdresses made of feathers came a whooping and a hollering and attacked the wagon train. When all seemed lost, in charged Buffalo Bill Cody to the rescue, his long blonde hair flowing behind him, and his Indian fighters firing their guns in the air, the Indian Chief, Sitting Bull, was captured and paraded around the arena. Joe thought it was all a bit tame; there was more excitement down the East End on a Friday night. Polly and Rose were overcome with excitement. Rosie would have got up and joined in given half the chance.

It was still light when they left, a glorious summers evening, and they strolled down the Crowtree Road to the Italian ice cream parlour. Joe ordered ice creams for the girls and an iced coffee for himself. The ice cream came in many colours with chocolate and nuts in a tall glass. A glass with ice in it was placed in front of Joe and a small hot black coffee. He lounged in his chair, one arm draped over the back tapping his cane nonchalantly on the floor. The girls were staring at him.

- "Aren't you going to eat?" he enquired.

They started with their long spoons. It became obvious to Joe that they were not used to eating in such establishments. Joe poured his coffee over the ice in the glass and drank it down in one. They were staring again. Joe took hold of Rose's hand and fed himself the ice cream on her spoon. He nodded his head as an expert might.

- "It's good ice cream."

The girls ate in silence overwhelmed by the reverence of the place, when they had finished Joe took out his Gauloise and offered them round. Polly was startled and shook her head vigorously. Rose leaned forward and took the cigarette. Joe struck a match and held it out as Rose leaned forward and lit the white tube held firmly between her reddening lips. Polly was aghast.

- "Come on Rose we'll have to go, thanks very much Mr Delaroche, the ice cream it was very nice, thank you."
- "I'll see you outside Polly," said Rose as she blew smoke out of the side of her mouth as though she'd done it before.

The glow of excitement had nothing to do with the smoking and everything to do with the daring. The clientele of the ice cream parlour stared and whispered at the affront, which added to Rose's thrill.

Alone they talked about the show and America; Rose said she hoped it wasn't like that in America because her auntie lived there. When she'd finished her cigarette she leaned towards Joe and whispered in his ear.

- "Next time you take me out I'll ditch our Polly."

She thanked him for the evening and the ice cream and with that she was up and away.

As the girls set off for home and Polly started, Rose stopped her in her tracks.

- "Listen here 'Holy Mary' if you say anything to anyone I'll punch your face in."

Joe had taken a fancy to Rose. For Rose it was much worse, from the moment she had seen him pass Miss Lomax's window she'd wanted him and she was determined to have him. The summer evenings on the prom and the trips to the theatre were followed by regular visits to Ayre's Quay Road. Mary Madden was a good cook, Joe soon had her recipe for soda bread and it sold well in Edward Binns restaurant. Joe loved the simple Irish country fare that Mary served up, it reminded him of meals in Normandy where the rich sauce from slow cooked casseroles were mopped up with warm crusty fresh baked bread. He especially liked the mushroom, chicken and rabbit stew with the pastry top. He also liked pan hegarty with its lamb chops, sausages and pearl barley. The seafood was always a favourite, often brought up to the house by one of the lads, the fish still swimming in the bucket. Country folk always knew how to find free food, be it caught, picked or poached. The bunch of canny lads at the Maddens made sure there was always plenty to go round. Joe was very appreciative of the hospitality and his praise was genuine. He never interfered in the kitchen. There was a strict demarcation between his work and his leisure, he also thought it would have been an insult; he wouldn't have wanted anyone interfering in his kitchen. The evenings at the Maddens became more frequent and relaxed. Rose's brothers became Joe's friends, drinking 'marras', and they and Bob Hill made for a regular crew.

Paddy had come over from Ireland to work down Lord Londonderry's mine at Seaham Harbour, with his brother Owen. Neither of them had cared much for underground work and Paddy moved on to Sunderland where he got a job at the Water Board where he'd worked for over thirty of his fifty odd years, so many years that everyone knew him as Paddy the Waterman. Owen married a girl from Crook who'd inherited a small farm near Willington and moved over that way.

Paddy loved his music, most of his children could knock out a tune on something or other with varying degrees of success, but Rose was a star on the piano. She could hold a tune in her head that she'd heard at the Gaiety or the Avenue and reproduce it on the piano an hour later. Rose and Joe made a handsome couple as they walked out together. Him, the suave Frenchman in his London tailor-made pinstripes, pin-tucked and pleated white silk waistcoat, straw hat, silver-topped cane and spats. Arm in arm with the raven-haired wild Irish colleen, the seventh child of Paddy the Waterman. To the Maddens Joe was the height of respectability, and so he was, up their west end of the river.

Down the east end, in the bars and the dives down by the docks, it was a different story and Joe and Bob didn't mix the two. Sunderland was a cosmopolitan town, full of sailors with plenty of money for drink, drugs, gambling and sex. Mixed into that heady cocktail, was the violence and retribution.

Many a drunken sailor was found, turned over, and floating in someone's down-stairs passage as the high tide flooded into the riverside houses. Corpses from the river ended up in the Death House, to be claimed, or more often disposed of. Joe liked the colourful side of Sunderland and he and Bob would join in with the various back room card schools on a regular basis. So as not to confuse the two sides of his life he kept tight-lipped with the gambling fraternity, with them he adopted the name Joe Roc and he only played in schools where he knew people. The bother he'd had in London, although a year past, was still fresh in his mind.

Joe also kept company with other Frenchmen, those who worked at the glassworks on the north side of the river. They swapped French newspapers and books they got off sailors who came in and out of the port. If anyone were going home they would take letters. Joe's family were not great writers but he liked to keep them informed as to where he was and what he was doing. One early evening in March the weather was foul, the rain off the North-Sea was lashed in on a biting wind. Joe had cut short his drink in the Howard Arms on Roker Avenue with his French compatriots, and made his lonely way down to the halfpenny ferry while it was still light. His overcoat and shoes were heavy with rain as he struggled up the other bank. Looking for a bit of warmth and respite he called into a bar on Lawrence Street to dry out. His digs were a cold and lonely place to spend the evening, whereas the pub was welcoming and friendly, especially after the strange sensation that had followed him up the hill and through the streets of the east end. Sunderland was a friendly enough place in the daylight, but there were some dangerous characters that stalked the dark recesses of the night. The chill in his spine needed the warmth of a whisky; his senses were heightened with an unaccountable loneliness, not homesickness as such, more a foreboding.

Through the din of the crowded bar Joe's ears pricked to the sound of the brass door latch, startled, he turned to see the unmistakable features of Jacob Peters. Peters came in to the bar bringing with him the outside, a coldness that radiated from his coat, his eyes fixed on Joe as they had done from the moment he had left the ferry. Joe's stomach sank; the short cropped hair and the snub nose were to him the hallmarks of fear. Jacob moved towards Joe and the look in his eyes rooted him to the spot. He felt the terror welling up inside and tried not to show it but Jacob could smell fear the way a dog does.

It hadn't been difficult to find Joe. Russian immigrants networked in all major towns and cities. A gang of Letts and Russians plied a lucrative trade in burglary round the posh houses of Hendon and Ashbrooke. Jacob Peters was nothing out of the ordinary in the east end. Boats from all over the world docked on the north east coast from the Yemen, Germany, Russia and France, a thousand different voices and shades moved like a flux melding together. The sailors from Sunderland in turn spread world-wide. Colliers were up and down the coast, taking coal from the Durham pits on a daily basis, picking up their cargo from the jetties at Millfield, they went to London and from there to the four corners of the Empire.

- "I want you to come with me for a chat, I have a proposition for you," Jacob said, his hand thrust deep in his pocket.

The blood rushed to Joe's brain he decided he wasn't going anywhere with Jacob, 'let him try and shoot me in a crowded pub,' was his first thought.

- "I've been following you for half an hour, I've known where you've been since you boarded the Isis in London. If I'd wanted to kill you you'd have been dead a long time ago."

Joe gave a small cough to control the voice that was in danger of being a squeak.

- "If you don't want to kill me why do you threaten me with a gun?"

A few people within earshot stopped and looked as Jacob took his hand slowly out of his pocket and placed a silver cigarette case on the bar; he opened it, and pushed it towards Joe. The black Russian tobacco was not to Joe's taste; he declined the offer and lit up a Gitane. The colour had come back into his face and his hand was as steady as his gaze. His boldness masked his caution.

- "What do you want? I owe you nothing."

- "Yes! You are right you owe me nothing, you have my respect Joe, I can trust you, you've got balls, and I just want you to do something for me, for a wage. Let me explain, there's a Russian money-lender lives in Harold Street, called Cohen, he also does a bit of, 'fencing'. I've got some jewellery I need to get rid of, he knows someone is coming and will have the money ready for me in an envelope. Herman Cohen knows me, and I don't want to be linked to this stuff."

- "Neither do I."

- "He doesn't know you and you can't be linked to it in London, there's five quid for you. Five quid will get you anywhere you want to go and anything you want, and you'll never see or hear of me again, that's a promise and I never break a promise."

Jacob flicked open the other side of the cigarette case where instead of cigarettes, there were folded bank notes. Jacob pulled out five one pound notes and put them in the top pocket of Joe's soggy overcoat. Joe didn't flinch, he thought either Jacob was supremely confident in his hard man aura, or didn't understand the nature of some of the people who frequented this area. His reputation counted for nothing in this town; there were those who would top their grannies for a 'pork dip' never mind the chance of picking up several months wages for dumping some foreigner in the Wear. There was no way Joe was walking out of the pub alone when he had five quid in his pocket.

- "Lead the way."

Joe followed quickly hoping no one had noticed the transaction or was too busy drinking to organise a plot. In his haste to get out he caught the edge of a marble table spilling an old lady's drink.

- "Pardon Madame," he said instinctively.

- "You're all right son," she said.

Joe was distracted for a moment, the old woman only had one eye, where the other one should have been was a small red hole, out of which, a tear ran down her cheek. He swiftly carried on, out the door.

The two men walked briskly, huddling their coats against the driving rain; soon they were in Harold Street. The green door of the moneylenders' house was in front of Joe. Jacob had parked himself in the shadows of an alleyway a few doors away. Joe pulled on the bell and heard footsteps approaching, the light tread of leather on the linoleum. Joe looked up the street but couldn't see Jacob Peters, instead he saw two women pass the top of the road; looking back at the door he could feel himself being observed through the spy-hole. He opened his coat and held the package Jacob had given him so Herman Cohen could see it. Joe imagined he looked like some sort of prosperous gentleman who may wish to part with some family jewellery to pay a gambling debt or sort out an unwanted pregnancy. The bolts were slid back and the lock turned, a small neat face with a waxed moustache appeared round the door. Joe spoke in French.

- "You are expecting some jewellery monsieur?"

- "Show me!"

Joe opened the leather pouch and the gems picked up the dim light from the hall.

- "I need to take them inside to examine them; if they are all right I'll bring you the money." Joe looked at him suspiciously.

- "It's alright you can trust me!"

Joe handed the pouch to the out-stretched arm. As Herman Cohen went to close the door, Joe put his arm out to stop it.

- "Leave it open."

The moneylender looked at him a while before turning to go into his front room office. Silently Jacob moved past Joe as if he were not there. Alarm bells rang in Joe's head and his legs started to take him away slowly, though his eyes stayed glued to the empty doorway that Jacob had just walked through. *'Don't run, don't run, don't draw attention to yourself, don't make a sound,'* the voice in his head was repeating.

Slowly Joe made his way past the bay window but the fascination of his eyes made him look through the gap in the curtains. He saw Herman Cohen walking to his desk, behind him was Jacob with an axe raised in his hand that he thwacked down on the Jews head with unbridled ferocity. The moneylender turned and staggering put his hand to the gushing crown of his head. A second blow from the axe chopped off one of his fingers and it went flying across the room. This horrific detail sent Joe running like a sprinter down the street. No memory existed of how he got there but he found himself in the toilet of the Lawrence Street bar, the shock of what he had seen had loosened his bowels and getting to the toilet had been a close call. His legs were cold as he stared fixated at the green wooden planking of the door. Had he dreamt what he had seen or had he really witnessed murder. Not many minutes had passed since he had first entered the pub, but any effects of the alcohol he'd consumed throughout the afternoon and early evening had vanished.

Joe's immediate problem was what to do next; the first thing to do was to stop shaking, he crossed the yard went into the bar and ordered a cognac and a milk stout, he didn't know why. Something in his subconscious had taken over. He realised why when he turned to look for a seat, there was one next to the old lady whose drink he had spilt earlier.

- "Pardon Madame, for you," his legs felt wobbly and the first sip of cognac had made him dizzy and sick.

He sat heavily in the vacant seat closed his eyes and rocked his head back.

- "Atamatta son?"

He opened his eyes and turned to and looked at the old lady. Sometimes he found it difficult to understand what Sunderland people were saying and this was one of those occasions.

- "Pardon"
- "You look like you've seen a ghost"

He looked at the woman's face for a while, transfixed by the small blood red hole where her eye used to be, as it watered she dabbed with a lace trimmed handkerchief.

At length he said,

- "I've just won a very large sum of money on the horses."

The money in Joe's top pocket burnt like a guilty secret as if it were cursed. He took it out and very deliberately gave it to her.

- "I would like to share my good fortune, would you take this to the bar and buy everyone a drink."

The pub fell silent as the old woman went to the bar where the notes were scrutinised and passed with a nod. The clamour for drinks was slow to start and then frenzied as the pints with whisky chasers were doled out with appreciative nods and thanks to the lucky French gambler.

The old lady sat down to wait for the change, should there be any, and no one noticed the Latvian gentleman in a grey coat re-enter the bar. He was offered and took his free drink, then asked the barman what boats were leaving the harbour that night. The barman told him that 'The Consett' was headed for Rotterdam and the 'Abechurch' and the 'Alu Mendi' were bound for Saint Nazaire. He noticed the blood on the man's coat.

- "What's that 'marra'? Is that blood? Are you all right mate?"

Jacob looked towards Joseph and raised his glass, drank it down and left.

The news of the murder reached the pub shortly after Jacob Peters and his blood splattered grey coat had departed. The barman said nothing; neither did the only other person who'd noticed blood on the grey coat of the stranger. Joe waited a prudent amount of time after Jacob Peters had gone then he said a good night to the old lady and slipped out of the pub. If there was any change from the five pounds he didn't want it. He made his shivering way home, passing groups of men and women gossiping on street corners, no doubt, about the brutal murder of Herman Cohen.

Joe was at work early on Tuesday morning, ashen grey with that sick feeling in his throat. Binns was abuzz with the murder; gruesome exaggeration fuelled each successive telling of the story, told with a relish. Joe was singled out by his silence; thoughts of Judas and the Garden of Gethsemane filled his head. He had led the assassin to his victim.

- "You were down that way last night weren't you Joe? You were seen in Lawrence Street flashing your money round I heard!"
- "Lend' us half a dollar, money bags."

Joe laughed it off, 'act normal,' he thought, 'I haven't done anything I'm not guilty,' but the more he said it to himself the more guilty he felt. A nagging doubt gnawed at him, fear and indecision filled his head. He couldn't go to the police; he was an accomplice, besides Jacob Peters would kill him. He was a man in torment. The week went by and stories of different suspects and arrests came and went. At one o'clock on Saturday afternoon Joe was finished and set off to the match putting his overcoat over his whites. He'd arranged to meet his French friends in the Red Lion, on Roker Avenue, for a pint before the game, but first Joe called into St. Benet's Church.

It was not an old church, brick built. Not like the stone Saxon building of St. Peter's the Protestant church he'd passed on the way. The day was as clear and bright as any an early spring day, and the sun shone in a kaleidoscope of colour through the stained glass windows onto the Italian marble of the Lady Chapel. Joe felt out of sorts, strange and apprehensive, the palms of his hands were sweaty, he felt guilty, guilty that he had been there that night. How had he come to know these people he asked himself? He wished he hadn't been there, in this town, in this country but that was ridiculous, what had happened, had happened. He had to deal with it; he had to do something to stop the screaming that was inside his head and the churning of his stomach. The going over and over again that kept him awake at night. This way he could unburden himself, assuage some of the guilt.

He screwed up his courage and went out of the church to knock on the sacristy door. With that action, the indecision that had plagued him all week, and nearly made him walk away had gone, and a spark of tranquillity calmed his soul. He asked the housekeeper who answered the door if there was a priest who could hear his confession. She told him to wait outside the confessional and a priest would be with him shortly. As he knelt in the church, the religion of his childhood rekindled inside him, without it he would have been alone. He clasped his hands behind his head and squeezed his moist eyes shut so as to stop the tears that were forming from coursing down his cheeks and prayed to the God he had ignored for so long to help him.

Father Declan Egan came out of the vestry with his biretta on his head, he kissed the stole around his neck before sitting in the pew in front of Joe, he turned to hold Joe's arm.

"Don't be upset my son," Joe looked up. "I'm ready to hear your confession."

Joe followed him into the confessional and started with the familiar "Bless me father for I have sinned…"

In the years since his confirmation and first Holy Communion, when his scruffy soul was claimed for salvation by the all embracing arms of Catholicism, Joe had only occasionally attended mass when dragged there on high days and holy days and now on occasions with Rose. Confession used to be at Easter so as to save his mortal soul from excommunication, but years had passed since the last time he had confessed his sins.

As one word of his sorry story followed another, Joe increasingly realised that he had not sinned; the telling of the events of Monday evening was like the shedding of a burden he realised, there was nothing to forgive, he hadn't done anything wrong, his mood lightened. How could he have gone to the police, he reasoned, doing that would have been suicidal, Jacob Peters was untouchable and Joe knew for certain he'd be killed.

For Father Egan Joe was not just another miserable sinner not prepared to face up to the consequences of his actions, Father Egan had seen Joe at church on the odd summer evening, when he and Rose had caught the six o'clock mass on their way back from the sea front. He was a ne'er do well mixing with decent folk. Maybe God would forgive Joe 'his trespasses' but Father Egan would not. The further the likes of the Frenchman were removed from decent God fearing girls like Rose Madden, the better. Father Egan absolved Joe of his sins and sent him on his way 'to love and serve the Lord.' Father Egan had an important phone call to make.

Joe's penance was to do a novena, not bad, he was sure he'd get around to it sometime. Maybe he could do it with Rose, she was a good catholic girl and it would impress her parents. Some of the things Father Egan had asked Joe he didn't quite understand like, how often do you abuse yourself? Joe was bored by then and wanted to get to the pub so he just said two or three times a day. And did he have carnal knowledge of any young women?

- "Yes I think so," he replied. He would have to remind himself to ask Rose what this meant.

As Joe made his way across Roker Avenue to the Red Lion, he recalled that towards the end of his confession Father Egan seemed as keen to get him out, as Joe himself was to go. He absolved him of his sins but questioned his contrition? Father Egan reasoned that it had taken the man the best part of a week to get around to owning up to his part in the murder and did the good Father believe all that stuff about not knowing what was going to happen?

Father Egan for his own part was too excited about what he'd just been told to hang about listening to the details of Joe's sex life. Quizzing penitents about the lurid details of their adulterous and illegal sexual affairs, and revelling in their discomfiture, was something he always considered a perk of his vocation. But this was better, he could live high on the hog for a good few years off this one, 'and what would you like to drink Father? That's very kind of you inspector I'll have a brandy,' he mused to himself as he made his way through the sacristy to the phone in the priest's parlour.

- "Operator, Get me Gill Bridge police station.... Inspector Webster if you please." "Ah! Inspector I've got that Mass card you wanted for that dear departed of yours, if you could be here within the hour...... That'll be grand. I look forward to seeing you then, goodbye inspector, goodbye God bless you."

Inspector Webster turned to his sergeant.

- "Carter, get the paddy wagon sorted and I want you and a couple of heavies."

With that Inspector Webster was on his way to Saint Benet's. When they got there Father Egan related the tale he'd been told by the French baker from Binns adding that,

- "Like a lot of these continental Catholics he's a Catholic in name only. The reason he came here today was to salve his guilty conscience. I'd be surprised if he doesn't come to church from one year's end to the next. And as for doing a Novena, I doubt it, therefore no absolution."

Although both men were of the opinion, that it would be God's will that a sinner should be punished by the laws of the establishment, a good hanging was more likely to cleanse the immortal soul than attending mass on the first Friday of every month for nine months.

Father Egan had had the foresight to get his housekeeper to see which way the penitent had gone, and was able to point the inspector in the direction of the Red Lion, they, in turn, pointed him in the direction of Roker Park.

The French lads were congregated on their bales of straw shouting, "Allez! Allez!" as the two teams chased the illusive

tell me what were you doing at Herman Cohen lodgings last Monday night?"

- "Last Monday I was with my friends on this side of the river then I went to a bar in Lawrence Street and stayed there the rest of the evening."

- "Well let's go over there now and see if anyone remembers you. Carter! You stop here and take some statements off those lying French bastards."

The two heavies remained in the back, while the inspector locked them in and rode up top with the driver. The journey down to the ferry and across the river was one of deep regret, this was not a situation of his own making, he'd lived his life like a cork on the tide with no control over his destiny. Joe had always been a fatalist, he had no other choice. Now, he could see no future, his mind raced as he tried different scenarios and concocted outrageous plans of escape from this horrendous reality.

Joe had an in-bred distrust of authority, these representatives of the state had arrested his body but his spirit was still free. No one was his better. Joe gave respect only to those who merited it. These policemen demanded respect for the uniform they wore, and the titles they conferred on each other, but they only merited his disdain. Although his heart spoke of disdain, his brain and voice spoke in the deferential tones that might appeal to those in charge of his destiny. A depression was closing in on Joe as the leaden, grey sky shrouded the houses of the East End that loomed up on the opposite bank of the cold dark river Wear. He didn't hold out much hope for his defence, for the simple reason they knew the truth. The inspector would have full knowledge of the facts from the good priest, but he had to prove it in a way so as not to implicate Father Egan. There was no reason for them not to believe that he was just an unwitting bystander, but for a conviction they could make him an accomplice or worse, this way the Slavs would not be implicated.

Inspector Webster marched into the bar like he owned the place. He was a commanding figure taller than his six foot one in his bowler hat, with his heavy Macintosh belted and buckled as if he had just come off parade. The presence of the three policemen, with their prisoner, brought a silence to the chatting in the bar. Joe was left to stand and feel the eyes of the place on his skin.

- "Does anyone here remember this man being in here last Monday night?" the silence reigned.
- "Barman, do you remember serving this man last Monday night?"

- "I might have done, it's hard to remember, we get a lot of passing trade, and I recollect there were a lot of people in on Monday night?"

- "I do believe he was in here on Monday night, but I am also of the opinion that he slipped out with an accomplice and perpetrated the brutal and horrific murder of Herman Cohen, the respectable Jewish moneylender with whom, I am sure, you were all very well acquainted. He then slipped back in here and continued drinking like the heartless bastard he is. Am I right or am I right?"

- "You're wrong!"

Inspector Webster's head turned like it was on a spit, followed by his body that didn't appear to think as quickly. The words had come from the little old lady Joe had sat beside on Monday night; she was sat in the same seat, a regular. Inspector Webster recognised the old lady and a look of resigned disappointment spread across his face. Removing his hat, deferentially, he sat down opposite the old lady.

- "Atamatta!"

- "Inspector!"

- "How is that wrong?"

- "He was sitting next to me all night. The man you want is a Russian, he came in here after the murder in a grey coat covered in blood and asked what ships were leaving the docks. Harry Boy there (indicating the barman) told him The Consett and Alu Mendi were sailing, he asked the Russian gentleman about the blood on his coat but he didn't answer, he drank his drink and he left. Isn't that right Harry Boy?"

- "Yeah! Aye! That's right I remember now that you mention it, it's all coming back now Atamatta, he was drinking whisky then he had a few brandies. He'd had a win on the horses and bought free drinks for everyone in here."

The barman's sudden total recall impressed the inspector, who although knowing the alibi was bogus, couldn't do a great deal. What the Frenchman had told Father Egan was true and the inspector knew Atamatta wouldn't protect a guilty man, they were both aware what was going on with the Eastern Europeans in Sunderland. The inspector didn't want to upset the apple cart, as long as they just kept killing their own and paying him for the privilege he wasn't too fussed about getting involved.

Leaning across to the inspector's ear Atamatta whispered,

- "If you're looking for a motive, try the caretaker at Villier's Street Mission. But leave the Frenchman alone, he's done fuck all and you know it."

With that, Inspector Webster got up.

- "Right lads, let's go."

And they left leaving Joe standing in the silence, the late afternoon light shone through the window and picked out the lonely figure. Looking around at the eyes focused on him he asked if anyone knew how the 'Lads' were getting on.

- "Beat Aston Villa 1-0, goal mouth scramble," said Atamatta.

Chapter Six

Marriage

Bob heard about the carry on at the match, and caught up with Joe that night in the Museum Vaults, just up from the Ship Isis. Joe wanted to know who this Atamatta was. Bob said his mother knew of her, so they went back to Hedley Street to ask her. She told them the story; apparently Atamatta knew everything that was going on in her parish. The old ladies reputation was legend. As a young woman, Bella Murphy, was the best looking lass in Sunderland, she'd married the cock of the area, a hard man called Laughton. They made a handsome pair and were the toast of the town for a while. After she'd given him two sons, he started to stray, coming home drunk and knocking her about. The beatings might not have been so bad had she not given him a fight. When the two boys were about nine and seven Frankie Laughton gave his missus such a hiding she ended up in hospital and lost her right eye.

- "Fair play to Frankie mind, he paid all the bills. He had a fair bit of money from the little protection business he had. When Atamatta was fit and well again and quite nicely turned out, she wore a patch in those days. The story goes that one afternoon he was late for his tea so she got all done up, dressed the two boys in their Sunday best and went down to the docks looking for Frankie. She found him with his mates down by the river, they'd just come out of the pub. She walked up to him, and without a by-your-leave she got a twelve inch carving knife out of her bag and stuck it up under his ribs and into his heart. She pulled it out, wiped it on his sleeve, and pushed him by the face into the river, then took the boys home for their bit tea. It was high tide so the body was taken out to sea, if it was ever found nobody let on."

Bob's mother said, to her knowledge no one has crossed Atamatta to this day, not even the police.

- "The story is, she took her boys down there to teach them a lesson and they seem to have learned it well, nobody gives them an argument, they took over their father's business and have done alright ever since. I've been told that that Jewish chap that was murdered down east end was one of their clients. I mean, a moneylender down the east end would need some protection wouldn't he. So it wouldn't have been anyone in their right mind from Sunderland that would have murdered Herman Cohen."

Bob was eager to get off, even though Joe wanted to know more.

- "The less you know around here mate the better off you are."
- "If her name is Bella Laughton why does everyone call her 'Atamatta'?"
- "It's her Sunderland way of saying 'what's the matter?' She says it to everybody, 'what's the matter son? What's the matter pet?' And they tell her, I think that's why she knows so much. And I'll tell you something else, she never forgets anything."

Providence had smiled on Joe whether it was God or good luck he was taking no chances. In future he intended to keep out of trouble and he looked for solace in the company of his girlfriend. The Maddens had taken to Joe and treated him with more kindness than his own family had. Joe began to join them for Mass at St Joseph's in Millfield on a Sunday; impeccably dressed he looked a pillar of respectability. Although his behaviour in church seemed odd, he sometimes sat with his arms folded and spent an inordinate amount of time looking ball up and down the muddy ground. During the half time Charles Pettifer said to Joe that he'd seen him coming out of the church. Joe told him he'd been to confession. Yves knew Joe not to be a religious type and looked at him concernedly.

- "I hope you haven't been up to anything naughty? Those priests down there can't keep a secret. My fiancée is the telephonist from the exchange and she said they were always on the blower to '*Le Flick*.' She reckoned that Father Egan there has put more men behind bars than Newcastle Breweries," the small hairs on Joe's neck stood off his flesh as a shiver went down his back.

He only had time to see his life flash before him and feel the rope tighten around his neck before he noticed his friends being moved out of the way by two large policemen. Joe was recognised by his 'whites,' and picked up by the arms and marched briskly to the awaiting paddy wagon. The interview was conducted in the back after the customary caution.

- "Joe, are you the baker from Binns? Inspector Webster asked.
- "Yes!"
- "What's your full name?"
- "Joseph Marie Delaroche"
- "Well Joseph Marie Delaroche you seem to have a canny little job at Binns and you bake a nice cake, so I've heard. So

around at other parishioners. When Rose asked him about this, he shrugged a Gallic shoulder and it was passed over as being because he was a Frenchman.

Rose on the other hand did appear to be very devout in Church. What she was praying for was mouthed in silent prayer?

The Madden boys all reckoned Joe only went to Mass for the fried breakfast afterwards, a read of the paper and a session down the Isis. Joe liked his fry up on a Sunday, and used to turn up with a bundle of bacon from a butcher friend of his and a couple of dozen eggs from the local farm. Joe used eggs at work all the time, but would rather throw them away than steal them. He expected the same honesty from the people who worked for him and did not tolerate pilfering, for him it was the thin end of the wedge. In other aspects of his daily life he was not so fastidious, rules were made to be bent, if not broken, and his life needed some frisson.

Joe had been walking out with Rose for about a year and life was sweet, he'd dropped off the bacon and eggs on Saturday night as usual and he and Rose strolled over the Gill Bridge to the Garrison field. But this evening something felt different, there was great pleasure in the way she held his arm and put her head on his shoulder. He looked at Rose and wondered if this contentment he felt with her was love, whatever love is?

Whether he was in love or not, he wasn't sure, but what he was aware of was the enjoyment of the moment and he felt at peace with the world. Another thing that puzzled Joe was that Rose had got the tickets for the Garrison field. A circus tent had been erected and the place was a throng of excited couples, young dudes, ruffians and children. The young Madden lads, horse dealers to a man were checking out the gypsies horses. They called to Joe who went to admire a handsome black stallion whose coat was so well groomed and shiny you would swear you could see your face in it. The raw noise of some battered trumpets, that sounded as if they could have been the ones that heralded Hadrian's entry into Wallsend, announced the show was about to start.

Rose had gone off with her sisters, and there was no way of finding each other as the crowd piled into the tent, so Joe went in with Hughie and Jimmy. A barber's chair sat alone in the arena. Moments later a motley crew wearing what looked like uniforms that had long since been discarded by some routed imperial army, quickly threw up a circular cage around the chair. The cage was opened to allow a man, with slicked down hair, in, he set up a table and put a box on it. A heroic tune blazed out from a single trumpet, slow and laboured it could have been from the Coliseum, a musical accompaniment last heard by a doomed Christian.

A tingle of anticipation ran down Joe's spine and the hairs on his goose bumps stood to attention. The tent had blocked out the sun and Joe realised he was cold, his hands were like blocks of ice, an uncomfortable pallor of realisation crept across his face, he shuddered as if someone was walking over his grave, something was wrong.

A man, dressed as a white hunter, entered the arena, he had a pistol at his side, a whip in his right hand and Rose in his left. They bowed to the crowd and Rose smiled and waved as they went into the cage. Rose sat down in the barber's chair. It was then that the lions raced through the tunnel that had been created at the back of the cage. The small ensemble of musicians now played fast and furious, while Joe's heartbeat provided extra timpani. The lion tamer's whip cracked, he fired his gun and moved the snarling, roaring lions around the confined space with the power of his will, while the barber worked at a steady pace combing, spraying and crimping Rose's hair into the latest style. Hughie said to Jimmy,

- "That fellow in the white suit could annoy those lions if he keeps on poking at them with that chair!"
- "Mind you she's got to be 'a daft lass' to sit there."
- "That's our Rose."
- "Is it? That'd be about right then."

Joe was in a cold sweat, the terrifying minutes passed by as the lion tamer did his act, the lions roared and pawed the air and jumped through flaming hoops. Joe was on the edge of his seat, then standing, the crowd yelling and those behind him shouted at him to sit down. He moved to the aisle, not knowing whether he wanted to get closer, or get out of there. The prospect of seeing the object of his desire being ripped apart in a feeding frenzy by the kings of the jungle seemed to hold a hideous fascination that had him fixated. Joe's worst fears appeared to be, what at least half the audience wanted, as they screamed out in an uncontrolled lust for the blood of his beloved. The Roman spectacle of impending sacrifice had the mob baying and pleading in equal measure. The lion tamer couldn't focus his attention on all six beasts at the same time. As he tried to impress his will on one bad-tempered individual, another would slope off and prowl menacingly round the cage behind him, until the screeching of the audience alerted him to his predicament. Joe was more concerned about Rose's predicament, at least the white hunter had gun, a whip and a chair, and all Rose had was a shifty looking crimper, with a comb and a pair of scissors, for protection.

Rose's logic for taking on the role as potential lion lunch, was simple, ever the follower of fashion, it was a way of getting the latest hairstyle for free; there was also the two free tickets and the one pound she would receive for her part in the show. She reasoned that Leo and his pals would all be drugged and well-fed prior to her coiffure, which had been started before she entered the arena, the bit in the cage only required a few minutes of finishing off. The few minutes began to seem like hours. Admirable as her logic was, Rose's knowledge of animal psychology and that of the big game variety was limited. Had she understood the nature of the alpha male and his territorial claims, she may have considered this venture less than wise. As it was she sat in her comfy chair, eyes tightly closed and ear-plugs blocking out a lot of the animal noises from both lions and the local populace. She couldn't help but sense the danger; she fought the fear and tensed as she heard two adult males disputing that small part of Sunderland each wanted to call his own. She had to admit that she had been alarmed before the event, when the lion tamer had told her not to move out of the chair or the lions might think she wanted to play and jump on her. She heard the cage rattle, as the two great animals, heaved and writhed in battle against the bars. She heard two shots as the lion tamer fired into the air. The hairdresser leaned over and spoke reassuringly in Rose's ear, his accent pure Lambeth and his breath forty degrees proof, "Relax darling, you don't want to upset the pussycats."

At that point Rose accepted her fate and was consumed with a feeling of power, it was then she decided that tonight was the night she would have Joseph Delaroche. Joe also began to relax a little, as the lion tamer appeared to regain control and at last started to get the lions out of the arena. The last one to leave, a big hairy beast, instead of going down the tunnel turned, stood proud, roared and swiped a paw at the lion tamer. The lion tamer cracked his whip and roared back at the lion, the lion realising he was beaten, bowed his head and disappeared through the flaps at the back of the tent.

The hairdresser put down his tools with a flourish, and he and the white hunter took Rose by the hand, she stepped out of the chair with her hair cut and crimped into a series of waves. Together they left the cage, and did a circuit of the arena; a twirl and a bow and they were off to the applause of a not too disappointed audience. The cage was struck and a baby hippopotamus with trainer bounced into the circus amid boos and cat-calls and general hilarity.

Joe was out of the tent and around to the business end of the circus in seconds. The intensity of the embrace he and Rose shared would have scandalised the catholic community. At breakfast on Sunday Rose was unusually quiet; she smiled coyly and had a glow to her cheeks.

Joe slotted into his new life like someone slipping on an old shoe. A few months after the circus and as a way of livening up a depressing cold and wet March Joe asked Paddy the Waterman for Rose's hand in marriage. It was all decided with a drink, a pat on the back, and an impromptu party. The diamond Joe bought as an engagement ring was a fair size, as he was never short of a bob or two and meanness was never a fault with Joe. The next night he was out with Bob trying to drink away his hangover down the Kings Head. Bob was shocked and appalled that his drinking 'marra' had succumbed to the wiles of a woman, 'canny lass that she was.' Joe confessed in hushed tones that he was worried in case Rose fell pregnant. At least if he was engaged it wouldn't look so bad.

- "Why! Are you not taken precautions man?"
- "Well, I pull out."
- "Ah! You're jumping off at Gateshead."
- "What do you mean?"
- "Well if you jump off the train at Gateshead you don't have to pay at Newcastle. What you want to do is see my mate. You look like you could do with a haircut. He'll fix you up with a rubber Johnny. After every time you use it you need to give it a good wash out and it should last you for years. It also protects you from the clap"
- "I'm not going to get the clap off our lass."

"Maybe not but you might get it off someone else. If you want to be extra safe you need to take a very hot bath before you do the business. It kills off all the sperm. The Romans used to do it, that's why they built baths all over the place. It was the only thing I learned at school that was any bloody use."

Armed with this new found knowledge and his rubber Johnny in its velvet lined case, Joe could sow his wild oats on a Saturday night, without reaping the harvest on Sunday morning. Joe's new found interest in history led him to discover from a very strange book in the library that the Egyptians had used natural sponge impregnated with soap, made from aromatic oils, inserted in the woman's vagina as a way of killing off sperm. Masturbation was also given religious status by the Egyptians as another form of contraception. It was remarked at the Maddens how clean and sweet smelling Joseph kept himself.

As friends and relatives paired off and walked down the aisle, or jumped the broomstick and babies turned up at regular intervals Joe and Rose continued on their merry way. Joe's money was good and he moved to better digs up Bywell Avenue. There were regular trips to the races at Blaydon and Gosforth, there was the boxing at St. James Hall in Newcastle and Joe would occasionally take in a cock fight down the east end.

Joe was living the life he liked, sometimes with his well-dressed good-looking lady on his arm and sometimes with his mates. The weeks and months passed by, Rose didn't mind too much, at first, she was having a good time, she had her man. As the years went from one to two and two to three the tongues started to wag. The question was asked more frequently, 'Have you named the day?' After four years of courting Rose began asking the same question, there was no doubt in her mind that Joe was the man for her, she was besotted with him. There was no way she would let him go, nothing she wouldn't do to keep him. As time went on, the wild child with the devil in her became more concerned about her mortal soul and the sins she was committing. She felt lucky, and blessed that no shame had been brought on her, or her family. But as she grew as a woman, she began to want to be by her man's side at night and in the morning and to have the security of her own home, and a child. When she broached the subject her pleas were answered with a shrug. When pressed, Joe would ask her if he didn't make her happy and that he needed to save some money. He didn't have much money saved because he spent it on having a good time. There was a void in Rose's life, a longing, to ease her sadness she turned to God. She had always kept the faith attending Mass and Holy Communion on a Sunday and confession on a Thursday, she gained some solace from the confessional box, but Polly had noticed she spent more time on her penance than the rest of them. She was mortal, and couldn't resist the normal urges of a young woman, but the growing guilt laid on thick by an oppressive religion was hurting too deep. It was obvious to everyone that it wasn't right apart that is from Joe. He thought marriage was all right for women but no good for men, he was comfortable in his life of hedonism. He'd seen his mates trapped into a life of work, and no money, as they struggled to bring up a family. He'd seen the despair as another ship left the slipway, the months of idleness, before the next contact was started. The savings dwindled; the wife took in washing or sold the furniture. The cycle of plenty and poverty didn't appeal to Joe. At least his work was not like that of the shipyard workers, or the dockers, sometimes you're in, sometimes you're out. Joe thought he could have his cake and eat it.

One Sunday morning after mass Father Kiely was outside St. Joseph's in his robes talking with parishioners. There was another priest standing next to him, a Redemptorist monk in his black cassock with the belt around the middle, although older, Joe recognized Father Egan. Father Egan was a big Irishman; he took Joe by the arm as though he were a naughty schoolboy and moved him out of earshot of the other parishioners. He spoke slowly and deliberately his eyes fixed on Joe.

"Mr Delaroche I haven't got a great deal of time for gamblers, drinkers and fornicators like yourself, but you've come to my attention as someone who needs redeeming from your sinful ways. I'm sure the love of God and a good woman will sort that out for you. I've taken the liberty of having had the bans read out at St. Benet's and expect to see you and Rose Madden there next Saturday at eleven o'clock mass. It seems to be the wish of the family that you get wed and they approached me to sort it out for them. God alone knows why they want to lumber their daughter with the likes of you but that's none of my business. Let me tell you this, young man, if you don't turn up for the wedding you better be a long way away, or I'll be forced to let it be known that you played a part in the brutal murder of Herman Cohen, God rest his soul. Do I make myself plain?"

Joe was struck dumb, white and shaken he returned to where Rose was waiting. On the way back to Ayre's Quay Road, Joe tenderly broke the news that he had arranged the date of the wedding. He announced it to the rest of the family over breakfast. They all seemed genuinely surprised apart from Paddy and Mary that is.

The twenty eighth of June 1914 was the day set for the wedding and it all went well. The reluctant groom done up in his best suit and Rose in a white cotton dress with a tiara made of wild flowers and sweet smelling jasmine, the trailing veil went down to her tight waist. They looked a handsome couple.

Following the ceremony, short notice though it was for a shindig, Ayre's Quay Road came alive. Hugh scraped his fiddle, Tommy piped his whistle and all manner of instruments accompanied the party. Polly and Rose danced up and down the cobbles, clacking their clogs against the stones with their kicks, cuts and twirls, arms by their sides and backs as straight as dyes. The whole road was bursting with energy, the whoops and the yells sent the dogs and the cats scurrying off and made the babies either cry, or stare in bewilderment as if to question the wisdom of coming into this world. In the intervals between one group and another striking up with a fresh jig or a reel, the hum of chattering laughter and the cackle of next doors geese kept the noise at a pitch. Indoors the table groaned under the weight of food, the cakes that Joe had brought and the pies and fare Mary Madden had cooked. The centrepiece being a three tier wedding cake Joe had baked, the sort that only the posh folk had. A barrel of beer from the Ship Isis sat in its cradle outside the front door. The blue sky of the warm afternoon slowly darkened, as evening crept on and a bank of cloud rose up from the North Sea.

Paddy Madden kicked up the dust of the street with the rattle of his step dancing at his daughter's wedding. As the drink took hold of the assembled company, the music and the dancing grew wilder, Joe spun Rose cross-handed, her hair loose and a glow on her face. Joe with his shirtsleeves billowing and his waistcoat and tie undone, flew round faster and faster until they broke loose on the verge of collapse.

Although the timing of the wedding wasn't of Joe's choosing, he thought that being married to Rose might not be such a bad thing, she was easy enough to get along with. Rose came over to where Joe was being held up and said,

- "We better go now before the fight starts."
- "What fight?"
- "There's always a fight, get your coat on we're off."

There was a round of goodbyes, a swig of whisky, and Janet Bennett, from next door but one, played her harp and sang, 'As She Moved through the Fair.' Mr and Mrs Delaroche climbed on to the carriage. Rose's mother had wrapped up the top tier of the cake and placed it in Rose's lap. As the carriage made its way through the throng Rose was still clutching the bouquet of wild flowers Kitty had picked for her. She threw it out, back over her head, and then turned to see if any of her sisters had caught it. Her throw had been high and hard but a cold gust of wind had caught the bouquet and blown it over the wall into the Gill cemetery. The sound of disappointment was audible amongst the cacophony of hooting and hollering as they headed off to Bywell Avenue. Halfway over the Wearmouth Bridge, the black clouds that had been building dropped a deluge of water on Sunderland. Rose was petrified, so was the horse as it reared to the crack of thunder and the flash of lightning that lit the sky. The strange iron structure that spanned the river was as alien to the beast as it was to Rose. Joe's reassurance that the bridge had lightning conductors didn't ease her or the horse's anxiety.

- "My mother always said that thunder and lightning was God being angry, do you think he's angry with us Joe?"
- "Us and the rest of Sunderland by the looks of things."

Once off the bridge Rose's unease subsided but she clung to Joe through the rest of the journey home. Once in the house it was still early and Joe unwrapped the top tier of the wedding cake he had made.

- "You can't eat that!" Rose exclaimed.
- "I was just going to have some with a glass of port."
- "No! That's for the christening."
- "You're not pregnant are you?"
- "Not yet I'm not." She said as she put her arms around his neck and kissed him on the lips.

   Next morning they went for breakfast at Ayre's Quay and sure enough there had been a fight. Alfie Blacklock had got stabbed in the neck by one of the lads from the Garths.

- "Who shouldn't have been there!" chipped in Kitty.

Hughie said,

- "Knowing Alfie, as soon as the bleeding stops, he'll be after taking a piece out of the young boy."
- "There's always one that wants to spoil the party, Alfie might have his revenge but what'll it do to that poor lad's mother?" said Mary, "That's the way it is with men! They're always wanting to fight, isn't there enough trouble in the world?"

Rose wasn't pregnant, even though Joe had stopped insisting on hot baths and his faithful sheath had been retired to the top of the tallboy. They'd had a few days off by way of a honeymoon and went to stay at Uncle Owen's farm. Rose had expected it to happen in an instant and although she knew it was unreasonable after a month of marriage her mood became low. Her mother gave her a medal of Saint Gerard, to wear round her neck, but as August came to an end she still wasn't pregnant, she felt she'd been cursed by God for her previous sins. Her mood, as if a contagion, affected Joe, he missed the carefree girl and his thoughts turned to his past freedom, the times he'd had in London and Paris. He thought about Claire who he'd left without warning, how different his life could have been? He felt his good times behind him; he who used to act on impulse now had to plan. He used to spend till it was gone now had to save for the baby Rose was desperate for. He'd had the chance to show a clean pair of heels, but he'd chosen to stay and not run away this time. Getting married seemed to be the easiest thing to do and anyway it was a good excuse for a party.

At times, over the years Claire had crossed his mind, and how he'd felt for her, courting Rose, being engaged and now married made him feel, however vaguely, as if he had betrayed Claire. She came into his thoughts more and more as the reality of married life dawned on him. After the excitement of the wedding, the weeks that followed were an anticlimax. His old mate Bob was still out and about with his bachelor pals but Joe felt out of place with them, his status had changed. The times were changing and news from abroad didn't sit well, war with Germany had been declared at the beginning of August.

Joe got a letter from his mother, written by a friend, he imagined it smelt of home; after the normal pleasantries the message was clear, Andre and Julian had joined the French army and his mother's entreaty to him was to stay where he was. The last line read "Don't come home to die for France, live and be happy with your new wife and family, Tu maman Ambrosine"

It pulled his heart out and inflamed his contrary nature, he felt the panic he had felt many years before, as he had stood on the Eiffel Tower and had to fight the urge to jump. He hadn't jumped, and now, he wouldn't go to France. He'd avoided conscription by leaving France when he had, unlike his brothers; he had no experience of the army.

All the talk prior to the war had been of the trouble in Ireland. Little notice had been taken of the war that had started between the Austro-Hungarian Empire and Serbia, but the Russians had gone to the aid of the Serbians, and the Germans had sided with the Austro-Hungarians. The Russians had a treaty with the French, and the Germans had a war on two fronts. The British had no real reason to get involved, but they had been losing power in the world, and saw the Kaiser as having ambitions to build an empire, an empire to rival that of his late Grandmother Queen Victoria.

By conquering France, Germany could concentrate on fighting the Russians, but the Germans had to invade France through neutral Belgium. Britain had a treaty with France and besides it was a way of halting German influence. On the fourth of August 1914 Britain was at war with Germany. The war had come with speed and from nowhere; hopefully it would disappear as quickly as it had arrived. In England Joe could sit it out for a few months and it would be gone. The British were not reluctant combatants, they didn't like the way the Germans had violated Belgium. They were also concerned about Germany isolating Britain by becoming the European superpower, too big a competitor in the market place.

The men had started to trickle out of Sunderland but it was the regular soldiers that arrived back by train blooded and battered from a battle at place called Ypres in late October. Joe was on his way home when he saw the crowd rushing towards the railway station in Union Street he got there and watched as men in ragged uniforms dragged their bandaged limbs to be greeted, hugged and held by family and friends.

Amongst the wounded were half a dozen Belgian families, refugees, who, by some quirk of fate, had found themselves in this far corner of an unknown land. A well-dressed young woman with a baby, stood with what looked like her father, a distinguished man with a large white moustache, with them was a boy of about four holding a parcel. Joe was moved by their plight, lost and confused without a friendly face in sight, he noticed the label on the man's suitcase 'Louvain,' and spoke to the man in French. Joe decided to take them home with him.

Rose was beside herself with the baby, and the story of the family's departure from Belgium, with all its attendant horror and misery was translated amidst tears and recriminations, filled her with rage. The woman hadn't heard from her husband for a while and had become resigned to not seeing him again. Rose was relaxed with Camille who was about the same age as her. Marcel, her son soon picked up enough English to get by. But it was the baby, Marie that Rose was most taken with. Joe spoke with Monsieur Suchard each night about the developments in the war. Rose looked at the two men as they sat and spoke in hushed tones, and at Camille, a widow? She prayed in her heart, that Joe wouldn't go. By the end of January, Monsieur Suchard and his family had moved out, he had found work and somewhere to live.

At about the same time it was confirmed that Rose was pregnant, something about the proximity of children had relaxed her, the baby was due in September and if a girl she would be called Marie. As the number of men signing up went from a trickle to a flood, Joe stopped in the house more and more, there were few men in the pubs. Bob and his pals had signed up. He felt the looks he got as a lone male in a town of women. Only young boys and old men mined the coal and worked in the shipyards, all the men had gone excepting, the feeble in body or of mind. Rose's brothers had signed up with the Durham Light Infantry. Joe was not interested in what people said or thought. He'd heard the stories Monsieur Suchard had told, he read the newspapers the lists of dead, and missing. The maimed were sometimes glimpsed, their faces as silent as they were themselves, they sat on the pavements in the sun, the dull mark of Cain reflected in their vacant eyes.

The war didn't appeal to Joe, but the possibilities it presented did, in his muddled dreaming, he thought it could be an honourable way of getting home. If not to start afresh then maybe a way of burying the past, assuaging his growing sensitivity about Claire. He also felt guilty about the men and boys who were out there fighting and dying. Appearances mattered to Joe, he had a man's vanity but he would not leave his wife and unborn child, he had an idea that when the war was over and the baby was born he might then visit France to put things right. Each night he read about France, and the idea wouldn't go away.

A baby girl was born at midnight on thirty-first of August 1915 on the cusp. Joe went to register the birth and she was christened Marie. With the birth, Joe's discontent blossomed into a panic of mixed emotions. Although he liked Rose, he was not happy with the role of the dutiful husband and father. The attention Rose had once lavished upon him alone was now shared with the baby. To his mind not even shared. He was no longer the centre of her universe.

The French authorities had got hold of Joe's address in England and he received his call up papers. The time they had taken to get to him meant that he had missed the date for turning up for recruitment. The solution that he and Rose arrived at was that he joined the British army, after all they were fighting the same enemy and the British seemed to be suffering a lot less casualties than the French. Anyway the war would soon be over.

It seemed the better option. Rose was reassured, she understood the male psyche. Joe went to the recruiting office but instead of joining the Durham's, as he said he would, he joined The Seaforth Highlanders.

After his initial training he was given a weekend pass. Rose's mother looked after the baby while Joe and Rose replayed their courtship. A spark of their love was rekindled as Joe, in his uniform, with Rose on his arm cut a dash around town. Joe was carefree, secure in the knowledge that on Monday he would be embarking for northern France, for home. The parting was harder on Rose, but the promise of a soon return sweetened the bitter pill.

Joe's attention span had never been great, he was easily bored, and that's why this new adventure excited him. The workings of his imagination often outweighed his intelligent reasoning. The idea of the routine life and the attendant responsibilities had filled him with foreboding. That dread of mediocrity had spurred him onto the unknown. Even being on board a troopship, with nothing to do, gave him a tingle of excitement, of apprehension. But after a few hours of floating precariously on a heaving sea as cold as iron, and with the icy wind sweeping in from the Arctic finding every gap in his clothing, Joe thought more than twice about what he had left behind.

The characteristic clack, clack, clack of windblown metal against metal, that sound Joe had listened to as a child by the harbour at Dieppe, was calling him back. The easy imaginings of the idle infected his open mind but his power to change events had been taken from him. His freedom was mortgaged, vacillation was not an option and decisions now were made for him, right or wrong. The gradual acceptance of his fate closed the door to any fanciful wanderings, for the time being at least.

The noise of the waves and the screech of the gulls, the smell of coal smoke and the salty sea air were poignant reminders of other times and places. Joe's reverie was occasionally shot through with guilt at the pleasure this strange feeling of liberation gave him. He swelled his chest as he took a deep breath of ozone into his lungs. At this moment he didn't miss Rose or the child, during his training he had felt alone for a while, but something must have changed in him, now he felt nothing, no love, only impatience.

The training that took him from confectioner, to warrior, was short and brutal and he had never felt as fit. The humour that men without women shared creates a bond, humour that necessarily grew from shared circumstances, a good humour that cheered him, stopped him thinking, and helped him forget. The friendship of his Scottish comrades was vital, another family, even though he found it difficult understanding what they were saying.

The ship's accommodation reeked with the stench of men's bodies, Woodbines, vomit, farts and feet. The air was blue with smoke and with the profanities of the men who swaggered to conceal inner thoughts and fears. The wind on the deck was cutting but at least it was fresh. The salt in the damp air stiffened his short hair, and a mist of water collected on his face formed droplets, heavy enough to weave a course down cheeks, as though they were tears.

- "Is that you Joe?" A voice piped from under a tarpaulin covering a lifeboat.

The black-toothed smile of Jock MacFadden beckoned Joe to join him in the relative snug of a lifeboat. Joe clambered over the ship's handrail and under the lifted tarp'. Jimmy, Wee Shuggy and Soapy lay about the space with a half gone bottle of whisky, which Jimmy offered and Joe was pleased to accept. The heat from the drink turned Joe's face red and he felt the rawness of his skin as the salty sea air tightened his flesh.

- "What's this France place like then Joe?"

- "I only know around Dieppe and Paris, I suppose Paris is the same as any big city, like London!"

- "What's London like," said Wee Shuggy?

Joe realised he was older and had lived a different life, these lads had never moved far from the confines of the village they had been born and brought up in. This was a big adventure, an escape from their predetermined life of hard work and poverty. Joe regaled them with stories of theatres, actresses, fine clothes, trains and wealth. His stories were interrupted with expressions like. "You're putting me on," and "Is that right?" The stories Joe told filled them with excitement and anticipation. The women, the wine, the sunshine, France became a rare place in their imaginations. They were escaping from their old lives of drudgery, which they accepted because they knew no different. In the army they were paid, fed and clothed, they'd put on weight, and up to now no one had asked them to do very much. For them it was a lazy man's life and they'd go home in a couple of months as heroes, clothed in glory, with stories and memories. This war they were fighting for freedom, their own freedom. None of them were more than eighteen; Joe recalled his own excitement of leaving Dieppe eleven or so years earlier and now he was going back older and wiser. Joe's ideas about war, death and glory didn't tally with the boy's. Joe saw the war as a mode of transport.

- "So you speak that language they speak in France then Joe."
- "Yes."
- "That's great that Joe, I'm sticking with you pal."

The whisky had done the rounds and the lads unused to the drink smoked their Woodbines, cuddled together for warmth and comfort, and dozed. Joe was left with his thoughts. He realised he'd made the decision to leave, albeit subconsciously when he'd gone to register the birth of his daughter. The beautiful blue-eyed baby had pushed him over the edge, he had to go now or the child would captivate him forever. The look in her eyes would be the final turn of the key that locked him in to a life of respectability. Respectability, responsibility, were not the things he craved, he still needed to feel that flutter of excitement in the pit of his stomach that made him a gambler that told him to take the risk. What he was looking for was intangible, illusive but he knew he would know it when he found it.

His was the coward's way, he couldn't tell the truth even to himself, it would hurt too many people, and it would mean burning his bridges and ruin his reputation. The dark secrets of his soul he told to no one. What would they think of him? What would that do to him? He had been accepted by them, partaken of their hospitality, they treated him like family. What kind of person would leave his wife and child? They trusted him and thought his motives were honourable, to fight for his home and family against an aggressor, they believed him when he said he'd joined the Seaforth Highlanders because he liked the uniform. It would have been easier to join the DLI but he knew people in the DLI, Rose's brothers, his pals. The eyes and ears of friends and relations would check his freedom. The man who never planned anything had plotted his escape; he had run away and used the war as an excuse.

The war was convenient, a catalyst for change, a conveyance out of Sunderland, a route back to France where he could lose himself with honour? Honour was important to him, if others thought him honourable maybe he could fool himself. He yearned to see Claire again, to see if she still stirred his emotions as she had done. It had also been convenient how his call up papers from France had got to England, how they had got his address? Serendipity had made his decision for him, made it easier to leave.

Jimmy stirred from his slumber.

- "I've been meaning to ask you Joe, you're an old bloke, why did you join up?"

- "We had some Belgian refugees come to stay with us in Sunderland and they told us of the horrors and atrocities the Germans had subjected innocent civilians to. I've got two brothers in the French army and a lot of my friends and my wife's family are in the DLI, fighting in France some of whom, God forbid, might now be dead. If I'd stayed at home,

I'd have felt like a coward so I left my wife and daughter to go and fight for my homeland."

- "Aye but why the Seaforths?"

- "I wanted to join the Highlanders because there's an old alliance between Scotland and France, and besides the Scottish Highlanders are the best fighting men in the world, and I wanted to be with the best."

- "Good on you man." He adjusted his position and went back to sleep.

Joe felt better now that he was clear in his own mind how he'd come to be under a tarpaulin, cold, halfway drunk and halfway down the coast of England on his way to kill some people he'd never met and see a girl he'd left behind.

Chapter Seven

The Western Front

Joe felt strangely out of place standing on the dockside in Dieppe. He half-expected to see his mother selling mussels, but the fish market was on the other quay. It was like he was in some kind of dream, a dream where he could see and speak, but no one could see him and he couldn't hear them. Soon they were marching and the sound of the boots beat a tattoo on the black granite sets. Joe's head was on a swivel that turned this way and that. He saw faces and places he knew but they didn't know him. The cobbler where he had bought his black shoes stood outside his shop. As the ranks approached him, the cobbler only saw an army like the last one, a uniformed body of men laughing and joking as they passed his way. The cobbler was solemn; Joe stared at him hoping he might recognise a familiar face. Their eyes locked and Joe shouted,

- "Monsieur Dore."

He saw the puzzled look on the cobbler's face as they passed.

- "Yes! Yes! Yes! It is me, Joe."

He nodded his head over his shoulder.

- "Tell my mother I will be seeing her soon."

Recognition came slowly to the old man's narrowing eyes.

- "Joseph? What are you doing with the Scottish?"

But they were gone. The cobbler ran after them and caught up with Joe.

- "Joseph! Joseph! Andre and Julian are dead."

- "Dead?"

- "Yes at Verdun at the end of February. I'm sorry my friend"

Joe looked back and saw the cobbler make the sign of the cross.

The feeling of optimism brought on by being home was replaced by deep regret and gloom. The last time Joe had seen his brothers they had been not much more than boys.

- "What was all that about Joe?" Jock asked.

- "He said both my brothers were dead!"

- "Fucking hell, those fucking German bastards, did you hear that?"

- "Hear what?"

- "Those fucking German bastards have killed Joe's brothers."

The word soon spread among the clan, and a collective anger filled the warrior's bellies as they marched.

When they eventually arrived at their estaminet behind their battle stations, Joe was in reflective mood, his thoughts and ideas confused, maybe the war would last longer than he had originally thought. It didn't matter to him how long the war might last, his intention was to live longer than the war. His focus now was on staying alive by whatever means he had. Judging by the evidence of his eyes and his ears the chances of staying alive and in one piece seemed remote. There looked to be four options; death, disability, desertion or defeat. Back from the front line the noise of the guns appeared loud and constant from both sides. On the journey from Dieppe the Highlanders had witnessed the movement of troops that formed a ragged pattern of lines going backward and forward, like city men in uniform, on shifts, heading to and from work. Some were muddy and blooded, worn out from sights and experiences, sombre. Joe's comrades in comparison although sobered by Joe's news found it hard to conceal their high spirits. Tomorrow they would move into the trenches and the immediacy of their predicament began to dawn on them. There was too much time to think, they were bored so they talked, shaved, played cards and drank. Some had never had a drink of beer before and most had never tasted wine. The early morning changeover would come hard to those who'd jollied the afternoon and evening along with too much gusto.

As the sun began to set in the evening sky, Joe turned his head to the sound of a throbbing engine as a motorcycle raced up the road to where they all were. As the motorcycle pulled up, the rider dismounted and ran his fingers through his hair to shake loose the dust. A crowd soon gathered to marvel at this machine. Questions came at the rider thick and fast, as the motorbike was inspected and touched with a reverence reserved for holy objects. The young rider lifted his goggles and lowered the silk scarf from around his mouth. The pleasure that gleamed from his face was unmistakable, as he basked in the reflected glory of his mechanical steed.

Lieutenant Murdo Macleod approached with a beer for the boy and asked,

- "Do you mind?" he straddled the machine.

As it turned out the boy was a despatch rider on his way to the front with the night's orders for the commanding officer. He said he always tried to get there before dusk so as not to make himself a target by using his headlight.

- "Best be on your way then," said the lieutenant as he dismounted and relinquished the machine to its custodian.

- "Thanks for the beer sir," he saluted, "it's a nice bit of straight road down there, I'll open her up and show you what she can do."

With that he pulled his goggles down and his scarf over his mouth and set off. They all stood and watched as he gained speed.

Further down the road a hawk had started to chase a sparrow, its eyes trained on its victim. With the silence and speed attributed to this bird of prey it zeroed in for the kill. The space between the two birds was clear. As the despatch rider opened the throttle his machine sped him into the gap and the hawk slammed into the boys head with the combined speed of animal and machine. The wings and what remained of the bird's body spun high against the blue backdrop of the sky. The sudden shock of what they had witnessed stunned the watching men into momentary inaction, and then they raced down the road to find the lad dead with what looked like his brain full of feathers.

Joe looked on, as a stretcher was organised and the motorbike wheeled back up the road. The next thing that would happen would be a call for a volunteer to learn how to ride the mad machine and deliver the despatch. Joe knew there would be no shortage of volunteers and he slipped into the barn to find a place to sleep, and hopefully a lucky sparrow, to take with him as a mascot tomorrow. The march and the drink had made Joe tired but sleep didn't come easily, his mind was in emotional turmoil. His thoughts turned to his two brothers, was their fate as bizarre as the boy on the bike? What strange set of circumstances had led them all to this place; he had to have a plan.

'How many kilometres was it to Belgium.' he asked himself? He'd heard the stories from men who had been at Ypres and Mons, and the slaughter at Verdun was all too real. He'd listened in disbelief at the stories men had told about going over the top into withering machine gun fire. Joe thought to himself, if I ever have to go through that, I'll just keep on going to Belgium. The possibility gave him little comfort, death or Belgium. He was exhausted and fell into a fitful sleep. It was still night when he was woken at four, to wash and shave and make his way, with the other grey shivering shadows, quietly in the dark along the communication trench, to the front line.

Joe thought this was as good a time as any to join the war. The summer was coming up and the weather was generally good at this time of year, apart from the odd shower, and the men had recently been issued with helmets. Stories of the past winter worried Joe, the trenches had been flooded, and men stood up to their thighs in water in some of them, their feet rotting with trench foot. To ease their aching limbs and dry out, both the

Germans and British took to lying on the top of the trenches and generally ignored each other. Some of them might have preferred if they hadn't, such was their misery.

The lessons of sending men over the top will surely have been learned and the war would end soon anyway. The thought of Belgium was put to the back of his mind. The routine of ten days at the front and ten days training near an estaminet was boring, but the casualties were low. An understanding grew up between the German and British troops in the trenches, you don't shoot us and we won't shoot you. They could hear each other singing and chatting, in the evening they could smell each other's food. The odd shouted comment came across the divide and was replied to. Joe developed a rapport with a German who spoke some French and English and supported Aston Villa. At the estaminet Joe kept his head down, obeyed orders, did his training, didn't drink too much or play cards; he read books, wrote letters, did drawings of his comrades who paid him a few coppers, he sent money home but some money he saved, in case it was needed. He thought his longing for Rose and the baby might grow but he was surprised how little he missed his wife, and the little girl he'd never really got to know.

He was settling into a routine, and enjoyed aspects of the life, where all responsibility for independent thought was taken from him. Apart from the excitement of the odd bomb exploding nearby, he liked the change of lifestyle, he felt good about himself. At the end of his second stint in the trenches, rumours started to spread. A big bombardment was about to begin. At the estaminet the training was focused on getting out of the trench and walking forward. The talk amongst the men was how to survive, each had their own theory. Joe kept his intentions to himself, the best way he thought, was to try to get across the first German trench and turn left, there was a hill not too far away.

For some reason the British had christened it Sausage and the valley to the left of it was called Mash. Joe knew the terrain there was a hamlet on the rise above Sausage and there would be a road, a route to Belgium perhaps. His mates asked him to find out the name of the hamlet, their interest was in the availability of girls and drink. In the long hours of boredom these topics seemed to be the only things on their minds. Joe dreamt of other things, the hamlet was La Boisselle and running alongside it was the Albert-Bapaume road. Joe's thoughts turned to how to get from there to Ostend, he had money, he thought he could buy a bike and if he dressed like a priest he could cycle through enemy territory. Being slightly balding made him look older than he was, too old perhaps to be of fighting age, anyway what German would stop and ask a rural French priest for his papers? He would take events as they presented themselves; the expected push might take them all the way to Germany and could end the war?

The artillery, well behind the front line started shelling the German positions and supply lines; night after day it went on, each day seemed heavier than the last. Joe thought there might be nothing left of La Boisselle, if he ever got there. The night before the attack the army was moved up into position. In the communication trench they waited, and watched, and prayed for the souls of the men who were suffering under the heaviest bombardment in the history of mankind. As they stood, and waited, and contemplated their own mortality the man with the grog went up and down topping up their tin cups. It was too early in the day for Joe so he gave his to Wee Shuggy. Looking out over the trench a pall of smoke hung like a shroud over the German lines. No one, thought Joe, could live through the last forty eight hours. His thoughts turned to escape, he'd never ridden a bike before, maybe, he thought, he could walk with it some of the time, till he learned how to ride, anyway the road to Bapaume probably didn't exist anymore, he might be better off cycling to Paris dressed as a priest? Most of the men had had precious little sleep over the last five nights, and the drink hadn't helped. Joe mused that he would not be the only one thinking of escape; nobody in their right mind would choose to be here, now.

Then there was heard what sounded like a blast at a quarry, the earth quaked beneath them as a wall of earth lifted along the line of the German trenches in front of them. 'No man's land,' that soft chalky soil had been tunnelled and exploded.

Joe still had cotton wool in his ears when at seven thirty a.m. the bombs stopped, the ringing carried on in Joe's head like the ghost of a symphony. The first wave of men went over the top to the shrill squeals of the officer's whistles. Clouds of black smoke had been pumped out to obscure their advance, but the distant rattle of machine gun fire, could only have come from the German lines. His mood of optimism evaporated, as the sun climbed in a bright blue sky. Why hadn't they attacked at first light? It was a long time of listening to the gruesome sounds of battle before the second Battalion of the Seaforth Highlanders ascended the ladders to the shrill of Captain Lewis' whistle. They set off walking, as ordered, up the incline through the blasted earth of 'no man's land.' Some of the men were laden like pack mules, and walk was all they could do with four stone of equipment. Joe quickly abandoned anything he didn't consider essential to his immediate survival, which left him with his Lee Enfield.

The distance from the German's trenches varied but as they came in range of the German guns the kilted soldiers started walking amongst the bodies of the first wave of the dead and wounded. The air filled with the lethal sting of flying lead. As the arc of bullets took down some of those to Joe's left, his instinct was to fall to the ground, knowing that if he did so he'd never get up. A moving target was harder to hit, running seemed to be the best option. He followed the movement of men falling till the German gunner reached the end of his arc of fire and started back the other way. The primeval urge to run spurred him on but defying logic he ran towards the danger aware that it was safer on the other side of the German lines. Joe was running forward and to the left as bullets danced and glanced and smacked their murderous way through fabric, flesh and bone of firing and fallen comrades. Joe kept looking for a gap in the lines of German trenches, where the wire was down. The firing from the Germans almost seemed to stop as he skirted the huge crater the earlier blast had made. He spotted three Germans manning a machine gun, crouched with idiotic bravery on the lip of the trench. One of them fell back, Joe saw the marksman who had hit him, standing legs apart with his Lee Enfield at his shoulder taking aim as if on the rifle range at the fun fair. The second man went down. The remaining gunner slowly arched the machine gun around.

Joe kept running at a steady pace watching his foot fall, absurdly afraid of going over on his ankle on the uneven ground.

He had to dodge the regimented walkers relentlessly moving forward, still moving, single-minded, conscious only of the space ahead, straight into the murderous mayhem. The fear Joe had felt had turned to terror, he had to focus on survival, his eyes were fixed on the marksman as he took aim and missed. Joe had no time to shoot; he was looking and waiting for the gap to open. A drummer walked past him, as if oblivious of the deadly hail of bullets, he was playing like he was on the parade ground. Joe had to pray a gap would open, and he prayed that his marksman friend would hit the machine gunner. A few feet more, Joe dashed towards the gun passing the implacable drummer boy. His marksman had to hit. Faster, faster, Joe ran then dropped before the barbed wire, looking up he saw the marksman's bullet exiting from the German gunners back, a handful of blood seemed to pull the machine gunner backwards, as if he were executing some sort of elaborate dive, head back and arms flung wide. Joe cut the wire as the drummer marched up and through the gap with a crowd of men who looked like they were trying to get the last bus at Park Lane.

Joe followed them and got to the other side of the trench. There was another trench not far away and not so heavily manned. Joe was in danger of being shot by the advancing British or the defending Germans. 'Keep low, go left and forward,' he said to himself. After what seemed like an age of ducking, crawling, running and weaving a few yards at a time, he was coming perilously close to the second German trench when to his left he saw a gang of men fighting like mad bursting through further up the line. Joe had somewhere to aim for and made haste to reach these new companions. To stop and fire his rifle would have made him an easy target and to fire while running would have been ineffectual, he never considered himself a good shot. German bullets were still flying too close for safety when he reached the screaming, yelling, band of orange kilted Ulstermen. He joined their increasing number as they struggled their way across the second trench carrying Joe along with them like some rugby maul. His heart was thumping in his ears, the sound of battle redoubled, as the supporting Germans retreated. The drummer kept coming, as the growing crowd raced on to secure the next trench. As the drummer made it to the third trench he stood on the parapet rattling out the charge as more and more rallied to him.

Unbeknown to Joe the advance was supposed to be to Thiepval, but with the Northumberland Fusiliers having no cover, they were cut down as they struggled across the rough ground, most of them were dead, some of them before they were out of the trench. With so few officers about there was a lack of direction and the sense of it all was lost. Joe felt relatively safe away from the deadly flying metal and in the confusion he decided to keep going to the left up Sausage ridge. His vague notion that he could get to Belgium and the coast, looked impossible amongst this chaos of men and murderous weapons. The best he could hope for in this madness was capture.

He could see La Boisselle on the high ground and running alongside it would be the road to Bapaume. As he picked his way up the incline with his new comrades, these Ulster boys had had a good day by their standards, this to them was what soldiering was all about. There was a slight dip before they reached La Boisselle.

- "Get down and crawl up the ridge, you never know what's on the other side!" shouted one of the Irish lads as they stealthily made their way. "You don't want to be silhouetted against the sky; you'll be a sitting duck."

Over the hump lay a bombed out farmhouse and further up the track, La Boisselle.

- "I'll go down and check that place out just cover me."

The leader of their little band zigzagged his way to the farmhouse while Joe and his new pals lay in the meadow grass with eyes trained on the upstairs windows. As their leader got closer so they moved up, soon the Ulstermen were in the deserted farmhouse. Joe stood by the fence as lookout while they reconnoitred the place, knowing that it would have been used by the Germans and could be booby-trapped. A crater lay to the side of the house, a shell had blown most of the wall away, part of the roof and all but a few of the tiles were missing. Joe looked down and next to him was a German boot. The foot and the lower part of the leg were still inside it.

The Ulstermen declared the place safe, and Joe scouted around to find where the chickens had laid their eggs, he collected a dozen or so and took them into the kitchen where he lit the stove. The shock of what he had just lived through had left him numb, light-headed, his body craved food. The normality of the surroundings, the minutiae of a farm kitchen, prompted him to act in a way that made him feel in control.

As the Ulstermen, and Irish, and Scottish Northumberland's started to secure the area more allies turned up, Manchester pals and some of the Highlanders, Ian Donaldson and Tex McCann with Lieutenant Macleod were with them strolling as though it was a day out. Ian told Joe that Jock McFadden, Soapy, Jimmy and Wee Shuggy were all either dead or wounded along with a long list of others. Joe had no time for grief, or the guilt of still being alive, he was on edge, like he'd drunk too much coffee. He had to do something to keep going, he found a pig wandering about; the Germans must have left it in their haste to abandon their post. There was a block and tackle outside and after stunning the pig with a lump hammer, Joe and Tex hoisted the animal. Standing over a tin bath he slit the pig down the middle, warm blood squirted on his tunic before it started to drain into the bath. Joe skilfully gutted the beast and let the innards fall into the pool of blood.

Macleod was in the kitchen with a map on the table. He looked up to see Suffolk's and Royal Fusilier's, and said, "I'm not sure we're supposed to be here. We're nowhere near Thiepval." When Joe came in looking like a blooded warrior he raised little attention as he calmly started to cook omelettes. A line was beginning to form either side of the farmhouse as the growing band of men started digging in. Macleod had made his decision. They would take advantage of this lull in the fighting to assess the situation, moving on to Thiepval or Beaumont Hamel was not an option. There were not enough men and no effective communication. With what was left of the main force, Macleod decided that the best option was to rest up for a while, then before the Germans could regroup, try to take La Boisselle. In the meantime Joe served up the omelettes. The Jocks had found the wine cellar and were putting opened bottles on the table, they sat outside; the building was too easy a target. Macleod gave a toast, "To the 'Ladies from hell' and present company." The Ladies from hell is what the Germans had nicknamed the kilted soldiers from Ireland and Scotland.

A hole in the wall of the farmhouse looked up the track, and as they ate, an observer with field glasses kept a check on the activity in La Boisselle: it didn't appear that there were any Germans there.

Food eaten in the open air tastes better somehow and food that you think might be your last has an intensity of flavour that can only be imagined. The wine tasted better than any wine that had ever passed Joe's lips but it made him drowsy. Macleod took out a pack of cigarettes and passed them to the others.

- "All I need now is a woman and I'd die a happy man." Turning to Joe he said, "You're the Frenchman in the regiment aren't you?"
- "Yes sir!"
- "Where did you learn to cook?"
- "At the Savoy, sir. Sir, there's a pig around the back, I was thinking we might butcher it and take it with us."
- "Great idea. Sergeant Campbell, make sure that pig comes with us, it looks like the only trophy we'll get today."
- "Sir!"

The pig was manhandled onto the table and Joe portioned it as best he could, the pieces wrapped in torn linen sheets taken from the beds upstairs. Joe collected vegetables, herbs and wine. The bundles were tied over their shoulders. An update from the observer reported, that there seemed to be some German activity in La Boisselle. Macleod had just given the order to advance, when a messenger on horseback arrived with orders from the

General to hold the line. The men stalled, "The front line is La Boisselle, we're too exposed here, and we'll be cut to ribbons if we concede the higher ground to the Germans." MacLeod said as he waved the men forward.

The observer with the field glasses had been right; La Boisselle was only lightly defended, at the moment. The Germans were busily reoccupying the bombed out buildings, as the ever increasing band of British soldiers made their way stealthily into the outlying houses of the hamlet even though some of them were still burning fiercely from the previous night's bombardment.

MacLeod remarked to Sergeant Campbell that the young subaltern might look the part, but being up there on his horse might not be the safest of places. Just then a German shell exploded nearby, and the horse reared. The subaltern decided it might be safer to walk. Macleod and the combination of, mostly Ulstermen with some Manchesters and Highlanders held the line, while Joe and some of the other Highlanders and a few French soldiers who were seconded as interpreters reconnoitred the rest of the hamlet.

Donaldson, McCann and Joe went into a bombed house. Making sure it was empty, Donaldson then started to clear away the rubble that was blocking the under stairs cupboard door.

"What are you doing?" McCann asked.

- "It's where we keep the booze in our house."
- "I didn't think you had any booze in your house."

He opened the door and found an old man, with a long white beard, sitting on a chair.

- "Joe will you come and have a look at this?"

Joe started talking to the old man, and then said,

- "We better get him out of here; this place could come down any minute."
- "Can you ask him where they keep the booze?"

They spoke some more, then Joe told them there was a trapdoor leading down to the cellar underneath him.

- "Come on Joe we better get him out of there"

They lifted him up in his chair and carried him out the front of the house.

- "Let's get him down to that kirk down there."
- "I think we'll just leave him here."
- "Why's that?"
- "Because those Germans look like they are setting up a Maxim Gun."

The three soldiers left the old man and went back through the house to the safety of their own lines.

MacLeod had received news that Captain Lewis was dead, and that he was now the senior officer. He was not best pleased that Sergeant Campbell had sent Joe off to reconnoitre the area.

And confided in the sergeant that he wasn't sure if the Frenchman knew his right hand, from his left, he sent Joe a good way back, with orders to cook the pork.

Joe and his two mates were stuck in a field behind a wall with parcels of pork and a variety of vegetables.

- "How are you going to cook that then Joe?" McCann asked.
- "Roast it, I suppose."
- "Why don't we dig a pit, get some of those stones off that burnt out house over there, they'll be mad hot, put them in the pit, pork on top, cover it over and just let the heat from the stones cook the pork."
- "Where did you get that idea from?"
- "A New Zealand geezer told me that's how the natives do it."
- "We'll give it a go."

The team got to work, a shallow ditch was dug and the stones from the burnt out house were knocked down and transported using two lengths of timber. The pork and the vegetables were placed on the rocks, and then covered with a sheet of corrugated iron, which was too hot to touch. More stones were placed on top and the whole lot covered in the excavated soil from the pit. Joe had poured water over the parcels of meat before they covered them thinking the steam might stop the meat drying out.

The three men sat behind a wall and slept for a short while as the battle for La Boisselle raged on behind them. As dusk slowly started to bring a halt to the fighting, camp fires were lit and tables set up. If the pork wasn't cooked Joe thought he would chop it up and roast it off in smaller pieces, but when the parcels were unwrapped the meat was cooked to perfection. More food and wine had been scavenged from houses. With flour, water, milk, eggs and salt, Joe made a batter and the small pancakes were fried in butter and oil on the men's shovels as they held them over the fires. Salted dough was rolled into long sausages and twisted around sticks and cooked on the fire to make bread. Lettuce, onions, carrots from the vegetable gardens made up a salad, dressed in oil, vinegar, mustard and honey. Joe couldn't resist a garnish of nasturtiums and marigolds. Some of the men had picked wild strawberries and the tartness was taken out of them with brown sugar.

At the end of the meal Murdo MacLeod outlined the plan. The next day they would improve the supply lines, bury the dead, get the wounded to a dressing station and reinforce the line. They would then make a frontal assault on the enemy while the subaltern would lead a force around the back of the Germans to cut off their supply lines. By day six of the battle the manoeuvre was complete and six hundred hungry, tired, blooded, embattled Germans surrendered. Macleod gathered together a hundred or so of the mixed regiments, mostly Suffolk's and Fusiliers, behind the new front line and had a photograph taken.

After two weeks at the front what was left of the Seaforth Highlanders regrouped and made their way back to their estaminet, it was hard to believe there were so many men to die. Joe thought it impossible for this carnage to continue. Files of fresh boys, faces wreathed in the nervous smiles of fearful anticipation looked on at these terrible figures, clothed as they were in bloody rags with sweat streaming down their faces.

They were the survivors, those not too shocked or exhausted to speak related tales of the carnage, of who was missing, who they had seen die and how. The drink flowed but didn't fuel their anger and silences crept on them in their introspection. Macleod turned up later with the young subaltern. "You've probably heard Captain Lewis was killed in action," he said. "Having reported to the colonel I've been given a battlefield commission and am now Captain Macleod. Subaltern Silvertop will be my second in command and aide-de-camp and the Frenchman is to be my personal batman. If you'd like to come to my quarters I'll inform you of your duties." Joe left with the other two men and was given his first task.

The next day was Macleod's birthday and he wanted to throw a party for those of them who were left. He had commandeered the kitchen of the estaminet and Joe would be in charge of catering. Joe slept in the officer's quarters exhausted in mind and body. The horror of it all too vivid in his memory for peaceful sleep, he dreamt a bloody dream not of war but of Herman Cohen and the axe smashing his skull and the flying finger. Then he began running, only this time he was running over bodies, his boots and putties covered in blood as the bodies melded with the earth. He was running, running through fences, over ditches, through the wall of the farmhouse then flying slowly, naked, a couple of inches off the distressed ground. His body floated effortlessly over the barbed wire and he felt the warm sun on his back as he swam through the long meadow grass then, nothing. He was awake, his eyes staring wide disbelieving of the events of the past weeks, all memory of a life before then was a blur, like the words in a book too far away to read. He had to learn take each day as it came, then forget it until it all stopped. At least he had something to do to occupy his time.

He picked his two mates to help him prepare Macleod's birthday dinner, but first he took advantage of the kitchen to boil the pig's blood and lice out of his uniform. Wearing whites borrowed from the owner of the estaminet they set about assembling the ingredients. In the evening the men sat down to a vegetable potage, and a casserole made of sweated horse meat, onions and legumes. White wine and wild mushrooms had been added; rosemary, parsley and lemon flavoured the dish, which was served with Lyonnais potatoes. Dessert was compote of early summer fruits covered in fresh cream. The meal was a success and as Macleod's batman Joe felt he was in a safer place.

The Battle of the Somme carried on with the front line moving ever closer to Thiepval. Every attack by the allies added to the death toll and was countered by the Germans who in turn were cut down by machine gun fire. The minds of men, who couldn't switch off, came to welcome an end to this torture and courted death with a nonchalant indifference, knowing their turn would come sooner or later, and the misery would end.

The summer that Joe had hoped for, the one of constant sunshine was one of rain and the men went up and down, passing the officer's dugout with their rotting feet encased in sodden boots. Those who knew Joe became fewer and new faces came and went. Boredom had ceased to be a problem for Joe, his skills as a cook, laundryman and cleaner were second to none. The meals he prepared in the dugout were of a quality designed to test his mental agility, and challenge the palette of any gourmet. Fresh meat was not served in the trenches but Joe managed to gain a plentiful supply from the dead horses that perished on a daily basis. Ingredients were stolen, cadged, bartered for and given. Joe roamed freely round the field kitchens trading with the Chinese cooks, the French Saphirs and Algerian Zouaves learning of new foods techniques and recipes. Many nationalities moved up and down the Western Front and Joe could tap into their cuisine. He experimented with the different nut oils used by the Chinese and the way they flash fried their own food. Spices he'd got from the Bengal Lancers along with recipes for nan bread and chapattis, he learned how they marinated meat in yoghurts with paprika. The new flavours found their way on to the plates of Macleod, Silvertop and a few others, extending their, and Joe's range of culinary experience.

In early August Joe received a letter from Rose. Hugh was dead: he'd died of pneumonia at the front in February. Harry had been invalided out. He'd been shot in the arm by a stray bullet from a target practice while on a ship bound for Gallipoli. There was the usual stuff about missing him, and news about the baby. There was also a letter, with a newspaper cutting from the local Dieppe paper, about the deaths of Andre and Julian, sent by Joe's mother; just a short piece. Joe felt the need to see his mother, to comfort her. He had some leave coming and he had already decided to go to Dieppe.

Rose also said she'd heard from her brother Jack, he was nearby with the Durhams. Jack was a skilled engineer in Doxford's shipyard on the Wear. Joe got Murdo to borrow him, and a gang of Sappers, for a few days to install a water heating system. The two of them swapped news of Sunderland, of those they had known some dead, some alive. Joe asked Jack if he knew what had happened to Bob Hill and no news meant good news to Joe's ears. Jack and his mates designed an ingenious set of pipes robust and portable. Murdo had been impressed by the German officer's dugouts he'd seen and wanted to build the same. A system for collecting water and pumping it was installed, the sanitation was improved. Silvertop claimed there were more men dying of disease then enemy fire. A small generator fed a battery to run a crude air-conditioned and ventilation unit, the air got stuffy that far underground. A stove fired oven with a back boiler, was supplied at the expense and the insistence of Silvertop. Long augers were used to make chimneys through the chalky clay and a bricklayer was found to make an open fire. Silvertop knew what he wanted and he was a good organiser. He said he'd seen the future at George Armstrong's house at Cragside in Northumberland. This was the same Lord Armstrong whose factories on the Tyne were supplying the armaments that bombarded the German Lines on a daily basis. Hot water baths and clean clothes, expertly ironed by Joe were the order of the day. This kept the infestation of lice down. The new Captain liaised with his fellow officers, Machyon and Macrae. Macrae had been convalescing at home in Scotland; he'd been wounded on the first day of the Somme. Between them they kept the men under their command busy

Captain Macleod's choice of Silvertop as his aide-de-camp had been inspired. Gabriel Silvertop was the third and only surviving son of Baron Silvertop, a pit owner from Northumberland. Gabriel's eldest brother Michael had just been reported dead in the battle of Jutland, about the same time as Gabriel was fighting his way through the streets of La Boisselle. Peter was lost at Mons. At nineteen, the Somme had been Gabriel's first battle. He'd volunteered to take the message to the Ulstermen's advance as he could ride and there was a spare horse available. Macleod saw the lad's potential, and soon secured his transfer from the Northumberland Fusiliers. Of course he needed a new uniform, and being of a generous nature, offered to get Murdo and Joe kitted out as well. A Jewish tailor was found from amongst the ranks and the measurements were sent to the Baron's tailor in Saville Row. The Baron arranged to have the uniforms delivered by courier a month later. The parcels were huge, and the fit was perfect, Joe especially liked his dress kilt. He decided he would wear it to visit his mother.

His parents had moved house, taking advantage of the many available properties that had come onto the market, they had bought a wheelwrights business. Joe had no difficulty in finding the new premises. Outside stood a cart shining in a fresh livery of paint, an intricate pattern of bright colours, in the local style. Joe knocked at the door, then tuned and faced the street; he wanted to see the surprise of recognition as he turned round. The door opened and as Joe turned the surprise of recognition was his. The blood drained from his face as he saw a boy of about sixteen looking back at him. He had Joe's face as if he were a carbon copy. Joe's mother came up behind the boy and putting her hand on his shoulder, told him to go back inside and help his grandfather. Then stepping outside she closed the door behind her.

- "Joseph, we must talk"

They went to a bar near the port where she told him the story. She began,

- "At the start of the war, this woman called Claire came to the door with the boy. There was no need for her to tell me whose son he was, I know my own. She left the boy with me; she said she didn't want him getting caught up with this 'war fever'. She sends money every month but hasn't been back."

- "What's his name?"

- "Leon. I don't want the boy to get to know you, then to lose you; there has been too much death and suffering. He is all I have."

- "You have me?"

- "When I had you I was young, you were my shame. I should have loved you like Claire loved Leon but I couldn't. I feel a love now for Leon that I should have felt for you, that is my real shame."
- "So Francis is not my real father?"
- "No!"
- "He was a father to me, the only father I ever knew. More of a father than I've been to Leon. There's no reason for me to get to know Leon, he's a man."
- "Francis is a good father and a good husband, he always treated you as his son, since Andre and Julian were killed his spirit is broken. He puts all his time and care into making and painting the carts and teaching Leon. Without that I think he would go mad. There is a pain to loss that doesn't go away, it aches inside you. I didn't want Andre and Julian to join up, to fight and die. No proper mother wants to bury her sons and I don't want to bury you. You must leave, you must go, no country is worth dying for, the soil doesn't need your life blood, and this country doesn't own you. You are a free man; you have a right to life, leave tomorrow and go to Spain. Please go to Spain."
- "I've arranged to go to Paris tomorrow; do you have an address for Claire?"
- "No."

- "Let's go home."

Joe now had a better understanding of his circumstances, but did not want to ask his mother who his real father was, maybe another time, another place. They went back to the house where the only father he had ever known embraced him, his long white beard awash with tears.

They ate the evening meal with the politeness of a family of strangers, Leon was too embarrassed to say a great deal, but he looked at his father, as if to study his face, the mask that he would one day wear. As soon as he had finished eating he went out to see his girlfriend, no doubt to restore some semblance of normality to his turbulent world.

The conversation turned to the war; Madame Delaroche apportioned blame to the English.

- "European wars don't last long, the French would have had the decency to stop this nonsense, this needless slaughter and depose bad leaders. But the English love war, their society is based on the fear of outsiders; it's only their pigheaded stubbornness and inability to admit that they are out of their depth that prolongs this war. The real enemy of the British people is the English aristocracy, who have led them like sheep, to this abattoir just to feed their vanity. The Germans and the English are the same, same face, same race."

Francis sat in silence and Joe was in no mood to argue with his mother's intransigence, but could not let her misplaced patriotism go unchallenged.

- "It's not the English or the French or the Germans that are the enemy, war is the enemy, man by his nature is full of envy and greed, war is about possessions, war is inevitable, war is theft. We don't get to make many choices in life, we can't turn off this war, like a tap, it's like a stampede that will slow and stop when its nature has taken its course."

- "When there's no one left to die. I can make choices, I choose to look after my own. Leon will not become part of this evil. And you; if you've got any morals, you'll stop this madness and go to Spain."

- "Things will turn out the way they turn out; tomorrow I'm going to Paris."

Chapter Eight

Paris

The next day Joe left early for Paris, it was still dark and the air was chilly, he felt as cold as stone, but things made more sense to him now. He thought about who his real father might be? What was he like, why had it been kept from him? How could he judge the father he had never known, now that he had met his own son?

The train still held a fascination for him. He looked out of the window and contemplated the movement of the clouds: clouds that knew no boundaries, which could change their shape and colour. He wished he could travel with them. The years since he had left Paris melted away as the daylight lit up its buildings. It had been a long while since he had walked down the boulevards and avenues of his capital city but it felt like he'd never been away.

He made his way to Hotel d'Alsace where he had advised Macleod and Silvertop to stay. Dupoirier was there, older and with an air of sadness that seemed to underlie this city, 'la belle epoch' was a thing of the past. Dupoirier was pleased to see Joseph, and gave him the reception suited to the prodigal son. Their relationship was different now to what it had been. Champagne was uncorked, salmon and oysters ordered. The previous night's revellers were still getting up, even though it was well past midday. Macleod appeared, looking remarkably fresh, displaying the powers of recovery afforded a man in his early twenties. This was the time of his life and he knew it. Silvertop was at Mass, he was a good Catholic.

- "He'll be on his knees in Notre Dame praying for the redemption of the souls of the dear departed," Murdo said mockingly. "Do you mind he asked?" as he slurped down an oyster. "Oysters remind me of Scotland," he said absentmindedly. "A girl stole my wallet last night, I've got bugger all left. I'll have to see Gabby for a sub."

Silvertop had indeed been to Mass and entered cap, gloves and swagger stick in hand.

- "Speak of the devil and she shall appear."

Joe asked Dupoirier if he knew where Claire was. He said that she might still be with the English portrait painter Augustus John but where he was he didn't know.

- "Most of the English artists have left Paris. Some enlisted with the Artists rifles and were in uniform. John used to come in here years ago but he and his friend Monsieur Condor preferred the company of ladies from the 'Boites de Nuit' in Montmartre."

He had heard of an Irishman called Orpen who had a French mistress and was making a good living both sides of the channel painting portraits of the generals and the like.

- "There is also a young British soldier, a sculptor, called Henry Moore, on leave, not far from here. He's staying with a Brazilian painter; he may know where Augustus John is."

Dupoirier gave Joseph the address. It was only a short walk, Macleod and Silvertop tagged along as sightseers, to take in the ambience of the city.

They arrived at the apartment come studio of Gilberto Gil, both he and Henry Moore were working from a life model. The sight of a captain's uniform opens most doors. Moore's own uniform coat was thrown on the bed and his transformation into a sculptor was achieved through wearing a wrap around overall. His hair was combed; he was clean shaven, with his sleeves rolled up displaying the stocky forearms of a sculptor, with their thick hands and fingers. The pipe that was clamped between his teeth gave off a smoke that smelt as sweet as ice cream. They dismissed the model, whose time was almost up, and he put the kettle on and made them all a cup of tea. Macleod's bearing and rank tended to bring deference from men who wore a uniform. Gilberto didn't, he was a pacifist, and sergeant Moore, who had been training soldiers in bayonet practice at the front, had the no nonsense grit of a pragmatic Yorkshire man. He spoke as he found.

Macleod was intrigued by the strangeness of the world these people inhabited. He was a career soldier who had joined a couple of years before the war and loved the life then as now. He had risen to the rank of sergeant in the first few weeks of the war and then on through the ranks with battlefield commissions to his present position. He had the gift of the chameleon and was able to change his demeanour to suit his environment. His Scottish Highland brogue was classless to an English ear. He hadn't lost his common touch and bore no resentment to the easy familiarity of these artists.

Joe explained who he was, and that he knew Walter Sickert and had modelled for Augustus John many years ago. He was trying to trace the whereabouts of a girl who had worked for the John family when they had all lived in Paris. Moore was too young to know any of these people personally but knew them by their work and reputation. As far as he was aware John was in England.

- "He shows a common sense not shared by soldiers, he's sitting out the war in safety, he will survive," said Gilberto.

- "Only spivs like you survive wars Gilberto."

- "And when you survive Henry, then you become spiv like me."

- "None of us will survive this war intact. What we have seen will be etched in our minds eye forever."

There followed an uncomfortable silence that was broken by Joe expressing an interest in seeing some of their work.

- "Are you an artist?" Moore enquired.

- "I was taught painting when I was younger by Walter Sickert."

- "I'm impressed, he's a good painter."

They showed them some of the work they had been doing. Moore had been working in clay, making life studies using the roundels of earth like thick cigar butts, to mould into the lively poses of the model. Gilberto had been working in a very loose way with pen and ink, filling in the drawing with large blocks of flat intense colour. At first the paintings looked like they had been done by a child, but they had a competent understanding of the rules of painting to be able to distort them with confidence.

Joe told Henry that he was showing the officers the sights of Paris. Henry asked if he could come as well.

- "And after the sights, I'll show you one of the most interesting sculptures in Paris."

He finished his tea, pulled on his army coat and cap and picked up a book,

- "Here," he said to Joe, "you read French. You might like that."

The 'allies' headed out the door leaving Gilberto to his painting.

Their quick tour of the city ended up in the Pere-Lachaise cemetery, they walked along an avenue of trees till they reached a sculpture of a winged figure. Moore told them that it was the tomb of Oscar Wilde. Joe didn't know who he was so, Moore explained about him being an Irish writer gaoled in England for being a homosexual. Joe was amazed, knowing that the British were famous in France for being homosexual and especially those in the forces. Moore continued to tell them that it had been made in England by an American Jew, Jacob Epstein. It was carved in Hoptonwood stone and shipped out to France. Joe went up and touched the stone; it was as smooth as a bar of soap. The strangeness of men and their endeavours would never cease to amaze him. This rock, a thing of natural beauty, had been cut from its home leaving, no doubt, a scar on the landscape. It had then been transformed into an ugly obelisk, then transported to rest in this foreign place, a cemetery full of sadness and grief, cold, dead, stone bereft of its craggy nature. Moore continued,

- "Up until the first months of the war it was covered with a tarpaulin and guarded by a gendarme."
- "For what reason?" asked Joseph.
- "The cemetery authorities and the Prefecture of the Seine police found it offensive because the genitals are on show."
- "No! This is France not England, there must be some other reason."
- "Well that was the official line, who knows what the real reason was, maybe it was to protect it for someone did throw paint at it once."

Joe turned and saw Silvertop transfixed by the power of the sculpture and its meaning.

- "It's like something I've never seen before, like I've been given someone else's eyes."

Henry continued his discourse.

- "That is why I am an artist. Art is like a disease that infects your soul; it squanders your time and money and takes away your reason. You are scorned and vilified while you're alive. Everyone has the right to comment on your work, to hurt and wound you, because you dare to tell your own truth and follow your own path. Then in death you are lionised, because you made people look at the world the way you see it."

Murdo was puzzled.

- "If he is lionised why do people throw paint on his tomb? Is it because he was homosexual?"

- "Could be. Could be because they don't like modern art or the Jew who made it. Maybe because it depicts the pagan Egyptian King Sesostris in the shape of a Sphinx with his cock and balls on show, Catholics might find it offensive in a cemetery. Only the anonymous person who threw the paint understands their own bigotry. All I know is that art has the power to inflame passions."

The afternoon was getting late and a thirst had set about Macleod. The men retired to a bar to warm themselves, they talked of the power of art and culture, none of them knew much about Oscar Wilde, his plays had not been seen in England for years but his reputation was known.

Macleod was keen to pick up any education he could; manners, culture, style, art, and his teachers were the young aristocrat and the worldly Frenchman. This was the best place in the world for food, wine, women and fashion. Murdo wanted it all, he wanted to transform himself. When this debacle was over his rank would give him the privilege in society he wanted. He was wise in the ways of war and had kept himself alive this long even though his chances of dying increased with each promotion. Officers were a target; he knew this, that's why so many had died through their irrational bravery, leading by example. What example could you lead by when you were dead? Hang back a bit was his philosophy. Don't show your rank, encourage your men from the side. Make sure your dugout is a little further back and a little bit deeper. Some of the German dugouts he'd noticed were thirty feet deep, they had carpets, electric lighting. He'd seen one with a brass bedstead and air conditioning. Don't be too hasty to move it forward with the line. Eat well, rest well, don't drink too much and don't smoke in the open. Keep your mind busy by reading a book and learn the language. Make sure you treat your men fairly. Good discipline will keep them safe and fair treatment may dissuade the odd deranged person from shooting you in the back. He thought even if he should die by fair means, or foul, or even if he were wounded, he and others would still say he had a good war. He'd experienced life; he'd walked with Gods and Demons.

Joe left them in the bar, it had been a long day and he wanted to take a nap and a hot bath before going out in the evening. He decided to take the metro. As he opened the door to the underground train he noticed a woman staring at him; this was not unusual, the kilt had a tendency to attract people's attention. Joe sat down a few seats alongside from her. He could see her reflected in the window against the darkness of the tunnel outside. Joe took out the book Henry Moore had given him, it was a poem by Oscar Wilde, 'The Ballad of Reading Gaol.' He stopped looking at the distorted reflection of face but the woman kept her gaze. The poem soon absorbed Joe's attention, as he read one line, 'each man kills the thing he loves and each man has to die......'the train slowed as it approached another station, Gare St Germain. The woman had gathered her things and brushed past Joe as she made her way to the exit, leaving a trail of expensive perfume behind her. The train moved slowly away. Joe turned to look at her. She wasn't walking along the platform, as you would expect. She just stood and looked at him. With her free hand she tidied a piece of hair from her face. With that gesture, he recognised Claire. The train moved back into the darkness of the tunnel.

Joe got off at the next stop and walked down the Boulevard St Michele. There was a chance she might walk that way. The missed opportunity upset him and his stomach churned with anxiety. He felt angry and ridiculous, he was tired, and the afternoon's drink had deepened the melancholy which had started in Dieppe. The thing was she had shown an interest in him, the girl he had known was a now striking woman, how could he have acquainted the two? Even now he might be wrong. This woman, the way she was dressed and carried herself, she was not of his kind. No? It was her, an opportunity missed, this time next week he could be dead. Then he saw her in the distance, looking in a boutique window, she went in. He reached the shop and waited till the woman emerged.

- "Pardon me Madame but do I know you?"
- "Yes! Joseph Delaroche."

Joseph's heart beat hard in his chest and the heat of embarrassment set his ears and neck aglow.

- "Can we talk?"
- "Yes! My apartment is around the corner, we can talk there."

The apartment was on the second floor; it was large and well furnished, the home of a well-to-do woman.

- "Café?" she asked. Coffee was scarce and expensive, "I'll have to make it myself the maid doesn't start till later."

She took off her coat and unpinned her hat then loosened her hair. The sound and the aroma of the coffee as it percolated excited Joe, he thought I must take some back with me. She placed the coffee on the low table and sat on the chaise longue with her feet up. Slowly she took a sip of her coffee and said.

- "What do you want to talk about?"

The words choked in Joe's throat, she seemed so self-assured, and it made him feel like a small boy.

- "I've just come from Dieppe! I saw Leon there."

- "How is he?"

- "He's good."

- "I knew nothing about him."

- "Why would you?"

- "I suppose my mother told you that I was in England?

- "Because I was away does not mean I didn't think about you. I've been trying to find you since I've been in Paris, you are the reason I came back to France."

- "It didn't take you long to find me, you've only been here a day."

- "How do you know I've only been here a day?"

- "Dupoirier told me you were here, he's a friend of mine, and he was very good to me when you left. He gave me a job when Leon was born. Augustus John and his family went back to England. My family didn't want to know me so I had to make my own way. It wasn't good for me when you left. I was heartbroken and destitute, and what did you care. You thought of me? I'm flattered, a letter, a reason might have helped. I must admit I thought of you, I hoped you were dead, I despised you. No, I would have heard if you had been dead. No! The reality slowly dawned on me that you had gone and left me because you are selfish and cannot face responsibility. So I lavished all my love and attention on Leon. But now you have come back for me, am I supposed to be grateful? Let me tell you, because I don't think you know, you haven't come back for me, I'm not me anymore, I'm not the person you knew, the person you loved and made me pregnant. Look around you; do you think I got all this from being a serving girl or working for Dupoirier? No! I'm a prostitute and I'd like to thank you for all the help you unwittingly gave me. I used to dream you'd come back and we'd be happily married and live above a small bakery, with rosy faced children running around. Women are fooled by their imaginations. It would have been more likely I'd be poorly shod and constantly pregnant while you would have continued your bachelor lifestyle, drinking, gambling and fornicating. You remember I worked for the English painter with his wife, and his mistress. He still went whoring, getting in drunk in the early hours of the morning. You don't need to tell me where you were going tonight, you're a man; you're a soldier on leave, led around by your loins. Don't give me that look, I can't tell if it's self-pity or condemnation of me, for what I do. Don't feel sorry for yourself, or pity, or condemn me, I enjoy sex and always did, I was always good at it you remember, and I've got better. Is that what you've come back for because the sex was good, because I was easy, because I was loving and generous with my affections? Because I loved you and it made you feel like somebody? Why waste all that on one man. I had my child and as he became more independent, I was still young and pretty and I could be free and easy. I could spend my days with him and have someone look after him in the evenings. I'd seen the women in Dupoirier's with their fine clothes and their carefree laughter, they pleased their men then they pleased themselves, even the married ones. It wasn't difficult for me and then the war came along and my work was not conducive to having Leon around, so I traced your mother. She took to Leon immediately and Leon to her. The war has been good to me, it's paid for all this, and when it's over who knows? Maybe, I'll find myself a good man, like your father, steady and reliable. Yes, the war has been good for me, but not so good perhaps for my clients. I only entertain English officers, they are charmed by the fact that I speak English, and they are gentlemen and generous, unlike the French who want to fuck for free. Some of them have come back but most times they don't, at least I've sent them to where ever they were going with some happy memories. I'm used to men not coming back; but for a lot of the wives - whose husbands do not return to them - it will be a shock. Like your wife! I know you are married and have a child. What do you intend to do? Disappear? You might yet, honourably, a hero perhaps? You won't have told your wife you were going to look for me?

Just left it to chance, have you? There's never a good time to tell your wife the dark secrets of your soul? They'll either bury them with you or you might take them off with you to someplace else. It's probably for the best anyway, she will learn the way I had to learn, and you were my first and best teacher. Don't look so shocked, sex is the only commodity a woman has, in 'a man's world'. An Italian general once told me, 'all women are prostitutes except your mother'."

- "When I left I didn't know you were pregnant."

- "What a happy accident. Look you haven't touched your coffee, let me warm it up for you before you go."

He took the hint and drank it as it was.

- "Can I see you again?"

- "Why? There is only a man who could say something like that. Joseph, you couldn't afford me, and it wouldn't do my reputation any good at all if I were seen with someone of your rank."

- "Just to talk."

- "What is there to talk about, old times? We have nothing in common."

- "We have a son!"

- "I have a son! Goodbye Joseph and close the door when you leave, I am going to take a bath."

-

He stood in the cold night air, the gas lamps were being lit, it was quiet, and Joseph thought he could hear the distant sound of shells exploding at the front. But it was the popping of the gas mantle, he was about to walk off when he felt a hand on his shoulder. He nearly jumped out of his skin; it was Claire, she was shocked by his reaction but soon composed herself.

"I'm sorry for what I said, I'm not the same person I was, and I won't apologize for that but I would like to see you again, next time you are in Paris. Stay safe."

She touched his arm and kissed him on his temple then turned and went back to her apartment. The small kindness of the touch of her lips took away his past and gave him an uncertain future.

Macleod had arranged to eat with some fellow officers at 'La Chartier' on Rue Montmartre. He strolled with Gabriel and Joseph past Notre Dame to the Louvre then up Rue Richelieu. Joseph and Gabriel went upstairs to 'Le Drout' and Murdo crossed the road to go to La Chartier. There was a queue of servicemen on the stairs into Le Drout waiting to be seated. Once seated, Joe was impressed by the Art Décor surroundings of the restaurant. Paintings adorned the walls. One was of tall slim women holding a brace of greyhounds on a leash. The expensive opulence of the place was wasted on the clientele, whose only thought was to spend as lavishly as they could, to experience all the world had to offer before they had to leave it. The food was good and Joe's mood of dark despair lightened. He did not want to drink too much and become morose. Silvertop was not a drinker; he had a spiritual air about him more suited to a monk.

The ranks of servicemen drank 'till all were well on the way to inebriation. Joe's introspection was noticeable, what Claire had said to him played over, and over again, and distractions would only relieve his torment for a short while. He thought; was he such a spineless person that he ran away from any commitment?   Was it in his nature?   The Brazilian that afternoon had said, "Only spivs survive wars." It is only natural to want to survive, he remembered his mother's advice, "go to Spain," but that would require making a decision, the wrong decision could mean death.

Captain Murdo Macleod sat down with three fellow officers of the Seaforths, Major Lancelot Waugh, Captain's Reginald Machyon and Archibald Macrae. The atmosphere in the Art Nouveau interior was an excited clatter as the waiters in their long white aprons hurried about the place. The talk was of women and drink and past times. They were all emboldened by their experiences and spoke of what they would do when it was all over.

- "When it's over we'll be out of a job," was Lance's observation.
- "I'm staying on only until Murdo gets to be a general," added Archie.
- "The way Murdo is going it should only be a few more weeks then. He already has an aide-de-camp, which I think is rather pretentious."

They were aware that Murdo had come up through the ranks and was not really one of them. The bastions of 'class' had been temporarily breached for the duration and the comment was received with good humour. For his part, Murdo didn't feel in the slightest uncomfortable. He'd seen enough death to know that the grim reaper paid no attention to breeding. In this conflict he had shown a preference for the privileged caste, the young officers, sons of the wealthy and the aristocracy.

- "The way Murdo is going he'll be ordering us around within the next few weeks." Lance continued. "By the way how's your back, Archie?"
- "Knocked a lump off the shoulder blade, still a bit stiff, the bullet stopped quarter of an inch from my heart but at least it gave me a couple of months up at 'The Hall'. If I find the blighter that tried to pop me I'd shake him by the hand - that is before I had him strung up, of course."
- "It could have been an accident."

- "No! It was probably one of those buggers I'd had tied to a cart wheel the week before the Somme."

- "You'd have a job stringing any of them up now, most of them are dead," said Murdo. "What was left of your company joined what was left of mine. How did you get on with that sergeant of yours, Campbell, I ended up with him at La Boisselle?"

- "A fucking good man, hard as nails, stood no bloody nonsense from the ranks."

- "He's too rigid; you can have him back when you get your new command."

- "No fear old man! I'd have him back tomorrow. I'd heard he's been giving your batman a hard time, is that it? Has your batman been crying to you?"

- "No, I wouldn't expect he's even noticed. He's used to having the piss taken out of him because he's French."

- "Like water off a Frogs back eh! I don't think it's because he's French. It's because he's a non-combatant, a fucking coward"

- "He's not off active service, he's my batman. Coward is not a word you should use lightly and certainly not one you should use about Private Delaroche. On the first day of the Somme he led the way, was in front of myself, you and your precious sergeant Campbell."

- "The only reason he was in front of me was because I was wounded in action. What's your excuse for lagging behind Macleod?"

- "The orders were to walk, ninety to one hundred yards remember."

- "Now who's being rigid? Your batman didn't stick to orders. Campbell told me he was running sideways like a crab and he'd lost his pack."

- He's got a very poor sense of direction and he told me his pack was shot off his back."

- "Poor sense of direction? Is that why you ended up at La Boisselle? You were following someone who didn't know where he was going. You're not sleeping with him are you? He seems to do everything else for you."

- "I say old man, leave off," said Reggie,

- "No, not my type old son he's too old and his tits are too small. The problem with you Archie is you're just jealous."

- "And you are a deeply unpleasant person." added Lance.

- "Being jealous might have something to do with it. Every time I'm near Murdo's dugout there's this wonderful smell of cooking. As for being unpleasant Lance, I defer to your rank and take that as a compliment. Since when was a war won by an army of pleasant soldiers, what do you think Murdo? "

- "I think this war is run on fear and food and I've got both in abundance, and my biggest fear is that I lose the best chef on the western front. So why wouldn't I want to keep him safe?"

- "I'll tell you what Murdo, if you stop one, I'm having him."

- "I'll be watching my back then."

- "What's the point, there's never anyone behind you."

- "Now we have better facilities, I don't see why all of us can't share in the advantage of having a gourmet chef amongst our company."

- "I don't know how you two can joke about it," said Reggie. "Don't you ever feel scared when you go over the top?"

- "I was more scared doing my finals at Cambridge," said Archie.

- "And what was it you were reading?"

- "Theology, I was going to take holy orders, probably still will do after the war."

- "I must admit I never saw you as a religious type, bearing in mind the fifth commandment."

- "What's that one again? 'Thou shalt not kill.' Whoever wrote those commandments certainly had a sense of humour, religion is a comedy written in blood. Breaking all the commandments and indulging in the seven deadly sins make you well qualified to becoming the Archbishop of Canterbury."

- "I'll tell you what Your Holiness," said Murdo, "I'll invite you all for Sunday lunch and you can sample the creations of the best restaurant on the front line, we call it the 'Dive' the 'Ritz' of Beaumont Hamel."

They all agreed it was a good idea. Murdo suggested next Sunday evening, as they would all be at the front.

- "Sunday afternoon would be better it's so fucking boring," said Lance, and so it was arranged.

The food at 'La Chartier' was good, so were the cigars and port that followed the cheese at the end of the meal. The four young men continued to fantasise about their hopes and aspirations and although Murdo was not, one of them, they admired him. He had achieved his rank because he was good at what he did. He didn't make excuses, success needs no excuse. The men serving under him, respected him, he had the charisma of a leader. If he could avoid putting his men in unnecessary danger he would, because of this he had their support.

Macrae, on the other hand, was reckless. Like a lot of his generation he thought he was invincible and charged forward into battle with gay abandon, as if he were bullet-proof. He had indeed been hit in the back by a stray bullet, intentional or not. If he hadn't been so far in front of the man who shot him the velocity of the bullet would have probably killed him. Murdo was sure he would die next time they went over the top.

Murdo found Reggie easier to get on with but was concerned about him. Like a lot of the young officers from wealthy backgrounds, the privations of the front and the sheer shock of seeing men die had affected him. More so than some of the lower ranks, some of whom had lived and worked in the appalling conditions in the mills and the mines of the industrial heartlands. Some of the ranks had seen this as a golden opportunity to have some fun for a short while. Accepting what came along as their fate, revelling in their freedom; the lack of a need to earn a living and support a family. A chance to live 'off licence' in a world without the rules, a world turned upside down. In two and a half years of fighting some men had seen only twenty odd days of action, others none. They trusted in the wisdom of their betters and went willingly to the slaughter.

After leaving 'La Charretier' they made their way to La Pigalle, Captain Macleod had no intention of spending the rest of the evening in the company of the young drones, reminiscing about Henley, Ascot and playing rugby and who knew whom, from who's school? Sad as it was to be with this dying breed on a professional level, he had better things to do than to hang out with them in his leisure time. A bottle of champagne and a comely young girl to help him with his 'French,' and provide some warm skin to wake up with in the morning was more to his taste.

Neither Joseph nor Silvertop felt the need to revel in the delights of the city, already their thoughts were on the future. Whatever fate was in store, Joe had decided to go with the flow. If the opportunity arose to flee this mad barbarism he would take it. If a German shell reunited disparate parts of his body with his homeland so be it. On their way back to the hotel a pretty young woman persuaded Joe that he needed her companionship more than he needed Gabriel's. Claire's prophesy was self-fulfilling, temptation by its very nature is something the weak give into.

Next day the three warriors were at breakfast, Silvertop again arrived late, having been to Mass. Murdo explained about the meal he had arranged and the men discussed a menu. It was decided that duck in the style of Rouen, after Joe had explained what it was, would make a fitting main course. This would be a meal to impress. Joe had his shopping to do before they went back to the battlefield. Dupoirier had packed them a basket of good wine, foie-gras, caviar and a few other delicacies for men with discerning palettes. He was sympathetic towards Joe's plight concerning Claire, he had not told Joe where she was, and he thought it would have been better to have left well alone.

- "There are no winners in this game, you are both good people, you have to live with your actions and play the cards the way they are dealt."

Joe appreciated his old employer's kindness and set off back to war in better spirits. Macleod always seemed in good spirits, whereas Silvertop seemed quiet to the point of being introverted. As the evening train pulled into Pont Remy Station Joe was aware Silvertop had been looking at him as he slept. Next morning they would be at the front.

Nothing much had happened in the few days they had been away. One of the men had been found wandering aimlessly behind the lines. A sixteen year old halfwit who had always stunk to high heaven and was ill suited to any task he was given. An army is not well-disposed to compassion for a runt and his treatment was merciless. Normally he would have been given some hard labour to attend to and be chained to a wheel at night, for a week, but being bloody useless Campbell had put him on a charge of desertion. The court martial was swift and Macrae offered scant defence for the boy, his execution by firing squad was arranged for the following day.

Silvertop was detailed to organise the firing party but feeling unsure about the whole affair asked Joe to accompany him for moral support. As the door to the cell was opened, the pathetic spectacle of a bruised boy, dressed in rags greeted them.

- "Stand to attention you fucking coward!" Campbell yelled.

The boy stood up, grinning, a black-toothed smile of bewilderment as his arms were tied behind his back. The chaplain walked with him chanting from his prayer book as the group made their way outside. A chair stood alone and as the boy was sat in it he looked up at Campbell with a puzzled frown on his still smiling face. Campbell pulled a black hood over the boy's head. In the silence before the order there could be heard a soft sobbing.

- "Take aim. Fire!"

An ear splitting volley rang out and the chair fell sideways with the weight of the slumped body. Silvertop went up to the lifeless bundle that lay on the ground in the foetal position and taking out his revolver fired a single round into the boy's skull. As they walked back to the estaminet, Campbell walked passed Joe and said,

- "You'll be next Frenchman!"

Silvertop who had heard what was said called him back.

- "What was that remark supposed to mean?"
- "What remark was that sir?"
- "If you don't apologise immediately to Private Delaroche, I will put you on a charge."

The men of the firing squad stood and watched as their Sergeant was made to apologise. After which he was about faced and headed off to the resting station.

Joe had Sunday's dinner to prepare and wasted no time in securing the services of David Jackson, a gamekeeper whose expertise with a hunting rifle was renowned as was his skill with the rod. They spent a day by a lake shooting duck and catching trout. Not an easy task in a land occupied by an army. They took their time; a soldier soon learns to do what he is told to, but to do it slowly. Joe built a little fire and cooked some of the fish by letting one side blacken in soy sauce and wild honey.

It was a pleasant day; the war was a distant memory for a few hours as the two men talked about their lives before war. Only the muffled noise of exploding shellfire sullied their peace. As they chatted over their meal of bread and fish Jackson warned him to be on the lookout for Campbell. Joe assured him that time would take care of Campbell. Jackson's spaniel, a soft mouthed gun dog, hadn't damaged the birds and the two men returned to duty with a couple of brace each. Jackson asked Joe, that if anything happened to him would he look after his dog, Joe said he would, knowing that Jackson wouldn't know either way what happened to his dog if he were dead.

Lots of the men had animals with them in the trenches, dogs, cats, rabbits, everything imaginable. One private even had a parrot. Joe had found some of these animals had made handy little meals when they became strays. The dogs were especially useful for trading with the Chinese for soy sauce and opium. The opium had been supplied to the Chinese for years by the British government from their plantations in India. It kept them placid as well as being a lucrative source of income.

Four-o'clock on the appointed Sunday afternoon was a quiet time in the trenches as Joe stood in his white apron, basting the plump ducks that he and Davy Jackson had got less than twenty four hours earlier. A real Rouennaise duck should be choked and the breast feathers plucked immediately but wartime forgave Joe these details. The homely smell of the roasting ducks excited the saliva glands of the men in the trench, huddled around their braziers with their 'billy cans' of grey boiled beef. It fuelled their resentment. They saw Joe's privilege as unwarranted, and this resentment, was stoked by the growing hatred harboured deep in the heart of the xenophobic Campbell.

Joe still had some friends who he'd started with and if he had any food left over he would serve it up. If he had the time he would knock up a meal for them on the quiet. Joe understood the importance of keeping a foot in as many camps as possible.

As the other officers arrived for their promised dinner they surveyed the stark beauty of the devastated landscape. What deadly power had they unleashed to cause such an unholy world and how many generations would it take before the evil was put back into Pandora's Box?

The tables were laid with white linen and there were jugs of iced gin martini. The small but adequate space was lit by numerous hurricane lamps and one dim electric light bulb illuminated the table. Murdo welcomed them in.

- "I say! Fantastic! A proper little Aladdin's cave we have here," said Lance.

- "Help yourselves to an aperitif"

- "Cheers old boy!" said Archie. "What's the sixth chair for? I thought there were only five of us Macleod?"

- "I've asked Joseph to join us as my guest."

- "Bit of a 'rum do' this, Murdo, eating with the servants."

- "Today is Sunday. It's his day off. Joseph is my guest."

- "What are you going on about, day off? We're fighting a bloody war here; it's not the annual altar boy's outing."

- "With your track record Archie, I thought you might appreciate having the cook eat the same food as yourself."

- "Point taken old chum, your party. I'll say no more."

Joe served the French onion soup. The sweetness of the caramelised onions had been enhanced by adding Demerara sugar. The flavour was enriched by cooking with a large piece of pork belly. The rest of the dinner was enjoyed in relative silence only punctuated with the odd 'I say' and 'indeed!' After the ducks, that had been roasted on a spit in front of an open fire, had been eaten and washed down with an endless supply of Merlot, Macrae spoke up,

- "Fair dues Macleod, that's the best meal I've had since this war started. Your man is a treasure indeed."

The lemon meringues were put in the oven, each in its individual tray then served with fresh cream. The tang of the lemon with the bits of zest brought them back to civilisation. The contentment and fellowship that good food creates was built upon with the cheese, the port, the brandy and cigars. The light from the door had faded as conversation proper broke out.

- "That's probably the finest meal I've had since Paris. Where did you learn to cook like that Joseph?" asked Lance.

- "Paris, London, Sunderland."

- "Joe used to work at the Savoy. He's even cooked for the King of England, haven't you Joe?" added Murdo.

- "Is that right Joe?"

- "Yes! The old King, I did a dessert for him many years ago when he was the Prince of Wales."

Reggie Machyon spoke,

- "You've obviously been around Joe. I have difficulty talking to the men; the uniform stops them from being honest with an officer. Understandably they tell you what they think you want to hear. You're older than we are and more experienced.

I haven't seen much action since I've been here and I really don't know what's going on and I'd be interested to know what you think. Charterhouse rules of course."

- "Steady on old man."

- "Charterhouse rules here Archie," said Lance. "No comeback and nothing said out of this company."

- "Joe's been where I've been, I value his opinion," said Murdo.

Joe spoke in measured terms knowing Charterhouse rules, whatever they said counted for nothing.

- "I think the war must end soon, Europe cannot sustain this killing, the lifeblood of the continent is mingled with the soil of France. It is the people who have brought about this folly who will pay the price, unfortunately that is you people," looking around at the company present. "You the ruling classes, the masters of war. This is the last time you will call on working people and order them to die. Before the war I never took any notice of politics, not many working people do, voting only changes politicians but not the status quo, if democracy existed it would soon be banned. Those that survive this war will want to change that, to break off the shackles that the unfair class system, with its greed and lust for power, has put on them. No man has the right to make a slave of another man. In my experience the United Kingdom is a land of slaves and masters. When I first went to England I was surprised that the richest country in the world had so much poverty. The soldiers that joined up to fight didn't do so to defend England, they did it to get out of England, the England that enslaved them. Those of us who go back will not go back as slaves but as equal partners with a share in the wealth, what's left of it."

- "Are you communist?" Archie enquired.

- "Let the man finish," said Reggie.

- "It's not important if I'm a communist or not, my priority is keeping my body and soul intact in this death trap. Luckily winter will be on us soon and we will stop the killing for a while."

- "That is until the soldiers turn their guns on us officers?"

- "It's a possibility, the French have already mutinied once at Verdun, whether it's the French again or the Russians. I don't think the English have the psychological make-up for revolution. The English behave like the lowest rank of dog in the pack, the one that is fiercely loyal to its abusive leader, as long as it is allowed a few scraps of meat now and again."

- "The French won't mutiny again not after what happened to the ring leaders, they were all shot. But what do you know about the Russians?"

- "I think it's already started, their army is starving, mutiny is inevitable, and one Russian has to wait till another one is dead before he gets a rifle. With no food or guns the Russians will be out of this war sooner rather than later."

- "What you're saying could be called treason."

- "Call it what you like, it's common sense. Whatever I say won't make any difference, what will be, will be."

- "Say what you like Joe," said Lance, "Charterhouse rules, and anyway I think we're all in agreement with the prognosis. Which one of us hasn't thought, at some time, that this collective stupidity cannot continue? It's a stalemate. How it stops is immaterial but it will stop. In essence this war is a family squabble between the offspring of Victoria Saxe-Coburg-Gotha. We are just the little lead soldiers they play with and when we are all lost or broken their empires will collapse."

- "How do you know what is going on with the Russians Joe, they're miles away," asked Reggie.

- "Just ask the Germans."

- "That's the value of reconnaissance," said Murdo.

- "All sounds a bit dodgy to me." Reggie continued.

- "It's the reality of the situation Archie. The first casualty of war is the truth. Maybe as we near the end the casualty is beginning to recover. Society won't be the same after the war, it will change, things will change, let's hope for the better."

- "Better for who?" said Archie. "I have no complaints and it's good to be reassured that your friend here has such a high opinion of his comrades, 'the lowest rank of dog,' what does that make you?"

- "I'm loyal, and so is Joe, and while we and the rest of us remain loyal you can cling on to your life of privilege. Don't try to pretend that you hold the fighting men in anything less than contempt, because I don't believe you. You were reluctant to even eat at the same table as Joe, referring to him as a servant. Anyway enough of that, I bought this hooker pipe off an Arab officer, along with a quantity of quality hashish for those who wish to partake." As the pipes were passed around Reggie turned to Gabriel, "You're very quiet Silvertop what's your opinion?"

- "I don't have one, and if I did I'd keep it to myself, some people don't play by Charterhouse rules."

- "I don't want to pull rank," said Lance, "but we are all honourable men here. The purpose of Charterhouse rules is so intelligent men can have a free and open discussion without fear of accountability or retribution. Civilised people need a degree of honesty and trust, without it we are a rabble. Nothing will be said outside of this place."

- "If that's the case I'd just like to ask Archie a question."

- "What's that?"

- "Are you enjoying the war?"

- "Some of it yes! You get to do things you wouldn't be allowed to do in civilian life."

- "Like kill people."

- "When I do something I do it to the best of my ability, if something is inevitable welcome it."

- "As a student of theology how do you reconcile, 'love they neighbour as thyself?"

- "I thought I'd answered that in Paris. God is on leave for the duration OK? But to clarify where I stand on the subject, I look on the Germans as my neighbour, my neighbour with whom I'm competing. It would be an act of disrespect to them for me not to compete with them to the best of my ability. It is an act of love to afford them that respect."

- "I think they are more able than we are and that we are going to lose, unless the Americans enter the war and save our bacon."

- "Yes! And we win, and to the victor the spoils."

- "I'll drink to that," said Murdo, "I'm sure we've all had a very pleasant afternoon and tomorrow it's back to what passes for normality, so let's not put a damper on the day. I think we should make this a regular event, if that's alright with you Joe."

- "I think it is a very good idea."

- "But let's keep it light in future, don't mention the war."

Each one of them had to deal with the situation in their own way but honour demanded they put to the back of their minds what had been said.

Murdo's intention was to make the most of his time. Every day above ground was to him a good day. He was certain that their society of diners would change over the weeks and months ahead, if that was the case, he vowed as long as he was in the party, he would only speak of them to remember them fondly.

The sweet smelling smoke from the pipe soon filled the small space. The food, the drink and the drugs had a soporific effect on the dinner party and they soon broke up. Murdo didn't partake in the hashish, he reckoned it dulled his edge. He went out to check on how his men were before catching some sleep.

During the night Joe lay awake not sure if speaking his mind had been a good idea. Macrae had a reputation and Joe feared him more than he feared the Germans, some of whom he'd grown quite fond. He heard Silvertop talking in his sleep and then he was awake. He looked over to Joe and said,

- "I'm scared."

- "What are you scared of?"

- "What I have become, it's not only Macrae who's enjoying the war. I want to die here; nothing in this life can top this experience. I couldn't live with what I've seen and what I've done; it would only make me mad."

- "If there's a sane person left in the world this place would cure them. We have all become mad but if we survive we will become sane again."

- "When I die, will you take my possessions to my father and tell him I died well?"

- "Of course I will."

- "Thank you. If you'll take some advice Joe, it's not always in your own best interests to speak your mind. Macrae is a very dangerous man. I'm cold Joe. Will you lie next to me?"

- Joe felt sorry for the young man and went to comfort him in his distress; their two grey coats over them gave them extra warmth and they drifted into fitful sleep.

They had lived and fought through the rainy summer and autumn. The early winter with its attendant mud made fighting the war impossible for both sides. They were reduced to fighting the mud: that all-embracing, strength sapping, mud which sucked at their very souls. Cruel weather had visited them like some divine punishment and they were all guilty. The rain was followed by the snow, the worst winter in living memory. The wicked beauty of its whiteness masked the imperfections of landscape, cleansing the souls of the men by making them do penance in frozen boots. The snow melted with the coming of spring but the war didn't melt away, and the soldiers feared more plagues from on high were about to descend upon them. More young men would be ordered to die for a country in which they were only serfs. Spring was lifting the green out of the scarred ground like evidence of rebirth and some men hoped for better days ahead.

The aroma of Joe's cooking wafted down from the officer's dugout across even to where the Germans sat thawing out from the rigours of the winter. The lines were close and neither side were inclined to kill each other having got out of the habit of it. Only the impersonal shells burst to keep alive the spark of a war that was looking like it would fizzle out through lack of interest. Joe had taken of late to getting himself invited into the German trenches to trade food, sugar and flour which he swapped for good German sausages and preserves. Macleod turned a blind eye to this practice because he enjoyed his food and was rapidly becoming a *bon viveur*. He also thought that it might make the Germans better disposed to his men next time they had to charge at their trenches. Macleod entered these visits into his log as recognisance sorties, as indeed they were; Joe did pick up the odd piece of gossip.

The night had been bitter and Joe woke up with a cold nose, it being the part of his face not covered by his balaclava. Gabriel had one leg draped over him. It was early and although Joe was stiff and fatigued he couldn't sleep. The constant closeness of death concentrated his mind; only the performance of ritual confirmed his existence. He had come to realise that it wasn't the luxuries that gave meaning to life it was the simple things, tasks that require no anticipation but are just there to be done as a necessity. The dull warmth of the stove radiated a heat you could just about feel. He raked the ash out of the grate before putting more paper, wood and coal on the dying embers, the fire would soon be warming the back boiler. He filled the kettle for tea, and put it on the hotplate, pulled up a chair and sat down to remove his boots and old socks and examine his feet. He cleaned between his toes and applied Tolnaftate powder. Silverfish were flashing around and under the stone hearth as Joe pulled a clean pair of hand-knitted socks off the airer above the fire. They were dry and warmed his feet. He cleaned the dry mud from his boots then polished them as best he could. He did the same for Gabriel's and Murdo's by which time the kettle was boiled, he pulled on his boots and made a pot of tea.

Making a taper from a piece of paper he lit a Gitane. The sun was rising as he climbed out of the dugout with his tea and cigarette. He walked down to the line to stretch his legs. In the mist he could see various bodies, sitting and lying about the place, huddling themselves against the cold in balaclavas and gloves. The dew stood off them like pearls and made them look like they were at one with their surroundings. Joe turned to the sound of a brazier that crackled. His eyes were met by those of Campbell staring at him with unabashed malice.

Macleod had managed to keep Joe out of most of the fighting at the Somme but that spring a new army started building. Beaumont Hamel had been a cosy winter billet but the Generals had plans to wake the men out of their complacency. The Seaforths were moved up the line and a bombardment more terrible than the Somme lashed the German lines near Ypres before the end of July. The sickening inevitability of the rise from the trenches echoed the previous year's disaster, one line followed by another. The predictability of the Somme was compounded by the rain that had flooded the battlefield, filling the shell holes with water.

Joe was well back in the order of ascent up the ladder and proceeded at a slow walking pace towards the enemy lines. As soon as the German bullets started to take their murderous toll

Joe made a dash for the nearest shell hole. Being newly created it wasn't yet full of water. Jumping into the pit he found half a dozen others engaged in various activities, some firing from the lip of the hole while others dressed the profusely bleeding gunshot wounds of two men. Joe didn't feel inclined to join in either of these pursuits and was content to keep his head down. He was in a reverie of self-pity contemplating the disastrous situation that he found himself in. Was this God's purpose for him? What had it been all about? Macleod dropped into the shell hole with a cheery, 'What Ho!' A couple of other chaps followed him down into the safety. Macleod soon organised the men. He had a bottle of laudanum with him that Joe had made up the night before. He took a hefty swig before giving the two bleeding men the bottle to share between them. Joe remembered his own bottle, he'd taken a drink before he'd climbed the ladder but the effect was wearing off. He didn't want to take too much in case it bolstered his bravado and made him do something stupid and heroic. He did as Murdo had done and passed it to the other soldiers with them. Murdo replaced men on the lip of the shell hole with the new arrivals while he and Joe comforted the wounded.

There was a lull in the fighting and Macleod ordered Joe to go back to the trench, get a brew on and fetch a few cans of tea back for them. He also told him that while he was there he might get some of cases of ammunition and alert the stretcher-bearers that they had a couple of wounded. Joe snaked his way back to the trench without attracting attention. He reported his orders to the staff officer and set about his duties. He followed on beside the stretcher-bearers with their white flag and Red-Cross armbands carrying the ammunition and tea on the stretcher covered with a blanket.

It wasn't far to the shell hole but when they got there they noticed the unmistakable smell of mustard gas. They saw it in the distance being blown around, this way and that, the distinctive yellow mist. Being heavier than the air the gas had sunk unnoticed into the shell hole. The two wounded men were dead at the bottom of the pit and the others were in varying degrees of distress. Gas held a terror for all the servicemen and the stretcher-bearers didn't hang about to feel its effects, Joe was dropped off with his tea and ammunition. They loaded the worst affected onto the stretcher and were off. He quickly donned his gas mask and sat looking through the round eyeholes at the devastation. As he watched his choking, coughing comrades spewing onto the brown earth, Joe felt lost and alone, his rifle lying across his legs. The offensive had moved forward enough for a colonel and his adjutant to ride out to see what had been achieved. Joe looked up to see this impressive figure riding high silhouetted against the blue sky. The gas had all but gone leaving behind its acrid taste. Joe removed his gas mask.

- "Take this man's name Lieutenant Jowett and make sure he gets a DSM," said the colonel. "Well done man holding this position single-handed you deserve a medal."

The adjutant duly wrote down Private Joseph Delaroche, Second Battalion Seaforth Highlanders and rode off.

- "Distinguished Service Medal for making tea under enemy fire," Macleod broke into a sardonic laugh before being sick again.

The rain had started and as the evening descended, the exhausted occupants of the shell hole, made their slippery way back to safety. On the way to the dressing station the men stopped to rest and sheltered from the rain under a railway arch, the track long since having been ripped up. In the dark Joe could see a half-moon of sky peeking over the sandbags at the far end of the arch. As his eyes adjusted to the light he noticed the sandbags weren't sandbags, they were bodies, stacked like bricks, floor to ceiling. The faint aroma of the decomposing corpses greeted his nostrils. One face stared out at him, a married man, his gleaming white dentures shining in a grim smile. The thought crossed his mind, that this might be his fate? Getting closer to the man he touched the cold forehead, it felt as smooth as stone. After a moment Joe turned and walked out of the blackness, as another cart full of bodies hauled by two donkeys pulled into the makeshift morgue. The reverence of this Golgotha was shattered as the driver's mate let out a scream.

- "Fucking hell you gave me the shock of my life. "You're not a fucking ghost are you?"
- "Yeah! I'm a ghost, have you got a light, this ghost needs a cigarette?"

Joe had to steady the trembling hand of the carter to light the Gitane. The smell of the smoke cleansed his nostrils of the sickly sweet smell of death.

- "Not dead yet mate, sorry if I frightened you."

All the survivors from the shell hole made it back to the dressing station in various degrees of blindness, deafness and choking. Gabriel Silvertop was missing, presumed dead. Davy Jackson said the last time he'd seen him he was leading the charge smoking nonchalantly on his meerschaum pipe. He said,

- "I heard him shout to one man, 'stop ducking it's not going to do any good and it only slows us down.'"

Macleod was off active service for the time being and so was Joe, gassed? Joe Roc DSM was on sick leave to recover from the effects of tea. He had a pass to go to Dieppe.

Chapter Nine

Dieppe

Joe felt a great relief at having the opportunity to spend some time at peace and not having his body in constant tension and mind in constant fear. A few more months might see the war over. The Russians on the eastern front had packed up and gone home. Russia was in turmoil. Joe's mother told him that it was rumoured that the French army were in mutiny again. America had declared war against Germany. Surely it must all come to an end.

Joe all but ignored Leon, it was not his intention to take on the role of father. But he watched as Leon worked with Francis shaving the spokes of a new cartwheel. In the evenings Joe would tell stories of the war and of things he had seen and done, of people, the good, the strong, and the dead. Nervousness compelled him to try to get people to understand. During the day he went out and he visited the places of his childhood, the beach, the fish quay, the harbour. One day Joe was at the fish market to meet his mother, it had finished early, there weren't enough people about. At a table outside a café Joe was surprised to see his mother sat with Madame Villain. Madame Villain was in black. Joe went and sat with them and ordered a bottle of Jenlan. The sun was shining and cotton wool clouds hung suspended in a blue sky.

- "Madame Villain has been reading a letter for me, it's from Leon's mother. She says you met her in Paris." Joe looked at his mother, she continued. "When she came with Leon I gave her your address in Sunderland. She says she informed the authorities. She said she wanted revenge but now she feels only guilt and wants to make amends. She says if you go to Paris she will hide you till the war is over."

- "Give me the letter I can read." He read what his mother had told him. The paper was expensive and perfumed and the writing neat and deliberate. He took out a match and set fire to the letter and envelope. "Is she stupid? I could be shot for that," pointing to the letter burning in the ashtray, "it's not worth it, chances are the war will be over shortly."

- "They've been saying that since 1914. Do you want to end up like that smiling corpse you told me about, I've already lost two sons, Madame Villain has lost all her boys. No more! Aren't you scared of going back?"

- "I'm terrified. I could say it's not the dying that scares me but if it's not that what is it? Being maimed, ending up mad and having to live with the horror and the guilt of having been part of this killing spree? Sometimes we even find the whole thing funny and laugh uncontrollably. You see there's a bond between us a bond of pride, a bond of shared experiences, I have a responsibility, a duty to my comrades."

- "You have a duty to your wife and daughter and go back to England in one piece."

- "How could I go back to England? If I were caught I'd be shot. How could you live with the shame?"

- "Easily. How can you live with the shame of what you've done and what you might do, the honourable thing to do is to go to Paris. Let those who want to stay and die, do so. This way you choose life and believe me you'd find a way to get back to England if you want to."

- "If I don't return for duty they will come looking for me. If my papers are out of date I'll be shot as a deserter."

- "Madame Villain has three boats, one of them is idle, and there are not enough men to man it. The boat is insured she can take it out to sea, open the sea locks, come back with her other boat and claim the insurance. Lots of fishing boats have been lost by hitting mines. No one would think twice about it. I could let it be known you were on the boat and a few days later I would make sure your burnt tunic was found on the beach. When you get to Paris you send me your papers, I will make sure they are found in your pocket. You would be just another dead soldier, no one would look for you you're not that important."

- "Of course Madame Villain would want paying.
- "I've got money, we'll see if anything changes by the end of the month."

As the end of the month came around Joe packed his bag said his goodbyes and told them he was going to Paris. As he sat in the railway station with his ticket in his pocket he noticed a one legged man about his own age, part of his face was damaged with one ear missing, he was selling newspapers. Joe walked over to him with growing recognition.

- "*Le Figaro,* please," it was Patrice. "Been in the wars Patrice?"
- "Yes, Verdun, I was there when Julian got killed, he dropped like a stone. I'm sorry, I never saw what happened to Andre. I

know what you're doing here, if you'd take my advice you wouldn't catch the train."

- "Why not?"

- "The redcaps are looking for you."

Over Patrice's shoulder Joe spotted two military police coming into the station. Joe took the ticket out of his tunic pocket gave it to Patrice.

- "Can you get rid of that for me? I was only going for the day."

Patrice looked at the ticket.

- "Maybe you should have got a return, this is no time to be thrifty. Just leave your bag here I'll get it back to you later. Goodbye and good luck my friend."

Joe nodded and gave Patrice a long hard look before heading off in the direction of the military police. Although his papers were in order, he was arrested but didn't know what the charge was and they were not at liberty to tell him. He was banged up and left there all day. The unpleasant stench of shit, urine and vomit permeated the very walls. The wailing and the screaming of the mad, the bad, and the drunk made it difficult to sleep. The guards who awoke him next morning marched him along the corridor to a room where three officers sat at a trestle table. A full colonel was seated in the centre and was looking at the charge sheet.

- "Private Delaroche, what sort of a name is that? The charge is fraternising with the aliens."

The blood drained from Joe's face.

- "It says here you've been living at the house of a French woman and not the billet to which you were assigned. Is that correct?"

- "Yes sir!"

- "We can't have this sort of thing. You were aware that fraternising with the aliens is an offence?

- "Yes sir!"

- "Do you have anything to say?"

- "Yes sir, the Frenchwoman is not an alien to me, Sir, she is my mother!"

- "Extraordinary! What are you trying to say, that you're French?"

- "Yes sir."

The other two officers on either side of the colonel confirmed that Joe was indeed French and that he had requested permission from his commanding officer to stay with his mother.

- "And how do you know this?" The colonel asked the officer on his right.

- "I am his commanding officer," replied lieutenant major Murdo McCloud.

- "That's the reason for the name then is it? Case dismissed. But before you go, why did you join the British army and not the French army?"

- "Sir, we are all fighting the same enemy and I wanted to be with the best fighting men in the world."

- "Who ordered the arrest of this man?"

- "My sergeant, sergeant major Campbell," answered Macrae, the other officer.

- "And he knew he was French? Bit of an odd thing to do if you ask me, wasting people's time, doesn't he know there's a war on?"

- "He's a stickler for the rules sir."

- "Case dismissed."

Campbell was standing outside the room as Joe left.

- "I'll have you for that you fucking bastard, you're a fucking coward, there are good men dying out there every day and I bet you've never even pulled the trigger on that fucking rifle of yours."

Joe looked Campbell square in the eyes.

- "Don't you dare look at me when I'm talking to you," ordered Campbell incandescent with rage.

- "Sir, I've been acquitted, if there's nothing else? Then I'll be on my way," Joe said as he walked off down the corridor and back to his mother's house; the next day he was to rejoin his unit.

That September 'The Line' had pushed forward to a land they hadn't seen for a while. A land with fewer craters, there were even areas of grass and a copse of trees was still standing. Macrae had got together a group of volunteers, an unsavoury bunch of known psychopaths that he'd sprung from different penal institutions. His intention was to keep both sides on their metal. As darkness fell this hapless gang of misfits full of drink and with the promise of more slipped under the wire armed only with coshes. The handmade coshes followed roughly the same pattern, a strip of lead wrapped around a stout wooden stave secured with heavy nails. The sojourn was short with an intensity that did not bear contemplation. Little to no sound was heard as the bloody handed assassins returned home to their reward. Next day the bereaved Germans would be less reluctant to shoot to kill.

As Macrae took his night raid thugs down the line Campbell had again come under Macleod's command. The obvious animosity Campbell held for Joe was palpable. It was the general consensus of opinion among the men that although Campbell was brave to the point of being foolhardy he was not a likable person. He was the sort of social misfit that thrives in institutions like the army, the prison service or the police force. A narrow-minded bigot with just sufficient intelligence to follow rules, the army was his mother and his father. His birth mother a Scottish woman had abandoned him in London and he had been brought up in an orphanage just outside London in the beautiful valley of Hanwell. Unlike the conscripts Campbell was a career soldier whose duty was to fight for King and Country, death was an occupational hazard. Other less enthusiastic heroes were of the opinion that he was mad, and concerned that he was likely to lead them to their deaths. Joe didn't want to be counted amongst that number but was aware that without the protection of Macleod there was every likelihood that that would happen.

As the end of October came around and the news of the Bolshevik revolution filtered down through the ranks Joe's unease grew. Campbell made no secret of the fact that he had Joe down as a communist.

As the autumn evening light faded Joe had been baking bread for the following morning. He had been distracted by the newspaper report of the storming of the Winter Palace and the bread ended up a bit overdone but too good to waste. Before starting a new batch he took some tinned sardines and a vine of Alicante tomatoes. He chopped them together with cracked black pepper and sea salt. He put on his coat, picked up a couple of bottles of wine and took the lot with the fresh baked loaves to the group of men down the trench. The men were appreciative and mopped up the tomatoes and sardines with the chunks of warm bread that had been roughly sliced and were dripping in butter. As the bottles of wine were passed from one to another, a German sniper sat in the cold arms of a tree. He picked up the smell of the bread that heralded Joe's arrival. Joe woke Campbell who had been dozing sitting on a firing step and filled his mess tin with what was left of the supper. Campbell was surprised and touched by Joe's act of kindness and unaccountably stood up to thank him. Joe's coat fell slightly open as he ladled out the last dregs; under his coat was his white apron. The sniper saw this through the gloom and drew a bead on the small slip of white. A shell burst in front of the trench and in the brief flash of light the sniper saw clearly the two figures and caught sight of the three chevrons of rank. Both men ducked in the instant of the shell burst and Joe pulled his coat tight to his body. The distant crack of a rifle rang out and Joe looked to its direction as Hamish Campbell fell, his head resting against the back wall of the trench leaving a good portion of his brain seeping onto the brown earth.

The meteoric rise of half colonel Macleod was no surprise to any of his men and with his promotion meant a staff job. He and Joe were out of the line for the rest of the war. Joe now had proper facilities and the right people to impress with his culinary skills. The war dragged on in its own bloody way with better machines, perfecting efficiency, with better bombs, better tanks and better aeroplanes. No one doubted the outcome of the war after the Americans had thrown their lot in with the allies but no one called a halt to the murderous juggernaut till a year later. The enormous bureaucratic empire that the British had built to administer punishment on its European neighbour was slow to dismantle. On the twelfth of November 1918, armies of men woke in the morning with no purpose to their day, their reason for being no longer existed and the efforts and sacrifices that had been made to turn them into killers would now be employed to turn them back into compliant civilians. The governments of the world looked towards Russia with trepidation; was this the shape of things to come? Would the establishment hand over power to the people? Or would they fight red in tooth and claw to hang on to their ill-gotten gains.

The bombs may have stopped falling in Flanders and Picardy but a more deadly vehicle of slaughter was raging through the populations of the world weeding out the old, the weak and the young. A flu pandemic that knew no front line and killed in the slums of London, Paris and Berlin, as it did in Peking, Delhi, and Nairobi. Men who had survived the trenches died, as if wearied by the fighting, they surrendered to the virus.

Illness had killed thousands of men during the war, meningitis had raged along with any contagion that thrives when large groups of people were herded together in unhygienic conditions. The war had created medieval cities populated only by men. Rose had lost three brothers, two with the flu and one with tuberculosis.

The first few weeks following the armistice were like a limbo, a machine geared for war had to reconfigure itself for peace. Servicemen in a collective sense of relief drank and cavorted and aimlessly waited to return to families who would never understand the life changing experiences they had had. Joe remained as Macleod's batman but had increasing freedom to come and go as he pleased. They were posted to Dieppe where Murdo and Joe acted as liaison overseeing the embarkation of the British troops. Joe developed a relationship and rapport with his family he had never known before. His son was growing up strong and intelligent. On days off Joe would take Leon out fishing on one of Madame Villain's remaining boats or they would collect mussels with his mother. The spring and summer of 1919 was like a blessing. A blessing designed to erase the memory of war, from the minds of those who had seen the iniquities of men, in their basest form. Only in the dark horror of his dreams could Joe recall how inconsequential his life and the lives of so many more had become for that bestial period of time. Each man dealt with what he had become in his own way, some with guilt at surviving, some with shame and some with pride.

Joe met a group of Durham Light Infantry veterans in a bar by the docks. The sound of the Wearside twang was like music to his ears. As infantrymen they had been in the thick of the fighting. Murdo had been talking to their commanding officer who had also commanded the Gurkhas. He told Murdo that the DLI and the Gurkhas were the best fighting men in any army, because they treated war as a job. Each day to them was a day's work. It was a spurious argument.

Murdo had never liked the English and their opinionated arrogance which hadn't been diminished by their inability to win the war. A war in which they had superior men and munitions, America the former colony had come to the rescue. Murdo felt the end of the war was unsatisfactory, the Germans had not surrendered. To his mind the armistice was no more than a drawn game, an agreement that the Germans could no longer fight on and not the unconditional surrender it should have been. It was of no interest to Murdo who were the best fighting men; from his experience it was the Germans whose stubborn determination to sustain a hopeless war on two fronts had been destined to failure. Now that it was over he doubted whether killing people was a job of work to be proud of. The memory of watching people die filled him with revulsion. How many men had felt only sheer terror as they had waited their turn to climb the ladder to go over the top, he himself had always pissed himself before a battle, a distinct advantage of the kilt. He recalled how they had laughed when Gabby had said he had not realised you could shit yourself while running. Murdo understood that this war was about individuals not generalisations and numbers. History would give us the overview, with the benefit of hindsight, but the individuals that shaped events did not have that luxury. Individual stories illustrate the incommutability of the human spirit, the inbuilt need for the species to survive, be it by luck or ability. The selection process was as random as the throw of a dice. It was better to be lucky than rich, brainy or privileged. It was as if the war had been designed by a Marxist god to destroy the stifling class system, and weed out the weak or unlucky. Armistice Day was the day of the clean slate, the dawn of a lucky new world.

A letter arrived from Claire; she wanted to see her son and would be arriving in Dieppe. She took rooms in the Hotel de la Ville. Whatever she had planned for the end of the war had now been changed. She had a woman's ability to change her mind. Paris had become unstable; poverty had descended on the city, a moral poverty that was exploited by the 'low lifes' that had appeared out of the woodwork. She knew it wasn't safe and had given up her apartment. She was pragmatic and knew now she had to make something happen.

Joe arrived at reception with Leon. Leon had the honesty that came with living the simple life. His face and arms were brown from working in the yard. Joe looked at the boy's shoes, they were good shoes and well polished. He was pleased to be there but knew there was no future for the three of them, they were coming from different places. The boy felt embarrassed by the woman in her fine clothes, he felt the hardness of the cold black taffeta bodice as she held his face to her shoulder. She released him and wiped a tear from her eye with a lace handkerchief held delicately in her gloved hand. This was not the woman Joe had known, this was the actress, and this was a studied performance. Leon had the look of a person who would rather be at work, he felt uncomfortable in these surroundings with his mother who he knew better in his memories.

Macleod was taking tea on the terrace and was impressed by the look of the elegant Parisian. Joe and Claire looked mismatched, an odd couple. Joe's receding hairline made him look old. Murdo invited them to join him. It was not done for an officer to be seen socialising with an enlisted man but Murdo defied convention. Joe was awkward in this situation and preferred to observe the protocol. The talk was polite and Murdo was magnanimous with compliments and picking up the bill for the afternoon teas. Joe made his excuses and left. Leon was keen to leave as well, to get back to his own reality.

As the weeks went by Leon became more relaxed in his mother's company but there was no doubting where he felt at home and with whom he identified. Joe's was ordered to rejoin the rest of the regiment in Paris for embarkation but Murdo arranged for Joe to stay in Dieppe on compassionate leave until it was time to sail. Claire had decided to go to Paris with Murdo and asked Leon if he wanted to return with them. Leon's answer was that, he had a job here and that he was getting married next month. Joe said he would do a meal on the Sunday before they left.

Joe and his mother went to the fish market on the Saturday and went round examining the catches with the discerning eye of the connoisseur. Only the best crab was good enough, wild and snapping with enormous claws. Joe had them tied before he put it into a hessian sack. The lobster was handled in the same way. Buying shellfish was an anathema to Joe's mother, her whole life had been collecting and selling shellfish never buying them. Avocado and soft white goat's cheese was got. Murdo had laid hands on some good pre-war German Riesling kabernet from the hotel and good year Taittinger champagne as recommended by Claire. An insulated metal box was to be hired packed with ice for the journey. Men from the regiment took off early on the morning to set up the picnic. Two staff cars had been commandeered for the trip. After coffee and croissants in the Hotel the party in their Sunday best set off to Varengeville. The day was bright and warm with a breeze wafting in from the sea. The hill top church was cool and the mass mercifully short. As the coloured lights from the stained glass window danced on the whitewashed walls Joe remembered how it had been before and how nothing would be the same again. Leon sat with his fiancée, Angelique, an orphaned girl from Mons. He was the only young man in a church full of women and old men, the young couple sat impassively as the banns were read out.

Parishioners and the priest talked to each other in groups as they had always done, old friends and memories were mulled over with a laugh and a tear. Too many young men were missing. Francis paid respects at his father's modest grave and left, passing the auspicious tomb of Roussillon.

The two open top Rolls Royce limousines had attracted considerable attention but slowly the people dispersed to their homes and left the picnic party to make their way down the cliff. Murdo had developed an aversion to eating out of his hands standing up or sitting on the ground as he had so often done in the trenches. So he had had pallets laid out on the sand, boarded and carpeted. The table was dressed in white Irish linen. Joe had instructed that an open altar fire should be blazing so as he could do the starter. The mussels had been bearded and left to soak in white wine and garlic overnight. Joe brought them to the boil in the liquor till they were open, he removed them and added the cream to the cooling liquid and they were served with cold champagne and Scottish smoked salmon. Joe and his mother had prepared the *Fruits de Mer* the night before and sleeves were rolled up to attack the feast. Joe had made a honey and mustard dressing for the watercress and avocado salad. The soft goat's cheese had been added to the crisp smoky bacon pieces, and spring onions gave it extra flavour. The new potatoes had been parboiled, were sautéed in olive oil, fresh butter and rosemary. The Riesling was cool and sweet with a slightly acidic taste and had a sharpness that cleansed the palette. Because it was not too strong their glasses were large and full.

When the debris of the meal cluttered the table the two waiters cleared the space to receive Joe's gateaux, chocolate sponge with schnapps, black cherries and cream. After the meal they sat around in deckchairs and talked, luxuriating in their idleness. The beach is never still, the shushing of the waves as they rolled up and back had a rhythm that sent Joe to sleep. When he woke he saw Murdo, Leon and a few young boys kicking a ball in some impromptu game of football. Claire had walked to the shoreline and was looking out to sea.

As the evening came on, the party left to go home. As the cars drove through Varengeville Joe was overcome with emotion. His head turned as they passed the patisserie that used to be Lenoir's and as the tears welled up in his eyes he wiped them away with his hands. Leon turned to Murdo and asked what was wrong with Joseph. Murdo looked away, there were too many answers.

Joe had decided to go back to the North East and the weeks dragged by. When Murdo arrived with the rest of the regiment from Paris he sent for Joseph. Their meeting was brief and cordial but there was a difference. Murdo had married Claire in Paris. He told Joe that after he had sorted out his affairs at the War Office in London they were leaving for Hollywood in California USA. Murdo said he could get work as a stuntman in the movies. Claire would stay for Leon and Angelique's wedding then join him in London. Joe said he looked forward to seeing him on the silver screen in a cowboy hat. They wished each other good luck then shook hands and went their separate ways.

Chapter Ten

London

Retracing of the steps you had walked when you were younger, remembering who you were and knowing what you had become is like walking with a ghost. On the train from Newhaven to London, Joe was filled with the same anticipation he had felt those years before, only this time there was no fear of the unknown. Just a strange nagging fear that fate may yet deal him the killer hand, each bang and hiss made him anxious. Visions of death hid behind his eyes, eyes that had seen too much as the train clattered its way through the lush green countryside of Kent. The smell of antiseptic filled the corridor, Joe and a medical orderly tried to disguise it with a shared cigarette. As they spoke their voices carried up to the next compartment. Someone called out,

- "Is that you Joe?"

Joe made his way to where the voice had come from and there sitting on the floor with his back to the side of the train sat Bob Hill.

- "We made it Joe, we made it."

The place was not right for joyous reunion, the seats either side of the compartment were silent with three wounded men. One lay on a stretcher, feebleminded and dribbling, struck dumb; the other two - one blind, one deaf. After the initial greetings and reminiscences of where they had been and who they had seen, who was dead and who alive, news of which sobered them both. Bob said,

- "How do we go back to normal life Joe?"

- "What's normal? I suppose we find some place in our heads to lose the memory of what we've seen and what we've done. Did you kill anyone?"

- "No, I joined up as a Quaker, it's against my religion. I started off as a stretcher-bearer. Now I'm an S.R.N."

- "And you?"

- "No. I only ever pulled the trigger at target practice. I thought if I shot at anyone they might shoot back, I didn't want to draw that kind of attention to myself. I didn't see much more than seven days action, I spent the best part of the war cooking for the officers."

- "There are a lot of people not coming back who saw less action. I saw them come and I saw them go. The turn up, stand up, and get dead brigade."

- "Things will never be the same again. Thank God! Russia certainly won't."

- "You always said the Russians would be the first to overthrow the government, how did you know that? You seemed to know quite a bit about what was going on, whereas I didn't take a great deal of interest. Recently though I got to thinking about that business with Herman Cohen, you were involved weren't you?"

- "What makes you think that?"

- "Just too many coincidences, the way you didn't get the same beating I got after the races when we were robbed outside the Coach and Horses. The way you turned up with that copper from Sunderland when I was going to see Piakow. And was it a coincidence that collier was heading up the coast the very next morning and you knew them?"

- "You have been thinking haven't you? I tried to warn you about Piakow but by then I was in too deep, it was the best I could do to get us both out of there"

- "Did you let Jacob Peters know where I was?"

- "No fucking way, I knew what he was capable of. I'd done my bit."

- "And what was that? I'm just curious as to why Herman Cohen was killed."

- "The Russians like to have a little leverage, they always think someone might be able to do them a favour, and you did, as well as accompanying me and a few crates up to Sunderland you were a decoy for Jacob Peters. As it happened it all worked out fine."

- "Not for Herman Cohen it didn't. What was in the crates?"

- "Well it wasn't toys from Hamburg like it said on the import licence. They were guns. If they had gone from Hamburg to St Petersburg they would have aroused some suspicion but coming from Sunderland, nobody's going to take any notice. While you were having a kip in me mother's house, a wagon had been arranged to take the crates down to Villiers Street mission. Danny Currie was the caretaker down there it was ideal, nobody ever took any notice of Danny, apart from, Atamatta, that is who took notice of everything."

- "So you were involved in shipping guns to Russia. It still doesn't tell me why Cohen was killed."

- "Cohen was the banker; he handled all the illegal money that paid for the guns, the shipments, and the hush money. He ran the money lending business as a legitimate front, it cleaned the money up. Banks keep records of the serial numbers of notes, so they can trace them. He'd lend out a couple a quid here and a couple of quid there, and get some coin back each week which he would then convert into clean money to finance the revolution. Money lending has its problems, like arrears. Cohen was also paying the police and Atamatta's two boys and as a result he had a cash flow problem. Rumour has it that someone from Villiers Street South Shul, who was in the know, told Jacob Peters that people weren't being paid. That by the way included me, and that Cohen was living the high life, drawing attention to himself, being indiscreet, not that he was. Chances are it was jealousy, just someone who had a grudge and wanted to take over a nice little business. At the time temperatures were running a bit high. News was coming out of Russia of the atrocities committed by the Black Hundreds. Jacob Peters was in the import export game so he had good cover and didn't find it difficult to move around. He wanted to send a message to his comrades that you didn't mess him about. It probably wasn't his wisest move the only people to benefit were those who owed money to Cohen. The police and the coroner had to bumble around pretending to be efficient while covering their tracks."

"So I was just caught up in this and could have been hanged."

- "Yeah but you weren't, were you? That's because I was looking out for you."
- "Sounds like you were looking out for yourself."

The words were what Joe was thinking but to Bob and Joe's surprise they were spoken by the blind man. In their conversation they had ignored their travelling companions the incoherent idiot, the deaf man and the blind fellow.

- "For some reason people think because you're blind you can't hear."
- "I wasn't looking out for myself. I believed in the cause and I still do."
- "Well you can leave me out I've done my bit, unwittingly." said Joe.

Wanting to change the conversation he turned to the blind man,

- "How long you been blind mate?"
- "Long enough to be able to see things differently. What pisses me off is when ignorant bastards like you ignore me, that just makes me feel so fucking lonely."
- "I've always wanted to ask a blind man…….."
- "This blind man's got a name, Chas Parker."
- "Sorry Chas! Pleased to meet you, Joe Roc. Are you black blind?"
- "Yeah"
- "Do you dream in colour?"

- "Funnily enough I do."
- "What about people who are born black blind? I wonder what images they dream."
- "I don't know. You're going have to ask someone else."
- "What's your favourite colour?"
- "Red."
- "What's yours Joe?"
- "Red."
- "Same as mine," said Bob.

The train pulled into Waterloo Station. Joe looked at Bob he knew he couldn't change the past. Back then he thought Bob was all talk, it didn't appear so now. As they parted, Bob said he was going back up north, to get involved in the unions or Labour Party. Joe admired Bob's sincerity, honesty and candour. He advised him to get rid of all three if he was to become a successful politician. Joe asked Bob,

- "If you see Rose, don't tell her you've seen me, I'm not demobbed yet and I want it to be a surprise when I get home."
- "What she doesn't know won't hurt her?"

London had always held a fascination for Joe. It had been years since he'd walked its streets, seen the sights and visited the

National Gallery. He took a room on the Kings Road he wanted to be near the New England Art Club. He had the idea of catching up with Walter, and what was happening on the London art scene, maybe, he thought, he could start painting again. The artists he had known had always seemed to live such glamorous lives, filled with good-looking woman and interesting friends. Why shouldn't he have some of that he mused?

Walter had had various addresses around the Camden, Whitechapel area but Joe had grown disdainful of that part of town, with its filth and squalor. What Walter seemed to revel in was not to Joe's taste, and they arranged to meet in the Criterion on Piccadilly. When they met, Walter told Joe that he had rented a house, the Villa d'Aumale at Envermeu, where he spent most of his time painting at the Casino, and Café Vernet, in Dieppe, so he was not often in London.

Although the peace had been signed in the summer of 1919, Joe was still being paid. He felt there was no need to hurry home or get a job. The opportunity was there to draw and paint. He took walks in the parks, down the river as far as Tower Bridge, each day he would sketch a different landmark and in the evenings he would hang around in the haunts of established artists. Walter had introduced Joe to several of his friends, older artists, some tolerant of his pretensions; others like Augustus

John, who vaguely remembered Joe from Paris, were more dismissive. Charles Jagger, who had been twice wounded while with the artist's rifles, was a fine draftsman and sculptor, and was starting to pick up important commissions. Although friendly, he was quiet and diffident, he was not a great socialite; the wounds he bore were not just physical. Joe found that the better the painter the less threatened they felt, and the more approachable. He liked William Nicholson a family man whose solid drawing and painting skills made him a livelihood. Joe felt awkward and patronised in their company, as though he was intruding on some secret society.

As the summer wore on Joe's isolation grew and as his ambition dampened he became edgy, the possibility of success frightened him and he shied away, embarrassed by the thought of failure. He visited galleries and looked on the works of other artists, less able artists. He knew he was better than them and became bitter and angry at the success of these lesser talents. He wondered if the artists he knew felt the same. Even though they complimented each other, behind their lying eyes there was jealousy. They resented and begrudged each other their triumphs and revelled in their disasters. Having more than one face might be an advantage, like some of those paintings by Picasso.

The peace conference in Versailles was over and William Orpen had just completed his commission to paint it. Joe met the Irishman one night in the Ritz. Joe was celebrating. His demob papers had come through. Orpen like Jagger understood the suffering and had seen the terrible waste at the front. He had an empathy with the common soldier; he was also a friend of Sickert. Orpen had no pretensions his reputation was built on a mastery of his craft and hard work. He knew Dieppe and talked to Joe affectionately about times he had spent there before and during the war. His favourite café was the Tribunaux. He asked Joe if he knew it. And what he intended to do now that the war was over? Joe told him he thought he might try to make a living as an artist in London, failing that he would go back to his family in Sunderland and open a bakery. Orpen told him to come with some of his drawings to his studio.

The next day Joe arrived with his sketch book in it were twenty four neat drawings of London ranging from St Paul's Cathedral, to Cleopatra's Needle. Figures, buses, cars, and horses merged down Whitehall. Sailing barges ploughed along the river past steamboats. There was a traffic jam on Tower Bridge. Orpen looked at each one intently. He said they were very good and asked if Joe had turned any into paintings. Joe told him he hadn't done any painting since before the war. Orpen told him that things were changing. With the popularity of photography, there was less credence put on good drawing and painting, and more on ideas.

"A famous French painter said years ago, that with the camera painting was dead. I disagree, people will always paint, but the images will change as fashion does. In the future an artist will not be special everyone will be an artist. Sit down," he said, "and I will give you a lesson, then you make up your own mind if you wish to join this doomed profession."

He placed a mirror behind the easel so Joe could see what he was doing. As he did so Joe could see the painter had a large boil on the back of his neck, it reminded Joe of something a long time ago. Orpen proceeded to do a one hour oil study talking as he went. He painted '*al prima*' the colours mixed and applied with a large brush; near the end of the session the detail was added with a smaller brush. As he did so he said the important thing about being an artist is to be confident, it also helps if you are of independent means and are charming. He took the painting off the easel and offered it to Joe. Joe shrank back.

- "It's a gift. Bring it back when it's dry and I'll varnish and sign it."
- "I can't accept it."
- "How long does it take you to make bread?"
- "An hour."
- "An hour for an hour you can bake me a loaf of bread."

- "It's not a fair exchange, a painting can last hundreds of years a loaf of bread lasts only one day."
- "I know what I'd prefer if I were starving. If you can make bread you'll never go hungry. I know plenty of artists that are on the breadline but I don't know any bakers who are. I became an artist because it was the only thing I could do and I've been very lucky. Be a Sunday painter Joe. Take the painting, it's my pleasure, its scant payment for what you and your comrades have gone through." Orpen wrote down his address, "Next time you are in Paris come and see me." They bade their farewells and as Joe stood on the pavement looking at the wet painting in his hands, a Rolls Royce pulled up, the chauffeur got out and opened the door for a beautiful young woman. Orpen was waiting at the door for her.

The painting was small. Back down the Kings Road Joe made a box to protect the wet surface, he wrapped it up, placed it in his knapsack, paid for his digs and left. He had realised he wasn't confident as an artist, nor was he of independent means, and his charm had suffered a serious setback over the last few years.

Chapter Eleven

Home

The great Norman cathedral and castle loomed over Durham city as Joe walked along the platform. He found the bus station and caught the bus for Consett. The steel works that had supplied the raw material for war dominated the town and a red dust coated the streets and houses. He changed buses at Consett and got another that went as far as Cartaway Heads up near the river Derwent. It was mid-afternoon and the early summer sun was hot enough to soften the newly laid tarmac that stopped just the other side of the Cartaway Heads inn. The lonely building stood in the middle of the rolling countryside as green and lush as any Joe had seen. He booked into the inn leaving his knapsack with the barman and asked directions before setting off down the hill. Farm labourers were working in the fields with pitchforks, harvesting. A muscular old man with a weathered face of chestnut brown stood high on a cart and joked with a gaggle of women, a sight as familiarly picturesque as it was backbreaking. Joe came across a pub at the top of a hill 'The Rose and Crown'. He had a thirst on him that needed satisfying so he called in for a drink and to check on his progress. The pub sold Magnet ales. The beer had a nutty taste and slipped down so easily he had a second pint, on the house, before he headed off. The landlord confirmed his directions. He passed a row of cottages as he descended Kiln Pit Hill before finding the gate he was looking for. It would have been easy enough to miss just wide enough for a large cart. Inside the gate, the gatehouse garden was slightly overgrown, a stream went past it and Joe crouched down and cupped his hands to wet his face. The water was crystal clear and as cold as ice. Standing up he adjusted the pack strapped over his shoulder before making his way up the drive between the large sequoias that formed the avenue. He could see a field of gooseberry bushes being tended to by three or four monks. He recognised the habit and the badge of the Passionists. It must have been half a mile before he reached the house, a solid building of honey coloured local sandstone. He put his tunic back on and tugged on the bell. The door was answered at length by an old grey lady who enquired as to his business. Joe told Emmeline, the housekeeper, that he had something for the Baron from his son Gabriel. She returned to invite Joe into the dining room. The room had an enormous bay window from ceiling to floor that was open onto a lawn. The baron stood with his hands behind his back. He was a tall man, lean, and when he turned his cheeks were high boned under soft brown doe eyes. His hair that must have once been black like Gabriel's, was now white.

- "You have brought something from my son?"
- "Yes!" Joseph replied, removing the bag from his shoulder, the bag that used to carry his gas mask.

He took out the grey metal box and placed it on a doily, making sure it didn't scratch the highly polished surface of the table. Joe delved into his sporran for the key and handed it to the baron. He opened the box that contained the usual personal items: letters, a fine hunter watch, the signet ring he'd taken off before the battle, he'd told Joe he didn't like the idea of having his finger hacked off by some avaricious corporal when he might only be partially dead. There was a gold chain with an enamelled medal of the Immaculate Mary. The baron held it in his hand.

- "His mother gave it to him before he left she gave each of them the same medal. This is the only one to come home."

He picked out Gabriel's wallet, inside were the photographs of the family and over one hundred pounds in white five pound notes. He took them out and handed them to Joseph. Joseph declined the money. The baron placed it on the table.

- "You haven't opened this have you?"
- "No!"
- "It's not my money it should cover your expenses. Take it, I don't need it or want it. You were under no obligation to bring this here."
- "I was obliged to your son, he was my comrade."

The baron carried on looking through the box in a distracted manner,

- "Take it, that's an order."

Joe picked it up and put it in his sporran.

The Baron was holding a letter addressed to himself. He looked at Joseph and said,

- "You'll be staying for dinner and the night. Emmeline will show you to your room and fix you up with a dinner suit. If you tell Thomas, my driver, where you've left your luggage, he'll go and pick it up for you."

Dinner was served on the lawn; Joseph had bathed and was groomed. The shirt was an 'Arrow', starched and pressed and gleaming white, he couldn't have done better himself. The estate had a farm that was now run by the monks, all the produce was fresh. The grilled, brook trout, had been swimming in the stream earlier in the evening. Its skin was crisp and brown and it was served on the bone. Joe squeezed the lemon with his left hand so as not to taint the flavour of the wine. He had hardly eaten all day so the supper was welcome; garden vegetables, home baked bread with a fine crust spread with butter churned that day. The chips were a generous size and had been parboiled before being twice fried in a mixture of oil and lard making them crisp on the outside and soft in the middle. While they ate Gregorian chanting came from the monks a distance away. The Latin words gave the meal the reverence of a holy ritual. The baron asked about where he and Gabriel had been and Joe told him the stories of the Somme and Passchendaele.

The main course was followed by a delicate fruitcake, heavy with juicy berries; the cake had been matured with an apple to keep it moist and was served as a dessert with a local cheese and an apple from the orchard. When the brandy was sent for it was Spanish, Carlos Primera. Their glasses were charged and the baron invited Joseph to walk.

They went past the field where the Friesians were grazing and then into the chapel. Brother Michael was playing the organ, Bach. Brother Michael he was told had trained at the Royal College of Music before joining the order. The smell of incense still hung in the air from the evening mass. Down the stone stairs was the crypt with several small chapels, each priest was required to celebrate Mass every day. The late evening light contrasted with the gloom of the building. The sun was just setting behind the distant Cheviots and the heat was going from the day. The fire had been lit in the library and a decanter of single malt stood next to two cut glass tumblers. The men sat in the leather wing backed chairs. The baron had spoken generally about the estate, the park, with its pathways and collection of rhododendrons, and the farm that kept the estate self-sufficient. It had been his wife's idea to hand the estate over to the Passionists. The baron explained how he thought it immoral to have such a large staff to serve one old man's purpose.

He told Joseph that after it had been confirmed that Gabriel, their third and youngest son was dead, his wife, who was a devout Catholic, had chosen to die a shaman death. After she had sorted out all her business she went and sat on the bench on the lawn and as the sun set she died. Her body slumped to one side. That was earlier in the year.

- "I think she lost interest in this 'Garden of Earthly Delights' and was looking for a more celestial sphere, she was a very spiritual woman. When a body is virtually finished with life, hearing clings on to the bitter end, the last thing she would have heard would have been birdsong. Hearing can give great pleasure and great pain. When I heard of Gabriel's death I put my hands over my ears to block it out. A futile gesture, nature takes its own course. No individual inflicted this cruelty on my family; it was just circumstance, the nature of events. We categorise emotions and give them names in an attempt to increase our understanding. In the natural world there are no words, no words for cruelty or evil. It is the nature of the beast to kill. Love and hate are two sides of madness."

Joe listened as the stream of consciousness unfolded.

- "Did you know my son well?" The baron asked.
- "He was an officer and I was a private, he was English I am French but we shared the same time and place. I knew him as well as I could, given our situation."
- "Would you say he was a good man?"
- "He was always good to me. He seemed to realise that he was going to die and asked me to tell you, that he died well."
- "And what is a good death?"
- "I don't know I wasn't there. I heard he was blown up by a grenade while leading the charge, I was a way behind and Major Macleod was behind me."
- "I can't say I knew him that well, he was more his mother's son. I read the letters he sent to her. I didn't realise he had so little regard for her feelings. In one he was thanking her for some bath cubes she had sent him in a parcel then he said he

was going to have to urinate in his helmet so that he could have a warm shave."

- "We had to shave every day that's what we did sometimes."

- "Did his mother need to know that? She was very upset"

- "He must have thought so. There is an enormous gulf between imagination and intelligence."

- "My children were brought up to a life of privilege and all three of them died in a bestial fashion; their bodies have no grave."

- "I think for him, it was preferable to die than to live in his world. He was a good catholic and thought he was going to a better place. Lots of men felt the same. Those of us that have survived have to live with the memories of those past times and the pain goes on."

- "The pain is worse when you know there is no better place. Take comfort in the embrace of your wife and children. I have neither; the only thing that can get me through this veil of tears is that I am responsible to the people who work for me, their wives and children. This country is facing financial ruin. It's people like me who can help to rebuild it. It is a debt I have to pay."

The look of utter despondency on his face belied these words of optimism the room fell into an awkward silence. Joe had seen the hollow look of emptiness on a man's face before as the baron stared as if transfixed by the glowing embers of the coal fire. Joe remembered the look, that look of lost love. He drained his glass quietly placed it on the occasional table and went to his room.

The grey sky of the morning brought its rain gently beating against the window, weather more typical of the region than the previous day's sunshine. It accounted for the lush greenery and full streams.

Joe had made his mind up to return to Sunderland An excited urgency gripped him, he wanted to get there today, and imagined it to be forty or fifty miles. If the buses ran on time he could catch a train from Durham to Union Street. This could be a fresh beginning with his wife and child, familiar places and old friends. His mind journeyed to the future, the money he had was already burning a hole in his pocket. He knew what he was like and was aware of his short attention span but now he had a project, he would open a baker's shop. He even imagined the location just up from The Red Lion on Roker Avenue next to the horse meat butchers. He pulled back the bed clothes and dressed again in his uniform. The uniform he had liked so much, the uniform that had been paid for by the baron; it suddenly felt strange as though it didn't belong to him now, it was part of his past or soon would be.

Joe went into the dining room. The metal box was still at the table more of its contents had been removed. A missal lay open with a thin strip of fabric lying across the '*De Profundis*' Joe began to read.

- "Out of the depths I have cried to thee Oh Lord."
- "Lord, hear my supplication!" The baron continued, as he entered the room.

He came over to where Joe stood and absentmindedly picked up the book next to the missal. It was a beautifully bound volume, in tooled leather, with gold inlaid writing. The sumptuous quality of the object looked incongruous next to the dog-eared missal with its thin well-thumbed pages. The pages of the book were thick, high quality, with an intricate border round each page. The name on the title page stood out Oscar Wilde. The memory of that day at Pere-Lachaise came flooding back.

- "Gabriel and I went to visit his tomb when we were in Paris."

He noticed the engraving of the author on the title page,

- "That's Sebastian Melmoth."
- "How do you know that?"
- "I met him in Paris before the war."
- "Oscar Wilde changed his name to Sebastian Melmoth and moved to the continent after his release from prison."

A shiver went down Joe's spine and the hairs stood up on the back of his neck. It was like he was back at Pere-Lachaise on that cold grey day.

- "Here have the book, I don't want it. You can read it on the bus, but I wouldn't let anyone see what it is. I thought we'd take breakfast in the kitchen this morning."

The kitchen range was on and the breakfast already started. Thick, fatty farm-reared bacon sizzled in the cast-iron pan. Joe's mouth watered in anticipation. Egg, sausage, tomato, mushrooms from the field and a fried slice were washed down with sweet milky tea. Emmeline served the meal with silent efficiency.

- "Do you know what I found in Gabriel's missal Emmeline?"
- "No sir."
- "I found his Ten Special Intentions. Can you guess what was number one?"
- "No sir."
- "I pray my father returns to the faith."
- "We all pray for you sir," she said as she silently left the kitchen.

The baron gave Joe twenty woodbines and instructed Thomas to drop him off at Consett. The sun came out as the bus made its way through Weardale. Joe found it more pleasant to stare out of the window than to read the book he'd been given, but he did look at Gabriel's book. The title intrigued him, 'The Picture of Dorian Grey.' He thought he would read it later.

Joe caught the train in Durham and it belched its way to a halt in Sunderland Station an hour or so later. As he strode down Union Street with a spring in his step he recognised the smell of the sea and the screech of the sea gulls. It felt good to be home. It was a short walk from the station to the new lodgings in Tunstall Terrace. Number four was opposite the railway line he'd just come in on. He knocked on the door and waited. A little girl, his daughter who he hadn't seen for nearly five years opened the door.

- *"Bonjour mon petit chou"*

She froze at the sight of this strange Scottish soldier, then turned and ran down the passage screaming for her mother.

J.P. Grinion

The Picture of Joe Roc

This book is available through mail order or from you local bookshop and newsagent please send Cheque/Eurocheque/Postal Order (Sterling only)

Please allow £1.25 per book for post and packaging UK. Overseas customers please allow £2.00 per copy for post and packaging.

All orders to: J.P. Grinion, Book service by post Eastgate House, The Street, Cressing, Essex CM77 8DG. Tel: 01376 583168.

Name ....

Address...

Please allow 28 days for delivery. Prices and availability subject to change without notice.